Realm Walker

by

Lori Francis

Cover Art by *Teddi Black*

The Wild Rose Press, Inc.
PO Box 708
Adams Basin, NY 14410-0708
Visit us at www.thewildrosepress.com

Publishing History
First Edition, 2025
Trade Paperback ISBN 978-1-5092-5733-1
Digital ISBN 978-1-5092-5734-8

Published in the United States of America

Dedication

This book is dedicated to two families; the family I built over the years, and to the family I was gifted. To Angela, Elissa, and Maureen who have always insisted I am worthy. Thank you.

To Lucy, who is the keeper of family history. There is a magic in the words and memories left behind, and you are the keeper of that magic. You inspire me.

And to the two people who always embraced my dreams and believed in me, even when I doubted myself.

My father gave me a love of reading and history and taught me to embrace the magic of the universe.

When I met my husband, he not only shared this wonder of words and worlds, but he also made time stand still. He still does...every time he looks at me.

Chapter One

The guard's shout heralded Teagan Deschamb's escape. The storm swelling over the sea that had threatened since morning's red dawn broke, cast shards of lightning to warn of the gale just as the guards warned of her empty cell. Synchronized discordance.

Darius struck the cart driver in the back of the head, then dragged the man beneath the overhang. He'd be drier and safer there than in the cart. Some solutions demanded brevity.

Reins in hand, he maneuvered the horses through the streets, toward the dock. He could only help her if he reached her in time.

He pulled the cart to a halt near the landing and leapt to the ground. Rain pounded the cobbles hard enough to make the streets slick.

An old man squatted near the end of the quay tethering a small craft.

A decent-sized skiff—easy to handle, if he could concentrate long enough to manipulate the weather.

The thunder rumbled as his boots pounded the wooden planks of the pier. The vibration of his own urgent steps resonated beneath him, scolding him.

If only the girl had waited. Another half an hour and he could have avoided all of this.

The scent of pitch carried on the wind. Someone had set fire to several of the village's outer buildings, including Ranulf Deschamb's house. Darius could see the rooftops from here. Someone sought to avenge the carpenter's death. Too late for Ranulf.

Darius closed his eyes as he advanced toward the boat and concentrated on the task at hand. A few whispered words, a sleight of will, and the storm began to slow. As he surged forward, onlookers scurrying from the quay slowed to a halt, some in mid-step. Rain fell—not in sheets, but in large plump bombs of spray—exploding in slow motion against whatever resistance they met.

The rowboat sat motionless against the dock. Its owner perched precariously on the ledge, one hand grasping the rope as he attempted to tie off the craft.

Darius slipped the rope from the old man's hand as he moved the motionless body away from the edge, then jumped into the boat, and began to row.

He hadn't stalled the storm completely, but he had slowed it significantly.

In the distance, against a swell of waves, he saw Teagan's boat. He meant to catch her before she put herself at dire risk.

Darius cut through the water as if it were nothing more than fog, bearing no resistance to each stroke. The girl had a head start, but he had skill—and time—on his side, slicing away at her lead with each movement of his oars.

He could see the small skiff clearly. He could also see the slight human form clinging to the plank seat, hugging the wood as the wave tilted, then upended the craft.

Sluggishly, the boat rolled with the water, each movement an isolated action. A blue streak spidered across the sky, craggy and ominous. Lightning reached for the skiff as it toppled, suspended in a ballet of flowing resistance until it met its mark, and struck the wood.

Darius heard Teagan Deschamb scream as the boat capsized. Each second passed like a human lifetime, until she poured from the boat into the water, the ocean greedily swallowing her.

Another three strokes, Darius met the capsized hull. He reached beneath the rim, to lift the vessel away from where Teagan sank. As he did, he saw her a hand slip beneath the waves.

Darius reached deep into the water, and yanked as hard as he could against the cold shank of her arm.

Ever since that afternoon in the courtyard, hovering in the crowd, a witness to her father's execution, Darius had known this ominous moment would be his undoing. He knew what it meant to intervene. Yet, he did not stop. Did not hesitate to wrestle with fate for her mortality.

Against everything he knew to be right, Darius pulled Ranulf's daughter from the blackness of death. Raising her up from the water, tearing her from the fabric of time, he created a void where her death should be.

He knew his mission. Find the clock. Destroy it.

Succeed or fail, he had just stepped across the threshold between right and wrong.

Darius Alwin, realm walker, had just stopped Teagan Deschamb's death.

****

Grandfather Mountain, North Carolina
July 2022

Mist enveloped Teagan Alexander like a shroud, protecting her from onlookers.

Rain, and mud, and crowds greeted her as she stepped from the bus.

Rain usually comforted her. Especially when she found herself nervous or self-conscious. *Nothing to see here. Just another tourist. No one worth noticing.* She tugged her bag close to her body.

The clanging of metal pots on campfires echoed through the trees as she sprinted through the campground. Even now, the wail of a fiddle sang mournfully to her, urging her to hurry.

Electricity charged the air–a palpable energy-amid these revelers-men and women, their clad in a variety of attire, each sporting clan emblems and brightly colored tartans.

Ghosts would be here today. The mountain always called. *They* always came. Ancient spirits of ancestors, both native and transplanted from faraway lands.

Teagan hiked up her skirts and sidestepped a mud puddle to circumnavigate a crowd of locals who huddled near the main gate, discussing last year's football season and the coming high school prospects.

Admission ribbon in place, she flashed her press pass and skirted past the attendant who smiled a welcome at her.

"Mornin'. You look ready for the day," the woman said, as she tugged at her wide brimmed hat. "It's too bad we've got rain."

"Rain just makes it more real. If this were Scotland, we'd expect a bit of soggy. Never too much fog. Never too much tartan." Secretly, she reveled in the opportunity to dress in costume. Plus, it offered protection from the damp.

"I hear ya. Have a good day, now."

Teagan nodded at the woman, then bounded across the gravel. Tomorrow, her patron's admission would allow her to park on the hill. Today, though, the bus ride from the parking lot had just added to the experience. Today, more tourists than locals wandered through the gates. Fridays were always slow.

Except for the dancers.

Since eight o'clock, teams of tartan clad highland dancers crowded the triple-tent structure in an attempt to keep their hair and costumes dry. The music kicked in and a teenage boy, already on the stage, posed in readiness for his cue.

Teagan's attention was on the cloggers who were practicing off to the far side, in the soft rain, instead of on the pathway when the collision happened.

First came the impact as she slammed into the man. Or rather, the wall of a man. Teagan lost her balance, and started to fall backwards when something equally hard met her back, keeping her from collapsing to the ground.

"Whoa. Take it easy," a brusque voice called. The wall reached out and righted her, nearly lifting her off her feet before planting her firmly on the ground.

Six feet of bright yellow tartan swirling from boot to shoulder caught her on impact. Tattoos covered the arms that clutched her as she vibrated from the ricochet.

Charcoal and burnt tobacco. The aroma of sweat, tobacco, and salt swirled around her. Bile rose in her throat as the scents mingled.

"I am so sorry," she stammered. "I, um—did I hurt you?"

A robust laugh bubbled up, and he smirked at her. Something more than mischief danced in the man's eyes as he licked his lips. "No, darlin'. But if you want, you can check me for broken bones."

Embarrassment flushed furiously from her neck to her scalp as she pushed away from her captor. Despite the heat in her cheeks, she managed a smirk. "No thanks. My mother warned me about Campbells. Always offering help or an invitation with one hand, while pilfering or pinching with the other."

Now his friends joined in the laughter, patting him on the back as he guffawed at her retort.

"Dang, Donny, that cat has claws," one of his friends quipped.

Teagan ducked and twirled out of arm's reach and skittered in the opposite direction.

"Yeah. I bet I could make her purr."

Teagan avoided the cat calls that the trio hurled at her as she widened the space between them.

Note to self—avoid the Campbell tent today.

Past the Patron's tent, and down the hill, Teagan rounded the corner and made a beeline for the cluster of trees just as the first band took the stage. She unpacked the waterproof blanket from her bag and spread it out on a large flat stone that jutted out from the ground. Miraculously, no one had yet claimed the driest spot on the hill, opting instead for the bleacher seats nearer the stage.

Next, she pulled out her camera, aimed it at the performers and clicked a few shots before the cacophonous warm up turned to melody.

The trees in the grove formed a suitable canopy for anyone who didn't prefer the clan tents along the oval track. Even the harshest rain had a difficult time penetrating the lush foliage. A deluge a few yards away on the meadow fell in sprinkles in the grove. Between the trees and three layers of cotton and wool, Teagan could stay comfortably set for the next few hours.

The Great Calling. This, the most recent in a series of events she had been asked to cover for a travel magazine, had been her childhood playground. The better part of her spring and early summer had been spent moving from one faire to another, capturing photos and moments from each. What better way to make a living?

She aimed the camera at a couple in traditional highland dress—he in great kilt, she in *earisaid* and white pelisse—standing at the edge of the crowd swaying to the music. The woman's long braid flashed silver-grey against the darkness of her plaid, hung nearly to her hips. Her husband wrapped his arms around her, and she leaned back against him. The perfect portrait of the timelessness of love, and the timelessness of this place. For more than fifty years, the clans had gathered here, revisiting history and heritage.

Teagan's throat clenched. Hadn't her parents stood that same way, many years ago?

Instinctively, she glanced over her shoulder looking for the ruins of faerie forts she built as a child upon the hill. Twigs and leaves, and bits of moss, and pebbles, crafted as an invitation for any woodland creature or sprite that might want a home.

Only moss and dirt. No forts.

More than two decades had passed since she had

played here with friends, toying with the fanciful ideas of a child's imagination.

Nearly a decade since her parents had left her alone.

The hair prickled on the back of Teagan's neck, and she shivered. Perhaps the faeries came still, like the other ghosts that gathered in the mists.

No such thing as ghosts. Her mother's voice echoed in her memory.

The bagpipe wailed a familiar note, and the crowd sent up a hoot of approval as the drummer beat a tempo for "The Gael", everyone's favorite tune. The rain had all but stopped, as if the music calmed the clouds to cease their tears.

Something prickled Teagan's spine again, and she flinched involuntarily. She turned her attention to the performers, once more. From the corner of her eye, she glimpsed someone standing against the trees to her right.

She turned her camera in that direction. He stood, casually leaning against the thick trunk of a tall oak. Dressed in black shirt and renfest breeks—not Highland attire—he merely stood, staring at her.

She nearly dropped the camera. Dark hair fell across broad shoulders, brushing the cloth of his collar. A wide band of leather, crossed from one shoulder to hip, matched the belt that wrapped his waist. From behind the opposite shoulder, Teagan could make out the glint of a sword hilt. A very large sword.

She drew the camera up and framed him in the shot, then clicked before he could move away.

He didn't budge. He merely held his stance like a statue, staring at her. Frowning at her. His expression as dark as his hair.

She raised a hand in greeting, which he ignored, and felt her muscles tremble at her effort.

What is he staring at?

An unwelcome familiar flush warmed her neck and cheeks. Damn, why did she embarrass so easily? She glanced around, checking to see if he might be looking at someone or something behind her.

Teagan's blush deepened, and she tried to ignore his gaze. She grabbed her bag and stashed the camera inside. Definitely a good time to go make the rounds at the clan tents. The blanket could stay where it was, holding her perch, while she escaped her voyeur.

She slung the bag over her shoulder defiantly, and raised her head, jaw jutting just enough to chastise his rudeness.

Gone.

The mottled bark of the tree trunk had been abandoned. To the left, and right, no sign of anyone who matched his description. As if he had simply vanished into thin air.

****

Darius fought the urge to march across the grove and yank Teagan Miller to her feet. Even here, how could he hope to protect her? Especially, when she insisted on planting herself like a target in the most inviting spot at the festival.

The only thing missing was a bright bulls-eye to help the hunters. Not that she needed one. A spray of sunlight shimmered through the trees against her hair, and she virtually glowed. A beacon.

Much worse than a bullseye.

The camera lens turned toward him, and he tensed.

She had seen him. He stared directly back at her, willing her to pack her gear and leave, while she had the chance.

While he had the resolve to let her.

Thought manipulation, however, never had been one of Darius's gifts. If it had, Teagan might be in more danger than she currently faced.

A wicked consequence for both of us. There were, after all, some advantages to his talents.

The vision of her planted on the blanket, like a present waiting to be unwrapped, reminded him why he lingered so close.

Too close for his own good. Or hers.

The music began, and she shifted her focus to the stage. Darius seized the opportunity and moved away from the oak, to disappear into the crowd. For the moment, the crowd protected her. They'd be gone soon enough. She'd be alone. She'd be vulnerable.

He'd be back.

Chapter Two

The branches overhead rustled in the breeze, and a cascade of raindrops peppered her scalp. Oak and moss drenched the air along with the clean scent of mountain rain.

Before he could return, she tromped down the bit of knoll, headed toward the tents. *Better the devil you know,* echoed in her thoughts as she headed into the throng.

By lunchtime, she had seen every familiar face that dared to brave the morning drizzle, including Susan and Robert Clarindon. The couple had been a part of the games long before she had even been a sparkle in her parent's eye. The Clarindons fronted the MacKinnon tent, meeting and greeting each year, inviting new members to join the clan association, and handing out goodies to anybody who slowed down.

A late arrival in Bran Elm last night, and an early alarm this morning weighed exhaustively on her. She begged off Susan's invitation for dinner, and returned to her rock, intent on gathering her energy and her blanket before heading for the bus stop.

The morning rain, combined with the afternoon surge in temperature, tempted her too much. She drifted off while someone on the stage sang a ballad.

Something flittered at her face. Teagan swatted at the bug that hovered too close, tickling her. Again, she twitched, and swatted at the intruder. Just as her hand swung out the third time, a muffled snicker penetrated her consciousness.

She sat straight up, eyes reluctantly opening against the dappled sunlight that struggled to peak through the trees. No more than four feet from where she lay stood the Campbell-clad man she had run into earlier. In his hand he held a long twig, tendrils of a cobweb fluttering from the end, close enough to brush her face.

Grinning from ear to ear. "I think our puss is awake," he teased.

Teagan slapped the stick away from her face. If she had indeed had claws, he'd be missing more than the hand that held the branch, right now.

"Ass," she mumbled.

"You know, you made a pretty picture, sprawled out on that rock," he said.

She grabbed her bag and found her camera gone. Opposite of where 'Donny' stood, one of his friend's stood holding her camera, aimed at her, and clicking a frame every few seconds.

"So you're not just insulting, you're thieves, too? Give it back. It's not a toy." With every click aimed at her, a horrible embarrassing blush crept up the back of her neck, threatening to reveal itself.

"No. But I know a game or two we could play with it."

Great. Assholes. Completely uncharacteristic for the games. She couldn't wait to get hold of Security.

She held out her hand expectantly.

"Toss it, Caleb," Donny called. Without a glance between them, Caleb tossed her camera to her tormentor.

Her temper flared. She pointed to his crotch. "Just because you have a penis, doesn't mean you have to behave like a dick. Give me the camera, now before I complain to Security.

His grin cracked a bit, and something cruel tinged his glare. "You've got a mouth on you, don't ya?"

Still stunned from waking quickly, she suddenly realized how quiet the grove had become. Between her and the bandstand, only a few people milled about. The tarps had been drawn over the bands' booths. The tech stand had been covered, as well. Afternoon break before the evening concert.

Any safety in numbers had dissipated, making her outnumbered, three asinine rabble-rousers to one very irritated freelance writer with a wicked, blinding headache.

She'd never had any trouble with anyone at the games. The predominant theme had always been safety and a sense of family ethics. The people who worked so hard here every year refused to tolerate anyone jeopardizing the integrity of the games or the town that hosted the gathering.

Apparently, these boys hadn't gotten that memo.

"Fine," she said. "Security!" She darted past the two men but tripped on a tree root and stumbled directly into the third man.

"Catch her, Jake."

Catch her, he did. Smaller than the other two, Jake's strength rivaled Donny's, as far as she could tell. Before she could get her mouth open to shout, he had clamped a hand over her face, pinching her mouth and nose, making it impossible to breathe, much less scream. She struggled against him, elbowing him, trying to break his hold.

"Let her go," an unfamiliar voice said.

She couldn't see who had spoken. She did see her camera fall to the ground as she stared through Jake's fingers. As quickly as he had grabbed her, he released her. She gasped a deep breath and elbowed him again, hard in the ribs, then looked up just in time to see Donny fall to his knees.

Charcoal and tobacco overwhelmed her, and she wretched. Almost immediately however, the air dampened with ambergris and sassafras and something she couldn't identify.

Behind Donny stood the man who had watched her earlier. The man in black. He held his arm firmly wrapped around Donny's neck. Caleb shuffled uneasily where he stood. "Hey man, be cool. We...Donny didn't mean anything. We was just teasin' her, you know. Just good fun. That's all."

The man in black apparently didn't agree since he still gripped Donny threateningly.

She scrambled to pick up the camera, her bag, and the blanket. All the time her face and neck burned. *How stupid. How utterly stupid!*

She drew her foot back in an attempt to kick her assailant in the crotch.

"Go now," the stranger said.

The simple phrase stopped her before she could strike. Donny, she noted, cringed in anticipation of her foot meeting its mark.

She stared at the man who held him. Behind her, Donny's accomplices scurried. No doubt, they thought the man had meant them, and they were willing to abandon tattoo-boy to his fate with this man.

She understood their wariness. Her rescuer held his free hand against the side of Donny's head. Something dark and dangerous smoldered in the man's eyes.

Something wicked this way comes…

"Thank-thank you. Look, I…I'm alright, really," she stammered. Pins and needles up and down her spine.

Donny looked up at her. Paralyzed with fear. No, more than fear. Abject terror.

"Go," the man repeated. He nodded at his prey. "This one won't bother you again. Grab your stuff and leave, Teagan."

Teagan. How did he know her name?

She opened her mouth to say something else, but no sound came out. She stumbled back, away from them both, unable for a moment to turn away from them. Afraid to turn her back on either man.

She should alert Security. Security would help. Intervene. Everything would be cleared up.

This one won't bother you again.

She met the man's gaze and realized immediately the words echoing in her head had not actually left his lips.

She didn't slow down long enough to find a security officer. She ran as fast as she could toward the exit, along the dirt path through the campground, and to the bus stop. As if by magic, the bus pulled up to the stop as she reached the boarding line. She hastily joined the short queue, found a seat near the back, and slumped into the worn leather seat next to a young kid who ignored her for his electronic game.

Seven hours ago, she had walked into the festival

with a light heart. Now she possessed all the confidence-crumbling fear of a mugging victim.

Why hadn't she found a security guard? Why hadn't she just screamed? Surely, someone would have heard her. After all, she had survived worse situations than three drunk jerks.

The bumpiness of the ride hid the trembling in her limbs. She held both hands tightly wrapped around her bag in an effort to keep her fingers from shattering.

The circuitous return to the parking lot relaxed her enough to stand without fear of collapsing once the bus finally stopped. The police officer ushered people across the two-lane road to the second parking lot. She slowed her steps and started to tell him—what? They were a mile away from a bunch of drunk guys who played "keep-away" with her camera, which was neatly stashed in her bag.

The officer nodded at her and motioned her across. "Can't block traffic, folks."

The mob swept her across the asphalt and onto the adjacent field. She rifled through her bag for her keys. By the time she had reached her car, plump droplets of rain pelted the windshield.

She climbed in, locked the doors, started the ignition, and leaned her head against the steering wheel. Like a tribal cadence, her head throbbed with each beat of her pulse. Only three miles back to the cabin. She would shower, grab a bite, lock herself in her room, and sleep.

Nothing happened. She was safe.

She regretted turning down Susan and Robert's invitation to dinner. She had a good mind to drive back to Charlotte and make up the article from childhood memories. No one would know.

"Now you're just being silly," she said aloud to herself. "There is no reason not to see this through. It was just an isolated event. I am woman. Hear me roar."

Concentrate. She needed to concentrate.

"Acetyl-salicylic-acid. Acetylsalicylic acid."

Chanting the clinical name calmed her. "A-cetyl sali-cyl-ic ac-id. Acetylsalycylic acid…"

Only three miles. Aspirin. And caffeine. And food. And safety.

She stepped on the brake, reached for the gearshift, and lifted her head. Instead of a roar, a scream escaped her throat.

Staring at her, arms folded across his chest, stood the man in black.

Chapter Three

Teagan reached into her bag and grabbed her cell phone. She dialed nine-one-one, and looked up, poised to hit "send", fully prepared to meet his gaze and let him know the cops were on their way.

Gone.

The space in front of her was empty. No man dressed in black. In fact, no one around her at all. She slowly, carefully, set the phone on the adjacent seat, then shifted the rental car into gear. Rain continued to pelt the car, warning her to turn on the wipers, as she maneuvered across the field and onto the highway. She glanced down the remaining rows of cars, expecting to find him hiding, like a wolf among sheep. She found only bumpers and tires.

The vision had been a trick. A shock response, brought on by exhaustion. That must be it. She just needed sleep.

In another two hours, the grove bands would be back on the meadow's field, setting up to play a concert.

More power to them. She had no intention of heading back to the festival tonight. She might not return at all.

The rhythm of the road and the misting rain required all of her attention and concentration to ensure her safe arrival at her aunt's house.

Relief washed over her as she arrived at the comfortable cabin. The events of the day gave her a newfound appreciation for the ordinary luxury of the place with its tidy rooms, sparse, simple furniture, cable, telephone, internet access.

The most enticing element was hot water. And lots of it. According to the bedside clock, she had stood in the shower for forty minutes, washing away the chill, grime, and hysteria of the day.

A strong cup of tea and two peanut-butter and jelly sandwiches calmed the growling beast in her stomach.

The huge wooden, double-seated swing lured her to the front porch while she ate. Elsa and Joe should be back on Sunday. Her Aunt and Uncle had insisted she use their cabin and forego the cost of a motel. Simple pleasures soon erased the confusion and fright of her day. A comfortable place to write. A family who cared. Good jelly. She sighed and allowed herself to relax. Finally.

The sun dipped behind the horizon—ribbons of pink and orange slicing the blue sky as night moved in.

"Beautiful time of day, isn't it?"

Sheer terror gripped her, strangling her scream as the words poured over her. Her heart and body leapt at the sound of the man's voice. That voice had spoken to her earlier today. The man in black from the festival.

She scanned the driveway and the hedge, her eyes, the only part of her moving right now, other than her heart which pounded like a kettle drum.

He stood at the far edge of the yard.

His face creased in amusement.

Three steps separated her from the front door, the safety of a dead bolt, and the phone.

"You'll regret stalking me" she ground out while she calculated her next move.

"I am not stalking you."

"Then, what would you call it?

A strange wariness played across his face. "Protection."

The word barely spoken, he vanished. Again. As if she had imagined it. What in God's name was happening to her?

Then his whisper brushed her ear. "Do you know what those men, those dogs, would have done to you if I had not saved you today?"

Teagan clawed the edge of the swing and struggled not to scream.

The man continued. "And for my effort, all I am offered is animosity? That hardly seems just, now does it?"

Despite the icy terror hardening her muscles, his voice burned at the nape of her neck, trickling like molten silver down her spine, reaching further still. Her cheeks flushed as did other parts of her anatomy.

He was imaginary. Not real.

"I am hallucinating," she muttered out loud. "Just like earlier today. You're just my brain's way of dealing with stress." Even she didn't believe the blather she was spouting.

"And yet, I am real. Tangible even." As if to demonstrate, he traced his lips along the lobe of her ear as his left hand snaked its way down her shoulder.

Teagan lunged, diving across the threshold in two steps, and slammed the door behind her. She turned the dead bolt, then raced to the back door.

Still locked. Good.

She grabbed up the house phone sitting on the side table next to the fireplace and dialed nine-one-one.

Completely unlike every scary movie she'd ever seen, she was not about to sit idly by, whimpering while some maniac stalked her.

"Nine-one-one. What is your emergency?"

"I have a stalker on the premises. An intruder."

"Where are you now?"

"I'm inside the house."

"Is the intruder inside the building?"

Teagan heard the tremble in her own voice. "No. I've locked the doors. But he's out there. He spoke to me."

"Spoke to you? Did he threaten you?"

"What? Yes! Of course, he threatened me. This is private property. He doesn't belong here."

"What did he say to you?"

"He said, 'I'm not stalking you.' Listen, what does it matter? I need police out here now."

The unwelcome pause that followed unnerved her more, driving her voice a note higher. "I'm here by myself. My aunt and uncle are out of town, and I do not have a proper weapon to protect myself with. There is someone outside this house! He wouldn't identify himself."

"What number are you calling from?"

"What?"

"Can you repeat the phone number where you are?"

"What the—are you kidding?" Teagan held the phone far enough away from her to read the number and repeat it back to the operator.

"We have a unit enroute to you now."

"Can I stay on the line? Can I just keep you on the phone until they get here?"

The operator's voice softened a bit. "Yes ma'am. I will stay on the phone until they arrive. Are you away from the windows?"

"I—yeah. I'm…" She moved into the laundry room, adjacent to the kitchen, a completely windowless room, smack dab in the center of the cabin. "I'm as far away from the doors and windows as I can be. I'm in the laundry room. With the door closed."

Minutes slugged by while she waited, standing in the center of the laundry room, listening for anything threatening, like glass shattering. Or footsteps.

Eventually, the operator said, "Ma'am, the officers are on the property. They've checked the perimeter and are at the front door. Can you go let them in?"

"What if it's not them?"

"Ma'am, I have the officer on the other line. It is safe for you to go to the front door and let him in."

Teagan swallowed the lemon-sized lump in her throat and did as the operator instructed. Two officers stood outside on the porch. One man, tall and lanky, the second a woman, not much older than Teagan, and considerably shorter.

The two stepped through the front door, and Teagan closed it quickly, as if to shut out anything or anyone that might be lingering outside.

"Ma'am, you called about a disturbance? An intruder?"

"Yes. There was a man outside there, in the front yard."

The male officer frowned at her. "And did you know the man?"

"Know him? Of course not. I don't even live here."

Two sets of eyebrows shot up, questioningly.

"Ma'am, whose house is this?" This time the woman spoke. She had one hand on her hip, precariously close to the holster at her side.

"It belongs to my aunt and uncle. They are out of town until tomorrow. I'm housesitting, and—"

"We need to see some identification, please."

Great. They think I'm the culprit. Deciding discretion was the better way to not end up in handcuffs, she retrieved her bag from the sofa, and presented the woman with a valid Commonwealth of Kentucky driver's license.

"And who did you say the house belongs to?"

"Elsa and Joe Miller. Uncle Joe was my father's brother. They're on a cruise and won't be back until tomorrow night. I'm housesitting. I came up for the Highland Games."

"Uh-huh," the guy, whose name tag read, R. Corrig, replied. "How do you know the person you saw isn't a neighbor?"

She didn't. Well, she knew he wasn't, but had no proof. "I saw him at the festival this afternoon."

The other officer, M. Ritter, said, "Not surprising. It's a pretty big event around here. Most of the townsfolk get involved in some way."

"But this is different," Teagan insisted.

Officer Corrig stared over the rims of his sunglasses at her. "How so?"

"He didn't look like he was involved. He just—"

"Just what?"

"He just—I think he followed me."

"Did you invite him back here?" Corrig addressed

his question with a wink. Teagan scowled.

Both police officers ping-ponged questions off her.

"Can you describe him?"

"Did he say anything to you?"

"Yes," she interjected. "He said he wasn't stalking me."

"Then what was he doing?"

She faltered. "Umm—He said he was here for protection. He came up onto the porch."

The male officer hooked his thumbs in his pockets and rocked back on his heels. "Protection. Ma'am? That doesn't quite sound like a stalker or an intruder. I suspect one of your neighbors is just trying to watch out for you." He paused and cast a scathing look in her direction. "Ya know, we know one of our own, when we see one."

"I'm telling you, he does not belong here! You don't understand. He's not one of my neighbors. Don't you think my aunt and uncle would have told me if they had someone checking up on me?"

"Well, we searched the grounds when we drove up. We'll check again. From what we can tell, so far, no crime has been committed."

Officer Ritter relaxed a bit. "If you're nervous about being here alone, why don't you stay at a hotel?"

Corrig shook his head. "Not likely, now. Every room between here and Charlotte is taken. Everybody's all booked up. Your aunt and uncle probably didn't want you to know they were checking up on you. But that's just how people are around here. It's nothing to be ashamed of. You did the right thing to call us. But everything looks good. There were no stray cars parked along the road when we drove up. I think your prowler is just a good Samaritan, making sure you're okay."

Officer Corrig double checked the upstairs rooms. As he descended, he stopped and pointed to the clock on the wall. "It's late. If you're going to the festival tomorrow, you'll be needin' some sleep."

Not likely.

The two officers lingered a few minutes more on the porch, then in their patrol car—probably laughing at her. Finally, they drove away.

Teagan, despite her best efforts, found herself standing in the battened-down cabin on a Saturday night, doors bolted, sweltering in ninety-degree weather. Alone. Shaken. Feeling every bit the *femme fatale* victim from a backwoods camp horror film.

Dusk had long since turned to boondocks-dark nighttime. She opted for air conditioning over cross breeze. She could write a check for the electric cost, if either Elsa or Joe complained.

Exhausted, yet too nervous to venture upstairs, she collapsed on the sofa and found the remote control for the television. British comedy won out over thriller on cable, and she pulled the throw blanket over her as she relaxed against the leather cushions. Her eyelids grew heavy.

"I've always known you were intuitive," her father said from where he sat stretched out on the opposite end of the couch.

Teagan cast him a glance from the corner of her eye. "Excuse me?"

He didn't even open his eyes. His hands were casually draped across his chest. He looked as if he was taking a nap. "I've always known you were intuitive. That you were special."

Teagan bristled at his matter-of-fact admission. "Well, why didn't you tell me?"

"Agh—now think about that. You know your mother. What do you think she'd do if she heard me say something like that? Remember the fit she had when I brought back the souvenir from Salem?"

Teagan bristled again and snorted. "Mom just knew that Beelzebub would come traipsing in with a pitchfork, followed by the neighborhood biddies, to ostracize us for the three- dollar necklace you picked up in a museum gift shop. Silly woman."

"Nah. Well, maybe. She was just scared, that's all, hon."

"Dad?"

"Yeah?"

"What do you mean, 'special'?"

One eye slid open just a hair, and he smiled over the rim of his glasses at her. "You used to say all the time, 'I've had this dream.' Or you'd tell us who was calling when the phone rang, before we would pick up. And of course, there was Juliet."

"Oh, I miss her." The beautiful Siamese had been her first cat as a child. "Remember how she use to sit on the chair and nibble on your ears?"

"Beware of creatures who nibble on your ears. You know, after that cat died, when you would say you saw her on the ledge outside the front door, your mother called it your imagination, playing tricks on you."

"I remember. But it wasn't my imagination. She was there. I could see her and hear her."

Her father reached a long, slender arm out and patted her hand. "So could I. It wasn't your imagination tonight, either."

26

At his touch Teagan flinched and snapped into a sit, blinking, furiously against the light. She kicked off the blanket and looked at the far end of the sofa.

Empty.

No ghosts. Father, or cat.

Her hand still tingled from his touch, though.

The air conditioner powered down, as she turned off the television. She listened to the silence for a moment. No sounds of impending doom. No scary music. No creaking floorboards. Only the yawn that escaped her as she sat there rubbing her hand.

The clock chimed from its corner near the back door, as Teagan stretched and stood up. So old, the cuckoo didn't even come out to sing, it just clanged out the hours. Even that sounded broken. Each strum echoed short, followed by a tick as if the striking mechanism needed oiling. Strange that her uncle hadn't seen to that. And it forgot to stop at twelve, striking twice more, after it met the midnight toll.

Teagan tromped upstairs to the guest room and collapsed, face down into the feather softness of the mattress topper. Hell, if the intruder were stupid enough to return, she'd just sic her mother's ghost on him.

"That'd teach him. That woman could lecture the spots off a leopard."

Her mother had once talked a gator out from under the canoe they were sitting in and clear out of the swamp.

Maniacal, over-protective, stalking neighbors wouldn't stand a chance.

Chapter Four

How long has the clock been chiming?
As if it heard her thoughts, the tinny drone of the hammer stopped. Teagan opened one eye tentatively and looked at the red digital numbers glowing from the clock on the nightstand.

"Damn. Eight o'clock." She had less than an hour to make it to the field for the parade of massed bands. Twenty-eight minutes later, she locked the cabin door behind her and jumped down the steps, paper cup clenched in teeth, bag over shoulder, hands fervently trying to lace the corseted bodice of her outfit.

Ten minutes to the intersection, four up the mountain, seven in the parking lot 3 line, gave her—eleven minutes to make it through the gate and to the grandstand area to see the opening ceremony.

Bleary-eyed and head pounding from lack of sleep and an adrenaline overload, she managed to beat even her own estimate. As if time had stood still for her, she settled down in front of the Chieftains' tent just as the bands were assembling.

Music wafted from every direction. Pipers were already competing on the end of the field closest to where she had parked. In the grove behind her she could hear someone tuning a guitar. From the far end of the field, the recorded music the dancers used whined gently from stereo speakers. When she concentrated, she could even hear the lilt of harps' strings from a demonstration tent outside the gates in the vendors' lane.

Sunshine would have been great for the photos she wanted to take, but the mountain had other plans. Today was drier than yesterday, but no brighter. Dark clouds rolled gently overhead, threatening rain. After all, what would a Scottish festival be without a bit of fog and rain? Ambience was everything.

She popped a couple of aspirin into her mouth, washed it down with the water still in her bag from yesterday, closed her eyes and exhaled. Yesterday and its horror had faded to the level of a nightmare, tempered by the deep sleep she had managed in the early hours.

Opening ceremonies commenced with speakers, introductions, applause, recognition of special guests, obligatory anthems, and welcoming prayers.

She breathed deeply and focused on banishing the headache and yesterday's bad memories. The drum cadence called her back to the present moment.

Snare and bass drum battled, setting the beat for the performers. Excitement crackled through the crowd as the first troop stepped onto the gravel of the track. The drum major floated along the path, wielding the seven-foot-long baton effortlessly. Spats and hat, and kilted magnificence heralded the rank and file of a pipe and drum corps. Then, at his command, the pipers, in unison, sounded the wail of the bagpipes.

The first note always unnerved her. At its best, the bagpipe could wake the dead, its soulful song floating on the wind, across distance and time, the sound hovering like a whispered memory long after the piper had finished. At its worst, the bagpipe sounded like a couple of snarling cats being strangled. From a distance, it appeared that way, too—the dark pipes extending out behind the piper as he pumped the air from the bag, like paws, beneath his elbow.

Here, though, there were no furious felines. Only the synchronous sound of celebration as the bands strode uniformly in time with the drummers.

She watched as the procession grew longer and longer, weaving slowly around the track toward the far side of the field. Overhead, clouds swirled in complement, as if dancing to the music. Fog rolled down from the mountain, unfurling itself like a half-time show flag across the field, blanketing it in mist. Nature's special effects, ordered just for this performance.

The mist enveloped the bands, holding them captive from their audience. The music paused. One soulful pipe wailed a familiar strain, and the usually hushed crowd began to cheer, as more than a hundred invisible compatriots picked up the melody of 'The Gael'. As the sound swelled, a movement glimmered in the fog.

A ghost in the highlands could be no more wrenching than the apparition of the drum major emerging from the mist, flanked by another, and another. On either side, like the spirits of souls long gone, the massed bands glided through the alabaster water molecules that cloaked them.

Whoever had managed to pull this off deserved an award. She would surely capture her editor's approval if she could capture this moment for her article. Teagan lifted her camera and aimed her lens to capture the shot.

The music stopped.

The marching stopped.

Everything stopped.

She lowered her camera and stared at the field. The bands were still there, pipers and drummers poised in mid step. To her right and left, the audience sat frozen, as well. Some in mid-clap, others perched in excited poses, one man half out of his chair as if he were attempting to stand.

Motionless. Silent.

Dreaming.

Even the molecules of water vapor had ceased their movement. The mist draped over the arm of the drum major, as if caressing his sleeve.

Teagan closed her eyes. "Wake up, now. You're missing it. Wake up." She slowly peeked.

All remained still.

Except for her. She scrambled to her feet and scanned the festival field and hill. Not one person moved. No bird chirped. No leaf rustled.

Yet *she* moved.

Sweat beaded her forehead. Her legs trembled at the sight of everything, of everyone…paused. She climbed up to the walking path. The crowd stood thick near the grandstand. Inside the Patrons' tent, a familiar face poured soda into cups for ribbon-bearing patrons. Only the soda didn't flow in this instant.

This is a dream.

Panic poked at her. *Wake up.*

"Hey," she called. "Somebody. Hello? Can anybody hear me?"

Not even a whisper of a breeze.

Across the path a young boy hovered—

weightlessly—waiting to fall to the ground. French fries, spilling from the paper carton he held, hung, waiting to continue their surge toward the ground.

Time suspended.

Panic prodded her again. The beads of sweat rolled down her cheek and neck. *Rolled. So, I'm not suspended.*

"Did you rest well?"

She whirled around and nearly knocked over an old man in military attire standing motionless.

Not ten feet from where she stood, she saw *him*. The man who had followed her yesterday. He sat on a picnic table, legs swinging casually. Moving. Not still like the rest of them.

This was no dream. It was a nightmare.

The stranger sat, arms back, supporting his body, while he rocked his legs, to and fro gently. His eyes, as sparkling as they had been yesterday, held no menace now. He wore the same outfit she remembered from yesterday.

Sweat. Panic. Hallucinations of dark men in renaissance garb adorning picnic tables.

She laughed despite her hysteria.

"Did you have sweet dreams? Or better yet, passionate ones?" His question hung in the air between them.

She couldn't even move her mouth to form the words, much less scream for help. All she could do was laugh at the inane sense of his casual question. As if they were having tea.

She couldn't find her voice, but she found the power to run. She turned and sprinted toward the slope where her car sat.

Halfway down the bend, something hard slammed her from behind, knocking the air from her lungs, pulling her backwards against a hard wall. Gasping and coughing, she fought to move forward. The pressure against her abdomen deepened, as she was drawn up against the barrier behind her.

Her body vibrated and jolted as if the wall were electrically charged. No burning, no pain, no scent of char, just the current passing through her. Then, it whispered, "I do like a good chase. However, we need to talk."

Not a wall. *A person.* And she knew that voice. The stranger had seized her around the waist and pulled her up short, holding her so her feet barely touched the ground. She clawed, kicked, and tried to catch enough air to scream—unsuccessfully.

In the stillness, his breath was warm against her ear, as was his grip around her torso. She hadn't realized how cold the panic had made her. Sweat still streamed down her neck, but she shivered against the warmth of her captor.

Ambergris and sassafras.

"Let me go," she managed to get out.

"Calm down. We haven't much…time. They know one when they see one."

The words, spoken gently did nothing to achieve that effect. She did not calm down, If anything, his voice panicked her more. She stopped clawing at him and tried to steady her breathing enough to make him release her.

The lightning charged air crackled.

She remembered the tattooed man from yesterday. The look in his eyes as he knelt, the dark man's hand firmly gripping his nape. She suddenly knew what he must have felt.

Her pulse thudded in her ears, like the droning of the bass drum. Her whole body vibrated so intensely she nearly fainted. Part of her hoped she would to escape the panic that threatened to consume her.

As if he realized her fear, the man released her, and she fell in a heap to the dirt. Her waterlogged arms and legs were no good for running or fighting. She was sopped with immobility. "What the hell—"

"Not quite. Somewhere in between, perhaps."

Hold onto whatever sanity you've still got. "Who are you and what do you want?"

From where she landed, the only thing she could see was the black boots, streaked with dust, that covered long, darkly clad legs. She craned her neck, deliberately not letting her glance stray anywhere. She met his stare with one she intended to make just as intimidating.

A smooth, serious jaw, finely etched cheeks, and dark lashes masked the ebony pupils that watched her intently. A facetious smile tugged at his mouth. "I told you yesterday. My purpose is protection. You chose not to believe me."

Stupid-assed nightmares.

Teagan lifted one rather numb hand and waved it at the statues surrounding them. "And this is all to allay my fears. Nice work."

"As I said, we don't have much time. I warned you yesterday. You need to get away from here. Now."

"What are you talking about? I just got here. Wave your wand, or whatever, and make this all normal again, or make me wake up, or something. I have an article to write."

"I assure you, if you do not do exactly as I tell you, that article may be the last thing you do in this lifetime."

"Once again, not endearing yourself to me. If this weren't a dream, I would so beat the daylights out of you. I would kick you so hard, you would never have to worry about Father's Day."

His eyes sparkled with ice or crystal, as if the irises were trimmed in silver. Silver and crystal with a dark coal center. A dare shone through, as well. He could make her regret her threat. Whatever it had been. Her words dissolved into the air.

"The men you ran into yesterday—"

"The ones you took care of? Are they dead now? Am I next?"

He didn't answer her question. "They were the first ones. There will be more. They know you have the clock, and that you are alive. Greed and revenge are very strong motives."

"Motives? For what?"

He pulled her to her feet. The air crackled, like it had the first time he touched her. She pulled away from him. "Motives-for-what?" she repeated.

"Motives for killing you."

"And you intend to kill me, too?" Teagan started to argue, then stopped. She looked at the ground, lifted her hand, and slapped herself instead. Hard. So hard, in fact, that her teeth rattled. Surely, that should have snapped—or slapped her out of this dream. Only, when she looked up again, he still stared back.

He cocked an eyebrow at her inquisitively.

"I need to wake up. Wake up. Wake up, now!"

He nodded, his features pinching to a sobering grimace. "Teagan, I am no dream." He motioned to those around them. "This is not a dream. Touch the people. Taste a french fry. This is real. Now, listen carefully to me."

"Why?"

"I told you. So you can survive."

An agitated edge crept into his words. His voice no longer sounded self-assured and calm. "There is a woman in the Donald tent holding a pair of binoculars which will be aimed at you, momentarily. When she spies you, she will make a phone call. By the time you get home, the clock will be gone. And with it, your future."

"See, I knew I was dreaming. The clock. I'm oversleeping." She raised her arm to slap herself again.

His hand curved around her wrist, sending a current through her arm and down her spine. "Get into your car before she spies you. Drive to the cabin as quickly as you can. Keep this with you at all times." He folded something hard and cold into her hand. "If you become separated from the cuckoo clock, at least you'll have this. Without the key, they cannot use it against you."

Teagan looked at the small metal key he'd placed against her palm. "What's this for?"

"It winds the clock. I took it last night. As I said, keep it with you at all costs. They cannot do anything without that key."

"You did what? How did you? Who can't do anything? Elsa and Joe? It's their clock—"

"Not your aunt and uncle. The others."

"What others? What woman with the binoculars?"

"Not here. Not now. Tick Tock. Get the clock. Get away from here. Drive to Charlotte as quickly as you can and get away. Don't go home. They will be waiting in Paducah, too."

"Who are 'they'?"

"The time keepers refer to them as custodians."

"Nonsense. Completely. And what do these custodians do, exactly? And who are the 'time keepers'?"

"They make sure that people leave when it is their time. Only you did not."

"Because I'm here for the weekend—"

"No, Teagan Alexander. You did not die. I saw to that."

The air wavered around her, as if the tension had grown too fierce, and the fabric was about to pull away from this dream.

"Of course, you did. And you are—?"

"A Realm Walker. I stole your death. Now go."

Light flashed. Cacophony blared in her ears. Music, voices, the sound of the air rushing in and out of people's lungs bellowed in her ears, pounding as loudly as her own pulse had earlier.

The french fries landed in the grass, as did the boy who had carried them. Teagan could hear him howl in pain as he yelled for his mom.

And the master of this circus? The realm walker? Gone, of course.

She looked over her shoulder toward the edge of the field where the Donald tent should be. Several women and a couple of men stood just outside the shadowed edge, watching the bands. One woman, wearing a red hat to match her red tartan jumper, shuffled through her shoulder bag and came up, hand held high, brandishing a set of binoculars.

Binoculars.

The woman aimed her focus on the field, watching the bands with a keen, vision-enhanced interest. After a moment, however, she turned her attention away from the field, and began to scan the grandstand area.

Searching for someone.

Teagan made a beeline for the hill. She made it to her car in less time than she had spent walking across the hill that morning. Before that woman could even guess that she was not in the stands, Teagan intended to be halfway to her aunt and uncle's cabin.

With any luck, when she got there, she'd find herself still alseep in the upstairs bedroom.

Next to a cuckoo clock chiming incessantly: End this nightmare.

Chapter Five

Darius tightened his hold on Caleb and asked once more, "How many more did she send?"

"I don't know the answer to that one," the young man answered. His bloodshot eyes turned and peered through the realm walker, as if he had cast himself invisible, which he had not.

"Do you know what happened to your friend, Donny, when he and I finished this game?"

Caleb twitched involuntarily at the mention of Donny's name. Pleased that he had at least some effect on the man, Darius lowered his voice to a whisper. "Whatever you were promised, I doubt very much you will survive their wrath once they realize you have failed. And they will realize it if you stay here. If you tell me what I wish to know, I might let you escape before they begin to look for you."

The putrid scent of urine filled the air. The boy had pissed himself.

"Shit," Caleb muttered.

"That's next."

"I-I don' know how many they sent. She-she just told Donny to get the woman. Said somebody else would worry about the rest. Dang it. I'm not in this, okay? Look, Jake and me was just out for some fun. That other lady said she'd pay us to do it. I don't know what Donny's deal was, but we just wanted our money.

Th-th-that's all."

Darius brushed his free hand across Caleb's eyes. Bourbon-soaked breaths rasped past dried cracked lips, and the young man's body relaxed into slumber. The half empty bottle of Jack Daniels on the passenger's seat didn't bode well for Caleb's early exit. With any luck, he'd be caught by the cops before any of the others found him.

Darius stepped away from the car. One selfish act of heroism, back to bite him on the ass, at the expense of a woman who hadn't asked for his help to begin with.

For now, he had hoped this morning's manipulation would enable Teagan to get to the clock before Zahra's people. If he hadn't gotten involved in the first place, neither one of them would be in trouble.

His mouth soured. Bitter. Metallic. Regret.

Too much energy surged through his body. His muscles spasmed from the constant impulse of static.

He hitched a ride back up the mountain, and made for the vendor's booth, arriving just as the woman with the red hat sauntered past.

"Oh, this is lovely," she said, pointing to an ornament of hammered silver with an inset of amber and tourmaline. "It's very unusual. How much?"

The girl behind the counter quoted a price which elicited raised eyebrows and a quirk of a smile.

"Allie, allow me to help her," Darius said to the girl who'd been manning the counter. "Unfortunately, that one is no longer for sale," he said to the woman and to his clerk. "Sorry, someone offered on it first thing this morning. I just forgot to remove it from the case. The buyer said he'd be back this afternoon to pick it up."

The woman in the red hat turned her attention to him. "Darius, don't you dare lie to me. I might just die if I don't have that ornament. I have the perfect place to put it."

He nodded to her as he removed the ornament from its perch.

"We'd hate to risk that, now wouldn't we?"

Lavender eyes sparkled at him, teasing him from behind tinted shades. Porcelain skin and a smile as sweet as honey. A winning combination for a southern woman. Deadly for any man not wary enough to avoid her.

"How about I promise to make one and ship it to you. A custom design. I'm sure I could have it finished long before the holidays."

"Oh, don't be silly. I'm sure it's just an impulse buy. Anyway, I'm looking for something a bit more practical. A clock, perhaps. You don't happen to have anything like that back there, do you, Darius?"

"Afraid I don't have a clue about clocks, Zahra. Perhaps over in Ashville you could find one." He pulled a watch from his pocket. Unless you're just interested in the time right now—"

Zahra drummed her fingers along the glass display case. Allie, confused and eager to make a sale, found another customer to help.

"Hmm—almost noon. Time flies, doesn't it?"

"And yet, sometimes the day just seems to drag so," she drawled, facetiously. "This morning, for example, time seemed to stand still. Didn't you think so?"

"I've been so busy I haven't stopped once. Haven't

even gone around the tents this morning. How is the rest of the old crowd?"

She cocked an eyebrow at him. "You haven't run into any of them this trip, then?"

Darius neither confirmed nor denied the question.

She leaned over the counter, to whisper conspiratorially, "Well, Averal is a bit excited to have a reason to be out and about. He prefers the North Carolina weather to the European climate. I suspect the others are just bored. Another day, another problem to be solved."

"A problem? What problems would Averal or any of us have?"

Zahra's eyes narrowed, slightly. "Face it, Darius. You lead a charmed life." She waved a hand at the metalwork. "Your work is your play. The world, your stage. Always an encore. Always another show." The undercurrent of her words ripped as sharp as if she had spit venom at him.

The scent of almonds drifted in the air. Her perfume? Or arsenic? Darius grinned at her. "Always another villain to foil. Everybody likes a happy ending, eh?"

Her lips pursed in mocking rebuke. "And yet tragedy is what Shakespeare is most noted for. After all, everyone knows Macbeth, Hamlet, Romeo and Juliet."

"Death and destruction. No happy endings there."

One nail slowly rapped against the glass, like water droplets crashing against a metal roof. "Precisely, Darius. No happy ending. Remember that. You started it. One of our own. And we will finish it. There will be no happy ending. For either of you."

****

Tobacco. Definitely pipe tobacco.

Someone had been here, in the cabin. Smoking a pipe. Recently. The odor was vaguely familiar.

She didn't smoke.

Was the intruder still here?

Teagan tiptoed through the lower level of the cabin, listening for any foreign sounds indicative of an unwelcome guest. Silly nonsense. Anyone in the house would have heard her unlocking the door.

Or should have heard her gag from the heady aroma that filled the den. The house creaked, and she jumped.

Was that a settling kind of creak, or an "I'm-waiting-at-the-top-of-the-stairs-to-get-you creak?"

Her aunt and uncle seriously needed a burglar alarm.

Too many summer cabin horror movies had taught her exactly where not to go. She sneaked to the back door where the coveted clock hung on the wall. What this had to do with anything, she couldn't imagine. Still, if the groaning boards upstairs were warning of an axe murderer or robber, she figured she should at least save the family heirloom.

Please let it be simple. Please make me invisible.

She gently wrapped her fingers around the pendulum and chimes, and inserted her index finger between the two elements so that no metal would clang. Her other hand delicately lifted the ancient frame from its nail on the wall.

Simple. Now for invisibility. She tucked the whole frame beneath the arm that held the chimes as she tried to unlock the back door. If she could make it out the back and down the deck, she wouldn't have to risk stumbling over her own feet inside the cabin and alerting the uninvited houseguest.

As if she'd said the words out loud, the floorboards overhead creaked again.

Someone moved across the floor.

She rotated the doorknob and sucked in a breath that echoed the sound of the air being moved as the door broke away from the rubber seal of the jamb. She fled down the back steps, not caring now if the pipe-smoking, axe-wielding boogie-man could hear her as she made her escape. She rounded the corner of the house, spied the rental car, and ran. Thirty hard steps and she slid inside, pounding the lock mechanism.

Divine intervention might have kept her from taking the key from beneath the planter on the porch and putting it with her car keys. Divine intervention definitely kept the robber upstairs. Of course, the robber probably thought finding the key and letting himself into the house qualified as some kind of advantage as well.

She turned the key without worrying about the sound now. Let them hear her spinning gravel. There were no cars for her to identify, but that didn't mean they didn't have one waiting half a mile down the road.

Movement behind the kitchen curtain caught her eye as she shifted into drive and floored the gas pedal.

Sure enough, as she fishtailed out onto the road, a man who looked a lot like Officer Corrig in regular clothes, stepped onto the porch, a pipe clutched in his mouth.

No axe. Just a cell phone to his ear.

Teagan rubbed her hand across the rough wood of the clock.

...didn't give him the time of day—
Fear always made her silly.
...just stole the clock and ran away.
Nerves always made her rhyme.

Crook or cop, her uncle and aunt could thank her later.

Damn. Elsa and Joe were due back tonight.

Okay. She would meet them in Charlotte. They'd have to make a connection there to get to Asheville. She could get a message to them, and they could meet her at a hotel.

Cop. Bad guy. Cell phone. Burglary. Well, she should have figured that one out last night. She'd be lucky if she could make it to the next town, much less the county line.

First stop, rental car agency.

Second stop, Charlotte Airport.

One woman with a laptop, a corset, and a cuckoo clock.

Too bad she didn't write fiction.

****

"I'll e-mail it to you in a couple of days, Miriam. Yeah, I know. No, but they need me to sign a lot of papers. I'll let you know. 'kay. Thanks. Bye.

She had just lied to her editor. This did not bode well for job security. Especially once Miriam got a call from the North Carolina state police.

Fiction aptly described her soon-to-be employment status.

The rental car agency had believed her story about the vapor lock problem and had replaced the car. Instead of a green Impala, which Officer Corrig no doubt had every cop looking for, right now, she cruised through Boone in a silver Camry.

With any luck, she would be in Charlotte in two hours and could figure out where to go from there.

Why would anyone want a clock that held no value other than sentimental? And why would anyone be looking for her? Especially in Paducah, Kentucky. She needed to get clothes, papers, and addresses.

No. Crazy hallucination or not, the man at the festival had been right about the cabin. She had no desire to test his theory about Paducah, too. At least not until she could get a bit of information about who might be after her, and why.

She dropped the car off at the airport rental return, grabbed her laptop and clock, and rode the courtesy van to the terminal. She had taken off the corset which made it easier to breathe and made her a little less conspicuous. On the mountain, a woman with a corseted bodice draped in plaid might not be out of place, but in the bustling international airport, she needed to look a bit less like a walking commercial for Rob Roy.

The laptop fit well enough in her shoulder bag, while the corset and tartan cloth now protected the clock, as she slid it into the shopping bag she salvaged from the rental car agency in Boone.

A check for her uncle and aunt's flight status revealed that they had not made their flight out of Tampa. In fact, the flight had departed half empty. The weather channel confirmed her suspicions. A tropical storm watch had delayed the ship's return to Florida.

At least they wouldn't be walking into a crime scene tonight. As soon as they docked, they would get her message about the burglary. She would explain about the clock later and they'd have a big laugh over the whole insane tale. Hopefully.

Right now, though, she needed to get out of town, so to speak.

Why not Paducah? Who in their right mind would head there? A small town, with little to offer espionage hunters or conspiracy theorists. That's what made it the perfect town to belong to.

Just like R. Corrig.

Humph.

She traipsed over to Southwest and scanned the screen for the next flight to Nashville. Six thirty tonight. Two hours. Perfect. Even better if she could avoid using her credit card or exchanging her ticket. Less of a trail.

Sheesh. Now, I sound like a crook from an espionage book.

There. Rhyming again. She had to get hold of herself. Caffeine. Caffeine always calmed her down.

She found the teller machine and withdrew as much cash as the bank allowed in one day, then headed back toward the ticket counter. Damn. She'd have to use her phone to buy the ticket. Airlines did not do cash.

Her skin prickled. Danger. Something's not right. No. *Someone's* not right.

The woman behind the counter hadn't been there a moment ago. The rigidity of the woman's posture, the deliberateness of her movements made the hair on Teagen's neck stand. Why was she so familiar?

Teagan's stomach roiled. *Always trust your gut.* At least, that had been her grandmother's advice. She looked at the line, and carefully averted her glance from the agent. From the corner of her eye, though, she glimpsed the woman looking up, following her progress as she moved toward the queue agent.

The curbside doors opened, and a sea of teenagers barreled into the terminal, nearly toppling Teagan as they swarmed into the air-conditioning, cases and duffel bags, and exuberance—all loud calls, and laughter. Bright orange jerseys branded them high school band students, headed straight for the group check-in at the ticket counter.

Breaking through the tangerine force field, Teagan used their diversion to disappear into the crowd.

The burning spot at the base of her skull told her that the woman stared after her, hoping to penetrate the legion of teens who had just saved her.

Nashville was no longer an option. No luggage. No clothes. No idea where to go.

She needed time to think, and time to sort out what the past twenty-four hours meant. How to do that? Disappear.

Where's Waldo? That's it. In order to become invisible, she needed to disappear in a crowd.

A skycap nodded at her, appreciatively, and she remembered her attire. White flounce and a jeweled metal belt on a blond was not definitely an invisibility cloak. First things first. She turned the corner and headed for the security check point, intent on getting through and to the shops.

Damn. No boarding pass.

Teagan had her eye on the security detail up ahead when she heard the clang. A custodial worker, rolling a trashcan with a mop and a broom, collided with her, tipping the bucket and its contents to the floor, along with her. One clumsy blonde, dressed-oh-so-conspicuously in white.

"Oh, ma'am. I am so sorry." The apology drawled effortlessly from the elderly worker, pressed and cuffed in his uniform as he righted himself and his equipment. "It just got away from me."

"It's okay. It was an accident—"

The elderly man's hands trembled slightly as he bent to retrieve her from the floor. "Watch yourself, ma'am. Here, let me help you up."

She grabbed at the shopping bag as she righted herself. He scooped scattered items up from the sprawl. "Here you go, ma'am. Don't forget this-—"

She turned to him, and he winked at her, pushing an envelope into her hand.

"I don't think that's mine."

"Oh? I saw you drop it. I'm sure. Don' mind me. I'll get this. Just slow reflexes, I guess."

She stared at the envelope, then at the man who winked at her again before he scooped up the mop and broom, remembered the bucket, and said, "You have a good day, now. Be careful, y' hear?"

An electronic ticket itinerary peeked from beneath the flap of the envelope.

She pulled the paper out just enough to spy her name on the top. Air Canada flight 451, six-eighteen departure.

Teagan slid the boarding card back into the envelope. Only a few steps separated her from the old man, who had his back to her now. She caught up to him.

"Excuse me, sir," she said as she tapped him on the shoulder.

The hunched figure straightened and turned.

Not the old man who had just handed her the ticket. In his stead stood a much younger man in his forties, with a dark shadow of a beard, and hard creases around his eyes.

"Yeah? Whatcha need?"

Teagan crammed the envelope into her pocket. "I-um-I'm sorry, I thought you were someone else. Did you see the other custodian?"

The man stared blankly at her. "I don't know what you're talking about, ma'am."

Of course, he didn't. "Could you...do you know which way Air Canada is?"

He squinted at her for a moment, then scrunched his nose as if he had sniffed something unpleasant. He pointed toward the directional signs. "Follow the signs. Air Canada checks in around the corner. That way."

Heat flushed her neck and face. "Thank you. Have a good day."

Teagan had never been lost in an airport in her life. What else could she say when he turned out not to be the man who had handed her the envelope.

I can't just get on an airplane and go to Canada.

Actually, she could. Whoever had bought the ticket had to have known she always carried a toothbrush and her passport with her. Didn't everybody? *Not.*

Teagan's grandfather had told her parents, "By the time she's two, she'll be able to book a reservation and cart her own luggage." He'd been right. Growing up with a parent in the business had taught her how to navigate the world, if not her own neighborhood.

The aroma of cinnamon and vanilla stoked her hunger, and she paused at the food court. She hadn't eaten all day.

All fear and no food makes Teagan cranky.

With one cinnamon roll and an order of to-go buffalo bites crammed in her shopping bag, she made a quick stop in a couple of the shops. A gray pullover and sage green shawl from one boutique, a pair of Bermuda shorts and sunglasses from another, and one last stop to buy a crossword puzzle book for the flight had Teagan dashing to the international concourse.

Since the band incident at the counter, she had neither seen, nor sensed anyone watching her. Crowds and strangers had never been a problem.

Yesterday and today, however, familiarity seemed to breed something contemptuous. Certainly, that the ticket counter agent would figure out where she was. She listened to the preliminary boarding call for her flight, then slipped into the restroom, and changed into the black shorts and pullover, twisted her hair into a bun and donned the black glasses before making her way to the boarding door. Just another tourist.

She reluctantly stashed the shopping bag into the overhead compartment, then slid her shoulder bag beneath the seat in front of her and settled in the window seat assigned.

Time to wake up, she reminded herself. So far, it hadn't worked. She grabbed the shawl out of her bag and removed the merchant's tag and wrap. Out of fashion for July in North Carolina, Teagan wanted the extra warmth the wrap could offer once the jet was airborne.

She had just cracked the spine on the crossword book when the flight attendant leaned over.

"Excuse me, are you traveling alone?"

Her hand froze, pen in hand, and she looked from the corner of her eye to see the young woman addressing her.

"Yes," she admitted, warily.

Fruity. The flight attendant kneeling next to her seat had either been handling fruit on the beverage cart, or she preferred citrus-based perfume. Sports. Tennis. No...running. Definitely a runner.

"We have a favor to ask." The woman stood up and motioned to someone toward the back of the passenger cabin, then smiled at Teagan and lowered her voice to a whisper. "We have a seating problem. We have two broken seats in the back and we're trying to seat a family together. Would you mind moving to another seat? I have a seat up front."

As the woman's words poured over Teagan, she could hear people bustling behind her. A baby cried, and people in the row behind her shuffled as a circus of soft-sided tote bags, a car seat, stuffed animal, wailing toddler, and stressed humans stumbled toward her row. "Uh, yeah. Sure. Let me just grab my bag."

"Come up front and let them get the car seat strapped in. I'll bring you the bag once they're settled."

The family surged toward her, scrambling to stash and stow, and secure the child seat as the cabin crew herded her toward the forward cabin.

She scrambled out of her nest, book and pen in one hand, boarding envelope, shoulder bag, and shawl in the other.

Up front meant past the bulkhead, into business class. The flight attendant stopped at row three and motioned her to another window seat.

The aroma of leather, oak and cork assailed her as

she sank into the seat. The flight attendant handed the passenger in the adjacent aisle seat a glass of wine.

Before she could even buckle, the lead flight attendant approached, asking, "Would you care for something to drink before takeoff?"

"Red wine?"

"Merlot or Cabernet Sauvignon?"

"Whichever is open is fine."

Almost instantly a glass with the heady liquid sat on the rest between the seats, a napkin beneath guarding against spills.

"Oh, thank you," she called, but the attendant had disappeared behind the galley curtain.

Teagan settled back, snuggled and buckled in the protection of the seat. The craft rocked gently when the push-back bar connected the plane to the push-back vehicle for departure. Available seats were verified, flight attendants double checked the overhead compartments were secure.

Teagan pushed the button above her seat, hailing the cabin attendant.

"What can I get for you?" he asked.

"I was moved up from the coach cabin, and I left my carryon in the overhead."

"We're ready for push back now, but I can get it for you after we're airborne. Do you remember what seat you were in?"

"13A. It's a large paper shopping bag."

"Thirteen-A. Got it. Don't worry. I'll take care of it."

Someone called him away, and she found herself alone once more.

She juggled recent events in her mind. She sat in

business class with a ticket she didn't pay for, on a flight to Canada. Along the way she had encountered a disappearing courier, a suspicious ticket agent, a burgling cop inside her uncle's house, and a purloined cuckoo clock.

Definitely not an average day, to say the least. This was the plot of a Hitchcock film.

A gentle jolt moved the plane as it began to push backward, away from the gate. Teagan took an indulgent sip of the wine and reached for the puzzle book.

"Just in time," a deep husky voice whispered as dark slacks slid into the aisle seat beside her.

Teagan smiled and nodded politely to the last-minute passenger. The man in black faced her, met her eyes, and returned her smile. She nearly spit wine all over herself. Then the engines roared to life.

Chapter Six

Wine burned Teagan's throat and sinuses. Her eyes watered as she fought against the cough that fluttered in her chest. She looked around, expecting to find that the world had stopped again. Instead, the plane disengaged from the ground crew's equipment, powered up and began to taxi across the tarmac.

She instinctively reached up for the call button.

A masculine hand closed over her wrist and tugged her arm down, locking it beneath his. "Don't bother. I'm fine. I don't need a thing. Besides, they have to secure the cabin and take their own seats."

The acrid taste of the wine mixed with fear, and she tried to get up. The damned seat belt held her firmly in place.

She twisted as far away from him as she could. A hissing sound escaped her lips. "You have no right to—"

"I beg to differ. I have every right to be here. I have a boarding pass that says so." He tapped the boarding pass sticking out of his jacket lapel. "So how do you like your seat?"

"How do I like my—" His eyes glittered playfully at her, and she shivered in spite of the hot July weather.

Though the cabin hadn't yet cooled down, Teagan suddenly needed the shawl, and maybe a blow torch to go with it.

"—gift?"

The pale grey linen jacket accentuated the silver rims of his irises, and the tiny streak of silver that glistened against the black of his hair.

"You bought my ticket to Nova Scotia?"

"I did."

"For a woman you don't even know. What if I hadn't had a passport on me?"

"You always have your passport on you."

Sassafras. He smelled like sassafras.

"How do you know that?'

"I know a great deal about you."

She bristled. "What are you? FBI? Homeland Security? I haven't broken any laws. You can't detain me without having a probable cause."

He had saved her life yesterday, yet here he was today, trying to detain her like a criminal. "Air Marshal?"

"I told you earlier. I am a Realm Walker, and an artisan. That's all. Finish your wine before the flight attendant comes back. Trust me, I won't let you get drunk."

"Trust you? You're not even real. Right now, that flight attendant is probably calling the captain to have the plane turned around so they can have the police cart me out of here for talking to invisible murderers." She craned her neck, searching for the cabin attendant. "Where is your big sword anyway?"

He smirked at her, offering her the glass, as he bent closer to her, and whispered. "Safely stowed away, I assure you. They frown on such long dangerous weapons on display in the passenger cabin."

Teagan's pulse throbbed in her veins. Her throat,

her wrists, her chest all heaved with the weight of each frantic beat. The blood rose beneath her flesh. She had meant the claymore. He, she suspected, had not.

His image floated in front of her, wavering as she stared up at him. The cinnamon roll sat in her bag, not in her belly. And she had just downed a glass of wine on a stomach empty, save for the double scoop of anxiety. Her head involuntarily fell back against the seat, and she struggled to focus.

"I don't understand any of this. I'm supposed to be listening to Celtic music right now. Not on my way to—"

"I know. I'll explain it as best I can. Right now, however, you need to eat. You need food and rest."

"In the bag. I have food, in the bag."

"Good. I'm starving."

He reached down beneath the seat and retrieved the food she had bought. Carefully unwrapping the package, he broke off part of the cinnamon roll.

Transfixed, she could do little more than watch as he pressed the layer of butter and spice-infused pastry between her lips. His fingers brushed her mouth as she warily accepted the offering. Sweet. Sensual. Like hot honey pouring over her.

She closed her eyes against her overactive imagination and let the hallucination consume her.

Ambergris, raw and warm. And once again, sassafras. Everything melded into an elixir of aroma and tastes. She couldn't refuse the second bite he offered her. Drunk. She must be intoxicated to allow this stranger to feed her. And in such an intimate way.

She should move her limbs. Resist. Feed herself. Where had the flight attendant gone? Why weren't they back at the gate yet? Surely, somebody would notice a crazy woman, talking to no one.

She swallowed another bite. What a decadent dream this had turned into. Electricity surged through her as it had this morning. Was it only this morning? She trembled involuntarily. This time the tingling sensation moved to two distinct parts of her body, neither of which needed to be responding in such a way.

"Water will be fine for me."

She opened her eyes to find the flight attendant nodding at her companion. The flight attendant could actually see the passenger next to her!

"And another wine for Ms. Alexander, please."

She pushed herself upright and retrieved the arm the man had captured earlier. "Again, how do you know my name? And why haven't you told me yours?"

"As I said before, I know a great deal about you. In fact, I know you better than you know yourself." He brushed his mouth against her ear. "Call me Darius."

"And why are you kidnapping me?"

He chuckled and settled back in his seat. "Not kidnapping. If fortune prevails, I might just save your life once more."

Teagan shook her head. "When I wake up, Mr. Darius, if I remember this, it is going to make one hell of a book."

****

Darius watched the rise and fall of her chest, his own muscles tightening with each breath she took. Aloof and disbelieving, Teagan Alexander had held her own today. And yesterday. She was worth the risk. Of course, he had always known that.

The warmth of her lips against the flesh of his thumb had nearly undone him completely. In another setting he would have suspended time as he had this morning, and would have made love to her, right here in Business Class, while the other passengers looked on, blindly. Thank goodness, he had some willpower left.

Of course, goodness held little persuasion with him. Except where Teagan was concerned.

Three hundred years had separated him from goodness. Except when he held Teagan so close. Whatever he might be to the rest of the world, he liked to think he performed some good deed in keeping her alive.

Even if he had broken universal laws. And his own vow of noninvolvement.

Teagan shifted in her seat. The second glass of wine sat untouched as she sank into slumber. What small amount of sleep she had managed to get last night had clearly been troubled. Now, however, her mouth curled into a contented smile as she exhaled deeply and snuggled against the pillow he had tucked between her shoulder and the window. Halifax might be warm enough for shorts. However, she would need something warmer for where they were headed, which meant another stop.

It also meant another opportunity for the others to find their trail.

*****

The three-bell signal chimed, and Teagan came swimming up from her nap, grasping for wakefulness.

"I'm up, I'm up," she stammered. Casting her arms out, as if shucking blankets away, she blinked heavily against the daylight in the cabin. Wide eyes and her blank stare revealed she had not yet worked out where she sat. Or why. She frowned at Darius and cocked her head to the side, as if trying to fathom the answer to a puzzle.

"Where am I? What day is it?"

"Still Saturday. And you are still on board an airplane. We're about to land in Chicago, where we will connect to another flight to Halifax."

Her frown deepened. "I had the strangest dream."

The flight attendant passed through the cabin and reached to retrieve her glass. "Feel better, sleepyhead?"

She blinked up at the flight attendant and nodded.

Darius fought to keep from laughing outright at her confusion. "I think she isn't quite awake yet. Don't worry, though, I'll take care of her."

She shrugged, and moved closer to the window, raising the shade to peer out at the city below. "Leave me alone. You're not real. Or you're not who you say you are."

Her body tensed gradually, the muscles tightening as her brain returned to wakefulness. She was so much lovelier asleep, and so much more vulnerable.

He spoke casually, deliberately avoiding direct eye contact. "You slept deeply, which you needed. We have less than an hour to make our connection in Chicago, so make sure you keep up with me. Let me have your envelope."

"No. Why should I trust you? I don't even know your full name."

His temper flared. "I don't have time for this, and neither do you." Not if they were going to survive.

"You do not have a choice. I am the only one who

can help you, Teagan Alexander, and you are not hallucinating. I told you before, my name is Darius. For now, that is enough for you to know." He grabbed her hand, and she flinched at the radiant blue arc of electricity that played between them.

He stared at her. *"I'll explain it all to you. But not here. Not in public. Not where we can be seen."*

His own breathing quickened as did his pulse. With each second ticking by, she became more frenzied, and he became less patient. "Soon," he promised her.

Terrified by his touch, and by his thoughts swirling in the air, like words spoken, her eyes dilated, her nostrils flared. Fight or flight. Which did she intend to choose?

A deer in the headlights. The engines hummed loudly as the plane drifted steadily down, playing on the air currents like a kite, until with a bounce and a shriek of rubber, the tires touched the runway. Reverse thrust pitched them both forward in their seats, and he gripped her hand tighter, deliberately easing his breathing as the craft slowed.

He held her attention as tightly as he held her hand. *"Can you hear my thoughts?"*

Despite the fact he had not opened his mouth, she nodded.

"Do you understand what I am telling you?"

Confusion clouded her expression momentarily, then she nodded, once more.

"A little while longer. That's all. If someone hears us, then, they could become part of our problem. That is why I will not discuss this anymore with you while we are in public. And this type of conversation is an exhaustion neither one of us can afford now. Just play

along."

She squinted at him, then opened her mouth to speak. "I feel better now. I'm a bit more awake."

"I hope so."

The loading bridge docked against the airplane and the bells signaled the all-clear for passengers to disembark. Teagan grabbed her bag, and her book and pen, and...

"My other bag!" She shot out of her seat, nearly leaping over the man in—Darius. "The flight attendant never brought me my other bag." He caught her around the waist. The jolt nearly cast her back into her seat.

"What are you doing," she asked.

"We need to be inconspicuous."

He stared at her from the corner of his eye. She had seen people talk without moving their lips. However, this was not ventriloquism. No one else could hear the man, except her.

Darius unbuckled and stood up, nodding to the flight attendant as he approached.

"Yessir?"

'My companion seems to have left an item in the coach compartment. May I?"

"I am so sorry," the man said. "I promised to get it for you while we were in flight, then someone threw up, and I got distracted. Hold on. Which seat again?"

"Thirteen A."

The attendant picked up the phone on the wall, and dialed to the back of the plane, to one of the coach-class attendants, asking her to check the overhead. While they waited, patiently allowing the remaining Business Class passengers to disembark, dragging their oversized carry-on bags, briefcases, and newspapers with them.

The flight attendant sauntered up the aisle swinging the bag as she strode. "Here you go. Thank you once again for your help." She handed the bag to Teagan and motioned her across the threshold.

The moment her fingers tugged on the handle Teagan panicked. The clock was gone.

Chapter Seven

Time could be altered. Hadn't Einstein made a career from strands of that concept? The faster an object moves, the slower the world around us seems.

That's what had happened, hadn't it? Time had moved too quickly. Just as it had moved too slowly before. The flight from Chicago to Halifax had happened the way it would in a dream. Time shifts and stretches over a week, until the snooze alarm goes off to reveal that a year's adventure only took ten minutes.

Teagan shivered and drew the shawl around her shoulders. Ten o'clock at night proved that Canada tested the global warming theory. Even in July, cool crisp air nipped at her neck and legs.

She had lost the clock. She had managed to lose a worn-out cuckoo clock while trapped aboard an airplane, thirty thousand feet above ground.

A very important cuckoo clock. Perhaps I'm dead and not just in shock?

Darius mumbled something to the customer service agent, then turned and frowned at her.

Could he read her thoughts? Did he hear the rhymes sounding within her head when she was nervous or stressed?

He strode over to where she sat, crumpled and cold, and toyed with the keys in his hand. "Let's go."

Since the discovery of a nearly empty bag in

Chicago, he had barely spoken to anyone.

As soon as she realized the clock was missing, the flight attendants searched the overhead compartments. Darius had charged up the loading bridge, trying to spot anyone carrying anything large enough to hide a wooden box.

No luck.

Two and a half hours of silence. For something she had, had little control over. Give up her seat or be proclaimed villain of the day by everyone else on the flight.

Well, no good deed goes unpunished. She had offered up her seat and had lost her grip. She had been warned to keep the clock close. She had let her guard down for one moment, and now a family heirloom was gone.

She grabbed the carryon bag she had managed not to lose and followed him out the door toward the car park.

"Why should I go anywhere with you? You might have made this all up. I'd be a fool to get in a car with you—a man I don't even know."

She saw his shoulders twitch. His pace slowed a bit, yet he did not stop moving toward the car. Nor did he grant her the argument that might have settled her nerves.

"Tell me why I am involved in this at all. I am as exciting as a pet rock. Why would anyone be interested in me?"

He opened the passenger-side door of the sedan and held it open for her. "Get in."

"No."

He sighed.

"I mean it," she spat. "I have no reason to believe any of this. Most of all that you want to help me because of some misguided sense of altruism. I want answers."

"And I told you, not in public."

"Public was fine for you this morning with thousands of people standing by watching."

"As I recall, they weren't exactly aware of our interaction."

"Where are you taking me?"

"Hopefully, somewhere safe."

"What do you mean, hopefully?"

"The longer you stand here arguing with me, the more time you allow anyone looking for you to find us. Whoever has the clock has us at a significant disadvantage."

"Ah," she said as she fumbled through her bag. "I listened to what you said earlier. Look."

She pulled out the small T-shaped key he had given her that morning. "You said they needed both, right?"

Some fleeting expression that might have been a smirk, brushed across his mouth. He motioned her once more into the passenger seat.

Far from satisfied, yet undaunted by his reaction, she sank into the leather seat as he closed the door and maneuvered to the driver's side. A quick check of the car's controls, and he started the ignition, shifted into gear, and pulled out.

"All right," she said, as soon as they were on the highway. "I did as you asked. Now you start talking. If you can make time stand still, then why do you need a car, and what's so important about an old cuckoo clock that doesn't even work properly?"

No acknowledgement. No answers.

She pulled out her cell phone, turned it on, and dialed Aunt Elsa's cell and hit send.

Before the display could reveal the network connection, Darius ripped it from her hand. He touched the control pad on the steering wheel with one hand, as he hit End on the phone. Without a word, he opened his window and tossed the phone out.

"What are you doing—"

"No."

No? What the hell kind of answer is that? "I'm calling my aunt, not the police—"

"No."

Darius accelerated, passed the truck ahead of them and kept his foot firmly planted on the gas pedal. The elevation of speed, combined with the shock of losing her phone, her last hope for help, sent Teagan's heart racing into hyper speed. It was all she could do to bite her lip and keep from screaming. No use alerting him to her plan. She didn't stop to think it might not be the best plan. At that precise moment, it seemed her only option.

She didn't care if he heard the click of her seatbelt. She unbuckled and lunged upward toward the open sunroof. If she died trying to escape, at least she wouldn't die a helpless, whimpering victim.

She managed to get the upper half of her body through the sunroof when the car made a sharp swerve to the right. The rebound off the shoulder of the road unbalanced her.

A muscular arm yanked her down with force. The car brakes locked. Halfway in the ditch, the tail of the vehicle left the ground and sent Teagan tumbling into the dashboard.

****

Quicksand movements. A strange sense of disorientation, disconnection came over her. She watched her own arms flail, saw herself reach frantically for the lock even as her body pitched back against gravity into the seat. In the darkness, an ominous shadow closed over her and held her in place.

Thought didn't enter into it. Teagan screamed as loudly as she could, clawing and scratching, as her body smashed against the glove compartment. Something hard stopped her head from moving, but her body fought, kicking and scrambling to unlock the door.

Click.

He brushed her arm and a jolt ricocheted through her. The tingling stretched up her arm and across her chest, spidering its way toward her spine. Toward her brain.

His right arm still held her in place, like a metal bar on an amusement park ride. His left hand tugged on the belt, tightening it against her abdomen.

"That was stupid."

"I'm not stupid, not by far. I made you stop the car."

Before she could stop the words, she saw his eyes narrow. Only the glow of the dash display illuminated his face. However, she could see every feature of his face. Including his eyes. Even in the dark, the irises sparkled. Dangerous. Compelling. Calculating.

Her chest burned, whether from the impact, or from the force he still exerted.

She so hated her life right now. Hated the rhyming.

Hated the choices she had made today. Summoning the pebble of will and strength that remained, she choked, "Move your arm, please."

Darius did not break his stare, yet the pressure across her chest lightened as he moved his arm.

"Child lock is engaged. If you really want to die, then I will let you out of here. I'm sure that whoever took the clock will catch up to you by breakfast."

"There's no way they could. The phone didn't connect."

Suddenly the car's temperature dropped about ten degrees.

"Don't worry. They don't need a signal to track you. They have your scent."

"What?"

"Like hunters, trackers, animals, the people after you can spot you in a crowd."

Teagan thought of the woman in the airport. "How?"

"Do you want out, here? Miles from anything?"

"I needed to call Elsa and Joe, that's all."

"Out or in?"

Moisture swelled beneath the edge of her lashes. *Absolutely not. Not a single one.*

"They aren't particular about where or how they catch you. One of them probably enjoys the thought of the hunt. In the end, though, they don't care about particulars. So, do you want out? Have I done all this for nothing? Or do we continue driving?"

No compassion tinged his voice. No care to what she had experienced in the past thirty-two hours. Not one crumb of kindness. No cruelty, either. Not like there had been in the tattooed man's voice.

She didn't trust her own voice to speak words, so she merely nodded.

Darius restarted the car and gently reversed the car out of the ditch, then maneuvered back onto the road, and slid into a comfortable accelerating speed. Cruising altitude more aptly described it.

"I wanted to tell them about the break-in. They'll be worried. They need to know I'm safe."

"You aren't. Yet."

She glanced sideways at him.

"By the time your uncle and aunt get back to the cabin, all that will be left will be some ashes, and a few pieces of charred timber."

So much for staving her tears. She blinked against the fear and aggravation in vain as streams of tears poured down her cheeks. She sniffled. She straightened her leg and pressed her right foot harshly into the carpet of the foot mat, as if doing so would change their velocity in any way.

"How do you know their house burned down."

"Because this is how Robert handled it last time. Arson is a signature device of his."

"Who is Robert?"

"Officer Corrig, who came to your door last night."

"You know him?"

"We've met."

"What do you mean by last time?"

"When the clock disappeared. To cover his tracks. To hide the fact that the clock survived and was stolen, he burned down the house where it was supposed to be."

"And just where was this house?"

"Here. Nova Scotia."

"Then why in the world are we here?"

"Clock or no clock, we have to find a way to make it right. To keep them from killing you for something that is not your fault. Never was."

"I don't understand."

"I know."

"No. From the way you've been talking, you don't know at all. I haven't got a clue as to what any of this is. It's like I'm in a nightmare I can't wake up from. It's like I'm in an episode of some sci-fi show. Only, I'm not. Have I gone crazy? Did I have some sort of breakdown, and I just don't know it yet? Are you really a psychiatrist or something?"

He actually smiled at her.

"No. Although that might be very much more appealing than the truth of this whole matter."

"I don't get it. What 'matter'?"

His middle and ring finger on his right hand drummed against the steering wheel. "The fact that you don't get it is a large part of what has kept you safe for so long."

"But why are we here? In Canada? Why Nova Scotia? I've never been here. I have no connection to this place."

"You have more of a connection than you think, Teagan. This is the only place where we can hope to sort this out. This is where it all began."

****

Flakes swirled in the night air, fluttering silently in the North Carolina breeze, to kiss the hovering clouds. Intermittent rain served the firemen well, helping extinguish the blaze that consumed the wooden structure before it crossed the road and threatened anyone else.

Robert Corrig tapped his pipe against the patrol car, expelling the ashes onto the gravel. "Did they find any bodies?"

Maggie Ritter shook her head. "Not so far as they can ascertain. George Whitby says it looks like the house was empty. Thinks it might have been electrical. Could have been smoldering for hours. By the time the neighbors noticed the blaze, though, the place was mostly gone. That's the problem with the overgrowth like that along the fence. Nobody could see it until it had nearly swept the place."

"Plus, it's Saturday night," he added. "Everybody's out to dinner or a movie."

"Yep. Including Teagan Alexander. George's guys aren't finished sifting through the rubble, won't be able to do much more until morning. But right now, it looks like she was not in the house."

"Didn't she say her aunt and uncle were due home tonight?"

Ritter nodded. "I've got a call in to the airline, trying to track them down, now. Their niece said they were due back tonight. Looks like they didn't make their flight."

"All the hotels 're booked up for the Games."

"How did things go over at the Ceilidh?"

"You know that crowd. A bit of toe tappin' is about as rambunctious as they get. Caught a couple of kids drinking in the parking lot. Confiscated the beer, kicked 'em out. That's about it. You want me to take over for you? So you can get home to the kids?"

"No thanks. Jim is on parent duty tonight. Sleepover after the concert. I don't even need to be a part of that. I've got this covered. Go on home and get some rest. Enjoy tomorrow off."

"You too. See you on Monday."

He climbed into his car and started for home. By morning, he'd have found Teagan Alexander. If she knew about the clock, then she had no doubt recognized him as well. Before any of the others could find her, he meant to get hold of that clock and destroy it.

Teagan Alexander's time had run out.

Chapter Eight

Darius popped the last log into the stove and closed the door. For the first time in a long time, true fear for her safety and her sanity clawed at his gut. How could he rationalize everything that had led them to this moment, to her? "I've put you in danger." Blue sparks crackled in the red heat of the cabin's only heat source. "Now, I have to try to set things right."

They shouldn't have needed a fire this night. July should be warm enough. Even in the middle of nowhere.

"About that," she muttered. "What did you do exactly that makes them want me?"

She needed answers. Admittedly. However, the answers he had to give were bound to create more questions.

"I intervened."

"Oh. Well, that explains it all."

Her teeth chattered as she spoke, and she grabbed the comforter from the bed to wrap around herself before plopping down into the only comfortable reading chair in the sparsely furnished wooden cabin.

When he didn't reply, she asked, "Where are we? Could it get any darker out there?"

"We are officially in the middle of nowhere. I've known the family who owns the inn for a while. They make the best breakfast in the northern hemisphere."

He motioned to the bedroom where two single beds flanked the white paneled walls, separated by a nightstand with a radio. "Right now, however, you need some real rest."

"You're an optimist. Like I'm going to be able to sleep. You said you would explain it all once we were not in public. This is definitely not public." She struggled against the yawn that consumed her. "Besides, I'll only make things up in my sleep if you don't tell me. Nightmares aren't restful."

So pale against the comforter, she could be a ghost. How could he confess the carnal pleasure he experienced being able to touch her, to hold her, to breathe in her scent?

"I-I crossed into your world once, or twice, when I didn't belong there, and I might have altered your future. A bit."

"A bit?"

"Close your eyes."

"What does 'crossed into your world' mean, exactly?"

He glanced toward the bedroom again, then at the frayed wingback chair where she sat, obviously relaxed. He dragged a straight-backed wooden chair from the writing table and settled in across from her. "Close your eyes."

"I don't think closing my eyes right now is wise."

"You wanted answers, and I am willing to give you some. However, you have to cooperate, so I can help you remember."

Her eyes flashed wider, defiant.

"Do you remember Chicago?"

"Yes."

"Now, remember it as it was when you were first there—"

She closed her eyes. "I was eleven. Mom and I went with my dad. He was there for work—"

"No. Not that time. Take a deep breath and concentrate. You were there much earlier than that. You were still a child, but older."

"Older? How could I be older, if—"

"New Years Eve, 1927. You had been invited to a party at the old Weller estate."

"I wasn't even alive in 1927!"

"Bear with me, Teagan. Do you remember the dream you had when you were in your third year of college?"

She opened her eyes and frowned at him. "More specific please…"

Closed eyes, please. "You were in your bedroom in your parents' house in Paducah, on winter break, when you had a vision."

Teagan struggled to open her eyes and failed. "How would you know about that?"

"Shh. Breathe. Concentrate."

Her breathing deepened and slowed. So did her pulse. The artery beneath her jaw fluttered ever so slightly with each beat—nearly iridescent in the firelight. Innocent and trusting.

"My bedroom fell away," she began, "like the ride at the carnival. I thought I was sleeping, but my eyes were still open."

"You hadn't fallen asleep, yet."

"My room disappeared. Like I was in a dream, but I was awake."

"And where were you, Teagan?"

The room I stood in was white, opulent. Marble pillars, and ferns. Tiled floor, lots of candles and lamps. Long garlands of spruce adorned the corridor. A party. I was at a party. I could hear musicians playing."

"And what were you doing?"

"I-I was just standing, sort of. I think…I think I saw my reflection, but it wasn't me. I mean it was, sort of, but I was different. I was wearing a long gown. Like a costume party—"

"And whom did you see?"

"There was a man. Blond. Older than I was, but not old. In his twenties. He had a tuxedo—the old kind, with tails. He had a mask in his hand. It was a masquerade party. He moved across the room, toward me. He looked like the police officer who was at the cabin. But that can't be right.

"He was there looking at me. But he was seeing someone else. Dressed in emerald green. I could see her in the mirror, blond hair flowing down her back. He looked right at me, only it wasn't me. He was seeing her. He called her Teagan. And she—I knew him. He asked her, I mean me, to dance, but I didn't want to. I knew he meant to hurt her. I saw it in his eyes."

"No. You knew it because you lived it."

"What?" Teagan struggled to open her eyes, to break the memory, but he brushed his hand lightly against hers.

So cold. Yet the current that arced between their hands could burn through paper. "Stay with me, Teagan. Breathe. Relax."

She inhaled deeply and the furrow in her brow disappeared.

"This vision is a memory. You knew what he

intended because you and that Teagan were one."

****

Teagan wanted to look him in the eyes. She struggled to open her own. She wanted to laugh at him. Yet she couldn't seem to lift her lids or move. Cold wrapped around her hand, yet her fingers burned. Frost bite. Nonsensical. Completely nonsensical. How could he know about any of this?

Snow crunched under her feet. She had gone to meet him in the woods near the beach.

"A week after the party, I…I mean she went to meet someone."

"You were infatuated with Malcolm Weller."

"But Malcolm Weller wasn't the man in my vision."

"No. A man calling himself Rudy Reitman, Malcolm's best friend, asked you to dance."

"Someone delivered a letter to the academy. I sneaked out of the dormitory and waited for him there in the woods. I waited for Malcolm."

"But Rudy showed up."

The nearly full moon shone through the trees, illuminating the snow, like diamonds glittering in the night.

Teagan had been waiting so long, the cold soaked her feet. Her breath warmed the dry wintery air, sending tendrils of steam heavenward with each breath. Butterflies as big as bats fluttered in her stomach as she waited. If he didn't show up soon, she'd have to start back. If the nuns found her gone…

She heard the ground and leaves crunch behind her. She turned, smiling, to greet him.

Chapter Nine

Rudy.
Not Malcolm.
"Where is Malcolm?" she demanded.
Rudy grinned and winked conspiratorially at her.
He laughed at his own cleverness, and that she had so
willingly sneaked out to rendezvous.
He had arranged everything. While Malcolm dined
in some club downtown, Rudy had taken the train up
from Northwestern. He walked from the train station.
"I knew you'd only show up for Malcolm. That's
why I sent the note with the flowers. You'd never be
able to resist any request he made, and I need to talk to
you."
"This isn't right. You shouldn't be here. I shouldn't
be here."
"You know Malcolm can never marry you. His
family will never allow it. Only the best dowry makes it
into the Weller family album. You barely have two
nickels to your name. Now if you even had a name he
could brag about, like Rockefeller--"
"You're wrong. Malcolm is not like that."
"Teagan, girls are foolish birds. Malcolm's family
is tied to east coast royalty. They're ready to marry him
off to someone who can further expand their fortune
and holdings. Do you honestly think he would waste his
time on you? You work for a living, darling. Unless you

want to be his mistress—"

Teagan's cheeks burned. "Stop it."

She retreated a step, and he stalked closer. His eyes burned, even in the darkness.

"It doesn't have to be that way, Teagan. I could change it, you know. If you let me. I could make your life so much easier. You and I could help each other. You may not have the money or status the Wellers want, but you would look dazzling on my arm. And I have no prejudice toward a working-class girl—"

"What?"

He stalked closer. "You're so young. No one has to know what kind of family you come from. I can give you everything that Malcolm never will. I could even love you."

Panic welled inside her. How could he say this to her? He shouldn't say this. "You're Malcom's friend."

"And?"

"Stop it! Rudy, I've never thought of you in that way. You know that. I-I'm leaving."

"He scared her," Teagan said. "I mean…me. He always had. The way he looked at me, I mean…her. The way he made me feel whenever he watched me."

Memory dragged her down again.

She tried to sidestep him, there on the path. He caught her arm and yanked her to him. "You can't leave yet. Not until we've settled this."

"There is nothing to settle. This is all a big mistake." Tears stung her eyes. "Get out of my way, I'm leaving."

Searing pain wrenched her arm, and she lost her footing. Snow crunched as she fell to the ground. She cried out.

Rudy was on top of her, his mouth stealing a kiss as his hands clawed at her coat. She rolled from beneath him, but he caught her leg, dragging her down again, into the snow to keep her from escaping.

He straddled her, telling her, "You are so beautiful. And so stupid. All you have to do is say yes. You'll see, though, that I'm right."

She swung wildly at him, trying to knock him off. She opened her mouth to scream, to shatter the silence of the woods. Somebody must hear.

He pinned her arms flat out to her sides as he slid his hips down her torso. His face darkened as he lowered his mouth to hers and savagely silenced her protest.

She thrashed against the weight of his body. Her lungs burned from the pressure, her throat burned from the smell of cologne, and hair oil, and...lust.

She couldn't breathe. His tongue, inside her mouth, probing, stealing what was not his to take. His hips rocking against her belly, then moving lower.

The ground beneath her refused to yield as his assault turned more vicious. Her legs were cold, her hair wet from melted snow.

She gagged, and he lifted his mouth from hers.

Cold air, putrid with terror and rage seeped into her lungs. Only a whimper made it past her lips.

"It's a shame to waste such beauty." His eyes glittered with a bizarre mixture of sorrowful regret and giddy resignation as his hands closed around her throat...

She fell onto the floor gasping. Gasping for release from the vision of that night. Of the snow. Of the attack. Fear stole the air from her lungs. Her muscles convulsed against her unseen assailant. Against the figure of the man in the vision.

Her voice wouldn't work. She tried to scream. She fought to get to her feet. Her legs, too, refused to cooperate. She had to get out of here. She had to wake up from this nightmare.

Strong arms wrapped around her and pulled her close against a broad chest.

She raised her fists and shoved at the chest. When her captor didn't budge, she hit him. Hard.

Still, he didn't move.

Terror screamed through her limbs and made them tremble. She blinked and stared up at the man. Darius's face swam into view, pushing past the vision of her murderer.

Darius extended his hand and brushed her cheek. "Shh. Breathe, Teagan. It's over. It's just a memory. Long gone."

No. How could any of this be possible? How could he have known about the vision? Teagan was strong, independent. She was not a victim. How could she and that helpless girl be the same person?

A garbled, feral moan escaped her throat. Like an animal trapped, she twisted out of his hold and lunged across the room. She tore open the cabin door. A brisk wind greeted her, lifted her hair and swept through the room.

****

Darius caught Teagan around the waist, his touch unbuffered by the sweater she wore. The air crackled as static electricity arced between them. He dragged her away from the door and turned her around to face him.

His gut clenched at the horror and memory

sparking her whiskey-colored eyes.

She hissed from the current that ran between them, fighting ever harder to free herself from him. Her mouth opened, and she inhaled, preparing to scream. He couldn't give her that chance, though.

"It's over. Wake up. Look at me."

She looked up at him, and he knew.

Too much, too soon. He had regressed her too soon. Panick surged through her. It radiated from her in waves. Shock poured over her and he saw her drowning the memories.

For an instant, he was once more in the skiff on suspended waves, holding her cold body, breathing life into her mortal shell.

A vow once made, ever held.

Magic to do. He needed to calm the storm that raged within her.

He closed his mouth over hers and claimed her pain as he claimed the kiss. As much as he needed to calm her down, he fought against the truth. He wanted this moment. He hungered for his own memory of her lips, of her spirit.

Molten energy.

The air sizzled as he held her there, against him, coaxing the breath from her, and with it, her fear and fury.

Hands that had beat at him an instant ago, stilled, then clutched the cloth of his shirt as she responded to his kiss.

All so wrong.

He wrapped his arms around her and gathered her to him as he sank into the kiss. The heat that swelled between them had nothing to do with the pot-bellied stove in the corner of the room.

He repressed the urge to carry her into the adjacent room and strip her naked and consume her fear with his own desire. He would not be a part of such a memory.

He had saved her twice with such a kiss. Now, he fought against her brain's violent desire to calm the feral heat that surged throughout her limbs.

Her hands snaked up the length of his chest to wrap around his neck, clinging to him. Death often sought life.

He lifted her slightly and carried her toward the bedroom, never breaking the embrace that held them magnetically joined, like the kissing dolls in a souvenir shop. Only when he had set her down upon the mattress did he dare move his mouth from hers. His lips strayed to that place just beneath her jaw that had throbbed incessantly as she had relived her vision.

Fire in her blood, ice in the air. He longed to cloak her in heated kisses to rage against history, and what had to be.

She trembled against him. His groin tightened in approval, urging him on.

Darius firmly pushed her down against the pillows and stepped back.

He had to stop. Now.

After all, isn't this how it all went wrong three hundred years ago?

Chapter Ten

Coastal Waters, Nova Scotia, 1758

The sea rumbled beneath the skiff as Teagan's father rowed furiously against the breeze. In the distance, the rock-strewn shore dipped below the roll of each wave, hiding behind the fog that taunted their efforts.

Sweat beaded Ranulf Deschamb's brow as he rowed harder. "What do you see, child?"

"*Ce n'est rien*, Papa."

"In English. You must speak in English. Never forget that. You cannot trust anyone. Not anymore. Do you understand?"

Anger burned Teagan's cheeks despite the cold morning wind. She nodded, curtly. "Yes, Father. I see nothing."

"Always. Always English now, *ma petite*. If you speak in French—even when you are alone—it could cost you your life."

She lifted her eyes to stare at the man sitting so very close to her. Fear and concern clouded his eyes as he stared past her. His hair, slightly grey at the edges, lashed at his worry-worn face. A frown of concern marred the gentle mouth that had until this moment, ever held a smile.

Her fingers ached from clawing at the dirt through

the night, digging away the sand and soil, then replacing it in the shadow of predawn.

On this day, however, the sun did not break the horizon. Only a few scattered streaks of crimson trickled through the gathering clouds as the tumultuous waves tossed the boat with each crest. They must reach the far-off ribbon of the mainland before the storm found them.

Between them loomed a dark stained grain bag, laden with silver. Behind them, the island that had held a secret for hundreds of years. Ahead of them lay an uncertain future at the hands of the English.

She placed a hand on her father's knee. "Shh, all will be well, now. You and I will be fine. You'll see."

Now, a fortnight later, Teagan stood beneath the eaves of the armory at Fort Louis, cloaked by the rain long after the crowd dissipated and stared at the gallows.

Treason.

For all her father's caution for her safety, he had never thought of his own. Now she and he remained in the rain. Two figures drenched in the tears of Heaven.

One alive, one dead.

For love of his home, he did not speak. For love of his daughter, he did not cry out.

The soldiers had made a good show of his hanging for the crowd, cajoling the audience to a frenzy. An easy spectacle—an old man. With his hands tied behind his back, and a noose around his neck, a rag stuffed in his mouth, Ranulf Deschamb had not been able to protest as they yanked his trews down for all the villagers to stare.

Vile maggots.

Her chest ached with the hollowness of loss. They had stolen all she had. Her head hurt from the tears, and the memory of the drums that pounded an evil cadence as the English commander executed her father. Her world.

A gust of wind swayed the body that dangled above the gallows. A movement near its base caught her eye. Something scurried beneath the oak planks, one leg dragging behind. An animal, injured, perhaps? Wounded by the soldiers more likely.

Teagan tugged her hat down to hide her face and drew the hood of her cloak over her head to hide her from any eyes that watched from shuttered windows. Beneath the folds of wool, she sought the handle of the dagger she had tucked into her belt.

Rain fell in sheets, ensuring no sensible person would follow her as she crossed the yard, and drenching her completely as she splashed through the mud.

Beneath the platform dry earth mixed with urine and the musk of wet wool. In the far corner, two embers glowed white hot, then blinked slowly. Nearly invisible in the shadows, white paws peeked out from beneath the mound of scrawny black fur that hunkered in a heat preserving crouch. One leg lay awkwardly straight, much like a white tipped handle, bushy tail curled protectively around the limb.

Cat? Or skunk?

"You do not stink like a skunk."

Once more the creature blinked at her.

The scent of urine stung her nose again until another wind gust swept away the reminder of what still hung above them.

"They will kill you," her father had warned, "if

they discover you speak French."

No one would harbor the daughter of a convicted spy inside their cozy cottages this night.

Damn them all. As they damned him.

What had happened to the courier? Why had he not been on the shore? How had the English found her father's skiff, hidden on the rocky shores, half a day's ride from Lunenburg?

As if they had known where to look.

Exhaustion and cold held her to the only dry spot in the inner yard. Here, there would be no prying eyes, no accusing looks, no conspiratorial nods. Only two wounded and wet souls sharing the sanctuary beneath the wailing clouds above.

She removed her hat and unclasped her cloak rearranging the layers of wool so that those most dry would insulate her from the chill. Across the small, cramped space, the cat inched closer to the wall.

"*C'est bien, mon ami.* You keep to your side, and I to mine. This night no one will bother either of us. *D'accord?*"

Wood, rope, and flesh creaked its approval from above as it swayed in the evening wind. Teagan curled into a ball and allowed the tears of loss to soak her cheek and hair. Ranulf Deschamb watched over his daughter one last time.

A dead man's keep.

****

Bright sunlight peeked through the white cotton sheers, nudging Teagan to consciousness. Somewhere outside a bird twittered, annoyingly, as if deliberately harping to wake her.

It should be raining. Shouldn't it?

The movie playing inside her head faded as dreams fell away to reality. Wood smoke teased her senses, fading quickly in the breeze that blew through the open window. Grass, newly mowed, and dried paint played with the scent of soap, exacerbating the pounding in her head.

Funny, she could have sworn she left the Celtic drums in North Carolina.

What had she drunk last night?

She opened one eye tentatively.

"Good morning," a husky male voice said.

Husky male. Headache. Morning.

She opened the other eye and sought the source of the voice.

Standing in the doorway, bare-chested, towel in hand, stood the man who had seduced her. Or kidnapped her. Or something like that. Looking very *secret agent* in the morning light.

Darius.

Black slacks unzipped, hung on his hips, revealing far more flesh than she needed to see. As dangerous a figure as he had cut in full black attire, the chiseled lines of his abdomen and chest were far more intimidating this morning.

He couldn't be real. Airbrushed. That was it. No man looked that good without photoshop.

"Meet me in the main house in fifteen minutes. I'll go and order breakfast.

She closed her eyes again. "What did you hit me with last night? A drug, or a sledgehammer?"

"Neither. Just a bit of exhaustion. Caffeine should help the headache. Coffee or tea?

"I don't care." She sat up as he slipped on his shirt

and shoes. "Um, I don't have anything to get ready with."

"Shampoo and toothpaste are on the sink. If you need something else we can ask at the front desk, after breakfast."

Before she could protest, he disappeared with nothing but the sound of the door latching behind him to mar the silence.

The digital display on the alarm clock read nine thirty-two. Four and a half hours sleep?

She tried to will herself back under the covers. However, the call to caffeine set her limbs in motion, dragging her toward the shower.

Twenty minutes later, she had dressed and made her way to the dining room in the main building of the lodge. To the left of the front desk, it sprawled beneath a raftered ceiling. Windows lined the room, one side looked down onto the cabins, the other side revealed a vast pasture sprinkled with cows. Wooly, highland coos, to be precise.

Within the hall, neat rows of rectangular tables, covered in white cotton tablecloths filled the room. High-backed wooden chairs stood duty at each table, like guards awaiting guests. Silver flatware gleamed in the morning sunlight framed each place setting, and Teagan realized each cup and saucer was different, as if each were part of a collection, rather than a set.

"Very Anne of Green Gables," she said as she slid into the seat across the table from Darius.

"Wrong Province," he replied. "Coffee?"

"Yes, please." He poured from a small pot, and she spooned in sugar and half and half until the walnut blackness turned to a honeyed oak, then downed the first cup as if it were a shot of whisky, and poured herself a second.

He lifted one eyebrow. "That bad?"

She eyed him cautiously. "You could say so."

Dark curls brushed the top of his collar, reminding her of the dark swirl of hair on his chest. She quickly broke that train of thought. Coffee. She needed more coffee. She prepared her second cup as breakfast arrived.

Cinnamon and brown sugar swirled in steamy wisps as the server placed a small bowl, and a much larger plate in front of her.

"Bananas in cream. And the house specialty," the young man explained, unnecessarily. "Poached eggs, homemade porridge bread, the chef's special house recipe, all broiled to perfection."

Her stomach rolled a little. "I'm not sure I can manage all this—"

Darius thanked the young man, then nodded at her. "You haven't eaten since the flight yesterday. Your body needs sustenance. Indulge me. Eat up."

She inhaled deeply, allowing the aromas to soothe her weariness. The tanginess of the cheddar cheese mingled with the smoked flavor of the bacon. Honey and oatcakes, tinged with…tomato? The edges of the oatcakes sizzled.

True to his testament, the house specialty exemplified culinary perfection. Bananas had never tasted so good as they did this particular morning, topped with cream and brown sugar and cinnamon.

Nothing had ever tasted this good.

"Is this Heaven, and you haven't told me?"

"You are very cynical, aren't you?"

"I'm pragmatic. All of this. The adventure, the weirdness, the—" She remembered a kiss of narcotic quality. Hallucinatory, even. Her lips still tingled at the memory of it, which immediately made her cheeks flush hot. "I'm not all that adventurous, that's all."

When she dared to meet his gaze, her cheeks grew hotter. Across the table, a perfectly charming smile tugged at dimples no earthly man should have.

"You're blushing," he challenged.

Her cheeks flushed with heat. So did her neck. "Um. Last night…did I, or we—"

"Did we what?"

The heat trickled toward her ears. "I, um, I was pretty wiped out. Did we—have sex?"

"You don't remember?"

His expression mocked her confusion, which pissed her off, and embarrassed her more. "Of course, I do. I remember the fire, and you talking to me about a dream, and—"

"And yet you don't remember what happened after I carried you into the bedroom?"

"That's not it—I mean…I'm just a bit foggy on that."

The napkin she had been wringing in her hands knotted into a ball. She tugged at it and lost her grip. Her hand swung out and clipped her cup, splattering coffee across the pure white linen tablecloth.

"Oh, no. Not the—jeez, they're gonna kill me."

His grin sobered, and he grabbed her hand as he lay his napkin over the spill. "It's only coffee. Don't worry. Nobody here will say anything. This was an accident."

"I'm too clumsy," she rambled as she tried to blot at the coffee with her other hand. "I can't do this. I can't even remember anything after the kiss."

"And you're rhyming again."

She stopped blotting and looked up at him. Silvery grey eyes, sparkling and cold stared at her with less amusement than she had hoped she would see. "I can't help it. I tend to do it whenever I get stressed. I think I just need more rest."

"I know you do. Come on, let's go back to the cabin."

He nodded to their server as they left the dining room, presumably acknowledging to add their breakfast charges to the room bill.

"Why? I mean, what are we doing today?" she asked as they descended the steps and headed toward a narrow stone path that wound along the front of the main house. Off to their right, two wooly, highland cows lingered at the fence, awaiting breakfast treats from tourists.

"Today, you sleep. I need you awake, alert, and on your game later."

"But you said they were close behind—"

"Don't worry. Nobody will be look for either of us here."

"Darius?"

"Yes?"

"I don't understand a lot of what happened yesterday, or the day before, or—"

"Don't worry, you will. Soon. That's why we're here. So we can talk. In the daylight. And so you can remember it all."

The aroma of ambergris and sassafras clung to him. She slowed her steps and breathed deeply. She closed her eyes for a moment and drank in his heady scent. It was like a smooth elixir. Her mind started to drift until the wind curled around her. She opened her eyes blurted out, "I—I'm sorry I don't remember a lot about last night."

Darius opened the white wooden door for her, and she ascended the steps into the cabin. Just as he moved across the threshold, a kitten scampered into the room, mewing and dancing around his ankles, begging for attention.

"You have nothing to apologize for, Teagan. There was no sex, so no need for awkward morning-after-regrets. Only a kiss."

"Oh." Her chest ached a bit at his confession. The scent of chlorine blasted her as she stepped inside. Someone had already tidied the cabin. *Muguet des Bois.* Whoever had been here had been wearing *Muguet des Bois.* Did they even make that cologne anymore?

She opened the window wider, admitting fresh air to staunch the smell.

"Last night, the thing about the vision—"

"Now, that did happen. What do you remember?"

"I remember all of it. How did you know about it, though? Can you read people's thoughts?"

"Something like that."

"Why can't you ever give a simple, direct answer?"

"Because in this situation, there is no such thing."

"Then give me a not-so-simple explanation that can serve as an answer."

She scooped up the kitten and cradled it as she sank into the chair she had claimed last night—and waited.

Darius moved the other straight-backed chair he had used last night to the opposite wall, sat and leaned back until the chair's front legs jutted out away from the floor.

Time to come clean. He swallowed his reluctance and stared at her, willing himself to tell her as much as he dared.

"I am a realm walker."

Teagan shrugged. "You said that the other day. I don't know what it is, or what it means."

"I step in and out of this world as needed," he explained.

She frowned. "This world. As compared to—what other world? A homeless person on the street?" She motioned toward the yard outside. "A farmer in the dell?"

He ignored her sarcasm. "A realm walker shifts between the tangible and the intangible. Between reality and dream. Occasionally between past and present."

Cynicism sparkled in her eyes. "And how does that pay?"

He couldn't blame her, but neither of them had time for lengthy explanations. And a true explanation would be very lengthy. "Last night I helped you remember a vision you had in college. You said you remembered that much."

The space between her brows furrowed for a few seconds before she let her shoulders drop. She squinted as if focusing on him, then nodded as the skepticism in her face faded. "Yeah, I remember. How did you—how did you do that?"

"Do what?"

"How did you know about that? I've only ever told a couple of people, and that was in college."

"What were you dreaming about this morning?"

Her expression went blank. She stared at him, clearly deliberately trying to conceal any emotion or surprise. Yet her pulse throbbed heavier, and faster than it should have. He could hear her deep intake of air.

"I—I don't remember."

"Shall I help?"

She sat back in the chair and rubbed the kitten behind the ears. "Do your best," she challenged.

"The cat under the gallows wasn't white, like this one. It was black. Its leg was broken, and it was as scared of you as you were of it when you first saw it. Your father hadn't been a spy. He had been something much more dangerous. You didn't know that though. Neither did the British.

"You thought he supplied money to the French troops, trying to help their fight against his own countrymen."

Her eyes widened with every word he spoke.

"Stop it."

"You didn't know his most prized possession had been left on the island. Or rather, hidden in the waters along the eastern shore."

"Stop it."

"I know what you dreamt this morning because I was there in 1758 when it happened. So were you. In 1758, you helped your father bury the clock. You planted it in the ground, beneath a metal plate and flagstone buried in the water. The clock replaced the money he removed from that hiding place. Silver. Enough silver to see you through...to get you safely away from the province. Away from the fighting.

"It's just a dream," she insisted.

"Then how can I know so much about it? About

you?"

"You're good at tricks. You hypnotized me, or something, last night, and you planted the whole scenario in my mind so you could have some fun this morning. I'll bet it would make for a great act in Vegas."

"Healthy skepticism is a good thing. However, consider what happened yesterday morning at the Highland festival. Explain that, Teagan."

"That could be hypnosis as well."

He slid the chair forward and stood. "Don't you want to know about the clock?"

Her silence betrayed her.

Darius moved to where she sat and knelt. "Raise your hand."

Her brows rose above narrowed eyes, but she he did as he asked, and released her furry companion to raise her right hand.

Darius lifted his left hand to meet hers, without touching. Two inches separated flesh from flesh. He kept his eyes open and concentrated on her hand. A thin blue thread passed from his hand to hers, wiry, and frenetic in its movement. Another spidered from it, and another.

Lightning. The electrical charge passed between them, sparking and crackling like the charge in a thunderstorm.

"That is not hypnotism," he chided.

The hair on her arm stood erect, like tiny scillae, wafting in the air. She lifted her eyes, her gaze questioning.

"Realm walkers are supposed to help preserve the balance between the realms, between the positive and negative energies," he explained.

"You're not human?" she asked, voice warbling just a bit.

"Half human. Half spirit."

"Which half am I staring at now?"

"Both."

She blinked. "I don't understand."

"Think of the shaman, think of the yogi, think of the clairvoyant. They are variations of my kind. Much more human than spiritual. Nonetheless, common in theme."

"So you're a dream in human form?"

He let out a chuckle. "Hardly."

"Are you real? Am I hallucinating?"

His chest tightened at the alarm in her eyes, as finally, the truth started to settle behind their amber depths. "Did I carry you into the bedroom last night? Did I drive the car here? Did I talk to the flight attendant on board the airplane?"

She nodded.

"I am real. I merely have the ability to move between planes of existence. Older than the druids, there have been spirits who walked the earth, guiding humans. When it became necessary, some chose human companions. Over the centuries, realm walkers emerged, a synthesis of the two. I am one of those."

She swallowed and shifted in her seat. "And so, how do I figure into this mythology of yours?"

"In 1758, when the British discovered you, and sentenced you to the same fate they dealt your father, I intervened."

"How?"

"As I said, we are supposed to maintain a balance."

He resumed his seat in the chair. "I did the one thing no realm walker is ever supposed to do."

"What is that?"

"I stopped a natural death. Yours."

"Mine?" Her eyes widened and she sat up straight, like a child in front of the principal.

"If I had been quicker, I might have influenced events in a way that could have saved your father. Or not. However, when I saw you, and I knew what your father had done, I couldn't let the British garrison commander kill you. I saved you from what would have been a natural death upon the sea. I halted time long enough to move you somewhere safe. The British presumed you died at sea, in an escape attempt, which would have happened if I hadn't helped.

"Why would the British want me dead?" Her tone mocked him. "What made you break the rules?"

"The British wanted you dead purely for your name. Teagan Deschamb. You were French. Your father, son of a union between a Frenchman and an English girl, led a double life. He had married an English colonist, yet supported the French autonomy that held portions of New Scotland. Your father's actions were to protect his legacy."

A blank stare gave him little indication of the thoughts running through her mind. For the moment, he didn't wish to intrude.

The kitten leapt onto Teagan's lap and she scooped the furry bundle into her arms again, as if grasping something tangible gave her something to wrap her mind around. She held the purring creature and stroked it gently.

He envied the cat.

"Ranulf Deschamb did not commit treason against his countrymen. He merely built a clock that could inevitably alter the future. He then tried to keep you safe from the people who wanted to destroy it."

She stopped massaging the kitten. Her brow furrowed and she leaned forward. "The missing clock?"

"The same one."

"But there's nothing to it!" Teagan insisted. "Why were the British even interested in it? Who would want to destroy it? It's just a bit of scrappy wood with a chime. It doesn't even work right. It chimes thirteen times, instead of twelve, the cuckoo doesn't pop out, and it just sits in the door. Who would even care?"

Darius took a deep breath. "Realm walkers."

Chapter Eleven

Teagan gripped the arms of the chair and readied herself. The man in front of her called himself a realm walker. The same people, or spirits, who were chasing her.

Enemy. Run. Escape.

Her mind shouted the words with each beat of her heart. But another part of her, deep in her gut, told her running would be futile. If he'd wanted to harm her he would have already. Instead, he seemed intent on helping her. Whether she wanted his help or not. Still, she had to ask the question. "Then, you're here to kill me? And reclaim a clock which someone else stole."

"Hardly."

The fingers of his right hand drummed against his leg, marking an imaginary cadence. As he had done in the car yesterday.

His expression darkened as he stared at her. Maybe he didn't intend to harm her, but any man who looked that devilish with a countenance that serious meant trouble. *One way or another.*

She took a slow deep breath. "Then what do you want with me? The more you tell me the more confused I get. First there was the story about the girl in Chicago, now you tell me a story about some eighteenth-century femme fatale who died in a storm with a clock for an albatross. Cut to the chase. I need to contact my aunt and uncle. I have an article deadline. And I have one hell of a hangover from whatever you slipped me last night."

"Elsa and Joe are safe. For now. The navigation system on the ship malfunctioned, and they were delayed a couple of days, that's all."

"But the airline said—"

"I know. Who are you more tempted to believe, right now? A technical piece of equipment dependent solely upon the data supplied by mortals? Or me?"

She frowned. "And my aunt and uncle... they're safe?"

"For now."

"That's not good enough! They have to be safe forever."

"Forever is unrealistic for mortals." His mouth quivered slightly.

She wondered if he tasted like sassafras. *Stop it,* she warned herself. "Explain the clock," she pressed.

"That's why we have to go to Smith Island." Darius's jaw tensed and he stood once more. "Without the clock, we will have to use the island as the portal."

"Now we're going to an island?"

He ignored that question, his gaze narrowed as he focused on his plan. "I think I know a way to set things right. But you—or we—have to revisit 1758."

"Yeah. Good luck with that."

He cocked an eyebrow at her. "Oh, I'm serious."

"And I, might I remind you, write non-fiction. I write travel, not time travel. Spirit walkers, magically traveling across the centuries—none of that is tangible.

"Neither was your vision. Or your dream this morning. But that clock is. And you yourself heard it strike thirteen."

She shrugged. "So?"

"Whenever the clock strikes thirteen, the portal opens or closes."

"You keep mentioning this portal, like I'm supposed to comprehend, miraculously. What and where is it, exactly?"

"What do you know about the lore of Oak Island?"

She hated questions answered with questions, but sighed, resigned. "Nothing."

"Originally, it was called Smith's Island. Supposedly, in the late 1700s, three young kids found evidence of treasure there. But they couldn't get the treasure themselves, because of the various traps set to ward off trespassers. Your father used the island to stash the clock he built."

"The clock that strikes thirteen and opens some door?"

"The clock that holds time suspended and protects the timekeeper, the holder of the clock."

"Impossible." She realized her protests were getting redundant but couldn't seem to stop herself from uttering them.

"Improbable. Yet not impossible. I was there. I was sent to find the clock. Two of us were dispatched to find it, and to destroy it."

"Why did the clock need to be destroyed?"

"Because, while a realm walker can play with time to some extent, no mortal should."

"Why not?"

"Balance. What Deschamb did once, he could no doubt do again. Such power would inevitably destablize the balance of the universe."

She stood, eager to move about and put more distance between them. "This is all way too science-fictiony for me."

He actually smiled.

Damn it. His smile was far too attractive.

"I doubt that. I know for a fact you preferred Jean Luc Piccard to James T. Kirk."

"Humph." *Of course he knew that.*

Darius ignored her obvious displeasure and continued.

"Deschamb carried with him some primordial memory or sense of wisdom from the ancients, as do most of us. His was of time. If the clock had fallen into the wrong hands, then the history of North America might be very different. America might still sing praises to a monarch, French or English. Who can say?"

"And so, just destroy the clock and the natural order of things plays out."

He smirked. "Easier said by you, now, than was the case three-hundred-fifty-one years ago."

"And why is that?"

"Because I used it to save your life."

She bit her lip. *Hmmm...so I didn't see that coming.*

"You managed to escape the cell where the garrison commander had imprisoned you, and you stole a skiff. Remember, Lunenburg is far north of Halifax. You would have had trouble navigating in the best weather, but this was storm season. You were close to a hundred miles from where you needed to be. The squall came up so fast, you had no time to prepare, or to avoid it."

"Enter superhero-realm-walker?"

"I found you already waterlogged, clinging to the boat."

****

Lunenburg, 1758

Clouds spiraled overhead like demons' eyes staring down upon her. Teagan gripped the oars firmly and pushed against the current of the waves, propelling herself farther out to sea. Behind her, on the coast, lay certain death in the form of a battalion of British soldiers intent on hanging her, or worse.

If she could get to the island, she could at least hide out for a few days, until interest in her waned.

Another wave broke across the bow of the tiny skiff, drenching her. The waves rumbled higher with each pitch and tossed her from side to side.

The oar in her left hand fell free from her grasp and disappeared into the blackish water. Cold as ice the waves lapped at the sides of the boat, taunting her to follow the wooden paddle. Another roll of the water and the skiff upended sending her sliding toward the stern of the craft. Like a giant sea serpent, the wave rolled beneath the vessel, leveling it once more, as she clung to the wooden slat seat. The other oar followed the first. Overhead, the clouds grew ever angrier, swooping and surging in a frantic dance. Sea and heavens engaged in a tug-of-war to see which could pitch her from the skiff first.

Teagan righted herself, and bent low in the hull, awaiting the next roll of water and wind. Lightning cracked the twilight sky, and she jumped from the closeness of the hit.

The sea and the clouds conspired against one another, and against her, thrashing her repeatedly, until her arms weakened. Numb from exhaustion and from cold, she sank to the floor of the boat, and prayed for a miracle.

If the ocean heard her plea, it ignored her cry as it roiled once more beneath the boat, capsizing the craft and pitching her once and for all into the cold darkness of brine and brimstone as a lightning bolt struck the hull.

****

The pieces were starting to come together in Teagan's overtaxed brain. "And so, these two deaths are linked to me because I'm somehow the reincarnated spirit of these two women whom you saved from certain death."

"Yes. Exactly," Darius agreed.

Giggly laughter bubbled up from her chest, swelling to hysteria as she sat there, staring at him. She tried, unsuccessfully, to stop the raucous response to what she knew must be a wonderfully romantic tale of self-sacrifice. Instead, the laughter boiled over again, causing her to gasp for air between fits of giggling.

"I'm sorry," she stammered, "I can't stop—"

Forty-eight hours of hijinks and little true rest had taken its toll. Teagan's arms and legs ached and trembled from the stress.

Potassium. I need potassium. Bananas for breakfast. Brilliant.

Badly brilliant. Only a genius would know that she would need bananas for breakfast.

Darius sighed loudly and stepped towards her. "Come on Miss Hyena. It's obviously naptime for you."

Unforgiving cackles tore from her throat at his calling her Miss Hyena. Visions of the cartoon characters in polka-dot dresses with hyena faces from an old, animated film swam through her head, sending her once more into hysteria.

Eventually, the laughter canister inside her chest emptied and her cacophonous revelry dissipated to a merely irreverent chuckle as he led her to the bed and she settled into it. He folded the blanket over.

She reached out and grabbed his hand. She hadn't meant to. The emotional release had left her unprepared, vulnerable…and scared. "Please don't. Don't go."

Darius perched on the edge of the bed, his hand still clasped in hers.

Her fingers tingled where their hands met.

His gaze softened. "You're afraid?"

She nodded. That was an understatement.

"Well, at least now, I know you've been paying attention to me."

"I'm still clueless as to what this all means. That's what frightens me most. Why did the guys at the festival–how did they know to single me out? What were they supposed to do?"

"You should rest, now. This is a lot to take in. We can talk more after you sleep."

She didn't want to sleep. Not yet. Who knew what strange dreams would follow? What new and unusual path her life would take when next she woke?

She squeezed his hand, hard. "I want to know all of it. Now. If I'm to accept this is all real and deal with it, really deal with it, then let's get it all out now so I can process and move on."

He considered her words for a moment, then nodded. "Tit for tat. Reckoning."

"Which means?"

"Someone convinced those men that they needed to either kill you or kidnap you."

"If you're the only one who knows that it happened at all, then who wants me dead? And why are you helping me?"

"Oh, I'm in trouble too. Remember, I am the one who stopped a natural death, originally. That is a huge infraction."

"But you're like some kind of immortal, spiritual creature, right?"

"Even spiritual creatures have rules. Realm walkers are not autonomous. We serve to maintain a balance. We answer to one another for our actions. What one of us does can affect the actions of the others."

"How many are there?"

"Enough. The world is a big place."

"Hey, if you're half human, then how do you exist?"

"Later. Now, you rest."

She closed her eyes and released his hand.

"Darius, do you bleed?"

"Of course, I do," replied.

"Do you die?"

He stared at her for what she perceived to be a very long time. At first he considered bending time just to hold her suspended in the moment. However, the swaying of the curtain quickly dismissed the notion.

He cleared his throat. "Everyone dies."

He brushed his fingertips across her forehead, playing with her hair. Then, he bent to kiss her lightly on the lips. She shuddered involuntarily at the shock that spiraled through her body when his lips brushed hers.

He stood and moved toward the door. "Ancients always carry their memories with them from one life to another. And we always recognize those we are meant to find. We always know one of our own."

Chapter Twelve

Chicago, IL

Dana slicked her hair back with her hand and sighed in disgust. "I can't do it. There's a piece missing."

"So, we'll get another piece," her partner said. "What is it?"

"It looks like there's some kind of key. The key is missing."

"So, get another key. What's the big deal? Hell, there must be half a dozen things in your old man's workroom that would work."

She shifted her gaze from her work to the creature who stood across the room, doing crunches. Bare chested, short wavy hair, he did present a beautiful specimen of male sexuality. No brains, just brawn.

She clenched her hands so hard, her nails bit into the flesh of her palms. "Don't be an idiot," she growled. "This isn't a regular clock."

The sound of crunching aluminum served as her only warning as he hurled an empty can in her direction. She ducked, and the crumpled beer can landed on the table next to the clock. "That's right. Break what we *do* have," she bit out.

"Don't call me stupid," he yelled.

"I didn't. I told you not to behave like an idiot."

She closed her eyes and tried to calm her thoughts. Eric, all beautiful muscle and lithe limb, did not possess the brain capacity of a thimble. There existed no stupidity in Eric, just as there existed no ambition. Just simple testosterone and an inexplicable fascination with spiders.

"I don't know what the big deal is anyway. It's not like it's made of gold or anything valuable. I could buy one at the flea market for about ten bucks."

Not likely. In fact, if her luck were as keen as her eyesight had been when she spied the thing in the overhead compartment, she wouldn't be frequenting flea markets for a long time.

She suppressed a laugh and turned to face him. "Lover, this is definitely not that type of clock."

Eric climbed off the sofa, stretched languidly, sauntering toward her, eyeing the timepiece she hovered over. Besides its aesthetic value, the damned thing had to be two hundred years old, or older. Something about it seemed vaguely familiar. Whoever had left it in the overhead, had been a fool, or just ignorant. The craftsmanship was exquisite. The internal gears were pristine, as if brand new. But Dana knew they weren't. She had never seen anything quite like it. A Christi's quality antique. She'd bet her life on it.

Something so familiar. Faberge? Bardiche? Her fingers gently traced the face once more, examining the intricacy as if it were a fine braille manuscript. Delicate carved markings, and embossed gold leaf appliques twined beneath her fingertips. Interestingly, each hour on the clock corresponded to a separate inlaid panel on its face. The tips of her thumb and forefinger massaged the grooves reverently, until she had completed the circle, eleven, twelve, thirteen...

Thirteen panels. An extra slot between twelve and one. She lifted the clock toward the light and squinted against the glare. So small. Seemingly insignificant. Something she should remember...something she'd read or heard—

Eric grabbed her around the waist, possessively and pushed toward the edge of the table, intent on kissing her. She pushed him away when his hands found her ass and pinched her.

"Not now—"

"Why not," he growled, sliding his hand up her thigh as he slid his mouth down her neck. "Now's a perfect time. I'm horny. You're aggravated. It'd be hot. You know it would."

Hot couldn't compare with what she had just found. "I said, not now. If you behave yourself, later, we can have some fun."

"Damn, Dana. Why wait?" His other hand found her breast.

"Because I am still working here. I need the key that fits this clock. Or I need to figure out how to make one. Now, go be a good boy and take a cold shower, or find some porn. Entertain yourself."

She elbowed him again, and he straightened. The bulge beneath his belt was barely confined by the fabric of his jeans.

"Hell, just take it to a locksmith. Maybe they could make one."

A locksmith wouldn't know the first thing about this.

"What is it that makes it so special, anyway?"

She inhaled and counted to five, then exhaled her

annoyance. "This, my horny friend, is sort of like an ancient security device."

"Like a burglar alarm?"

"More like a force field. He cocked his head to the left and stared over her shoulder at the wooden and metal trappings. "So what do you need it for?"

"This could make all our dreams come true. If I'm right, and I suspect I am, then this clock could make us richer than Midas."

"The muffler place right?"

"No, my dear. The king from Greek mythology who turned everything he touched to gold."

Now, she had his attention. "We could go anywhere we wanted, take whatever we want, and no one would be able to stop us."

"How come?"

"Because," she began as she turned and fingered the delicately carved clock face, "This clock is magical."

He snorted. "Yeah, I'm magical, too. I got a wand for ya—"

She cut him off. "Look at the clock face, Eric. It isn't drawn like a normal clock. There are fourteen lines, meaning thirteen spaces on the clock."

"So?"

"So, I heard a story once, a legend about a device that could bend time. Now most clocks are divided into twelve hours, am I right?"

He shrugged.

"Then why would this one have thirteen sections?"

Another shrug. "It only has twelve numbers."

"That's right. But if you look closely, right there, is a shadow on the clock's face. It's almost completely faded. That thirteenth slot is when the magic happens."

"It just looks like a regular old clock to me."

She bit back her frustration at his lack of interest in their find. "Look at the markings on the outside edges. That's not scratches a cat made. Those carvings have a meaning.

"I still don't get it."

"You don't have to get it. You just have to believe in it. Let me do the work. You just do what I want, when I tell you to." She stepped back from the table. "You might be onto something, though. We could have a key made. A locksmith wouldn't know where to begin with something like this. Although, a watchmaker might. Or better yet, I might know just who could help us."

"If you didn't have the key, why'd you steal it?"

"I told you, I didn't steal it. Exactly. The woman who put it in the overhead compartment just left it there. I bet she's regretting it now. Something as important as this should never have been let out of her sight."

"Maybe she got it at a flea market. Thought it was just a plain old clock."

"Trust me, babe, whoever she was, she didn't have this because she's a lucky shopper. She had this because she knew someone or she had a connection to something powerful. Like I said, I have a feeling this is big. This could be the answer to all our prayers."

Eric laughed, tugging at the leather tab on his belt. "Not all of 'em," he said as he ran his gaze up and down her body. "You're still dressed. And the only thing sexier than you greedy, is you greedy and naked."

****

Corrig waited for the security guard to motion him through the magnetometer. When she smiled and him and handed him back his gun, he slid it back into its holster and shrugged his sports jacket back on as he followed her to the gate for check-in.

The agent looked at him, then at the photo on his identification. Tall, thin, cropped hair; he looked every bit the policeman. A wave of the paperwork, and a few murmured words between the guard and the customer service agent and he had a window seat in the back with early boarding priority.

Teagan Alexander wasn't doing much to cover her tracks. An All Points Bulletin had found a hit within a couple of hours. Catching an international flight did nothing to keep her hidden from pursuit.

Corrig left the Millers' house to Ritter. Ritter could handle the reports and arson investigation once the couple returned home. As far as Officer Ritter knew, his departure was just official business; extraditing a possible suspect in an arson case.

Law enforcement had its advantages.

The flight crew showed up, and he introduced himself to the captain and first officer, then to the lead flight attendant. Another perk. The lead flight attendant's eyes glistened appreciatively when she looked at him. Shame he didn't have a long layover in Chicago that he could take advantage of.

Perhaps he'd indulge in a little realm walker dream diving tonight.

She whispered, "What do you like to drink? I'll bring it to you after we're airborne."

His mouth twitched as she licked her lips, slick and red from her lipstick. She did know how to work it.

What a shame. He would have enjoyed her.

Business before pleasure this time if he meant to catch up to Teagan Alexander.

"Scotch."

"On the rocks?"

He shook his head. She winked at him and wandered up the aisle, walking a little more slowly, swishing her hips carefully as she made her way toward the small crowd of people filing into the passenger cabin.

He needed to keep his mind on the job, and mischief on the back burner.

With any luck, he'd find the flight attendant again, once he finished his job. And he wanted to finish this particular task. He wanted to get to Teagan before Zahra or the others found her.

They could have Darius. Corrig intended to destroy the clock, and the girl, and have both problems solved before any serious questions arose. If he destroyed the clock first, then she would no longer be protected. He smiled, thinking of the wicked fun he could have before he wrung the life out of the silly girl. Resolved, he closed his eyes. First things first. The clock before all else.

Three hundred fifty years ago, he had lost the damned thing when Deschamb died, and the girl disappeared. Now he would correct that mistake. This time, he'd make certain the clock and its owner stayed lost for good.

****

"Realm walkers didn't take the clock," Darius said, squinting at the bright morning sun as it streamed through the window of their cabin.

Teagan paused stirring her tea. Her eyes were wide when she looked up at him.

She looked better for having slept the day away. He had let her sleep through the afternoon and into the night, setting a cup of soup out for her in case she woke in the middle of the night, hungry. The cup sat half empty on the dresser, and she had traded her shirt for the print shawl she bought in Charlotte. Craftily tied, it clung to her curves, distracting him a bit too much.

"How do you know?" she asked.

"Someone called the airline asking about a lost luggage claim. Said something about picking up the wrong shopping bag, not realizing until they got home."

She frowned. "That's ridiculous. The bag wasn't missing. Whoever took the clock left it behind on purpose."

She retrieved her cup and sipped the tea. Steam curled around her whiskey-hued eyes, giving her the appearance of a faerie.

"I know that, and you know that. However, the agent who got the call didn't. They called my cell phone this morning."

"You've got a cell phone? I've been cooped up here for two days, worried sick about Elsa and Joe, and you've had a cell phone this whole time?"

He ignored the barb. Clearly, sleep had also invigorated her temper. She was much easier to handle, exhausted.

"Wait," she continued without waiting for his response. "How do you know it's not a realm walker who has the clock?"

He smiled at her. "Trust me. Realm walkers wouldn't be calling baggage service to return it. If a realm walker had the clock, we'd know, because you'd be dead."

The cup trembled in her hand. He suspected she might lose her grasp altogether, but she swallowed and straightened her spine, gathering her composure. She finished and set the teacup lightly in the saucer. As he watched her struggle with nerves and the China, the blood drained from her face. Only her eyes retained their color. Her complexion faded to the color of the tablecloth.

Those same eyes watched him, wary. "You're serious. Aren't you?"

"Unfortunately."

She let out an exasperated groan. "Then why are we even here. Drop me off at a morgue somewhere with a good book, and I'll just get some reading done while I wait for the inevitable."

"Don't be melodramatic. I said the realm walkers wanted to set things right, and I had saved your life when I shouldn't have. I never said that we couldn't figure out another solution."

She squinted, and her lips pursed in a frown. Eventually, she found her voice. "So, then, what is the answer? What is your solution that will get me back to my oh-so-boring life, where the worst thing I have to contend with is the German shepherd that chases my car whenever I drive down the street?"

"For that, we have to take a little trip."

"We're on a little trip. Wait. Do you mean one of your little trips in and out of whatever world you live in?"

"You have a lot to learn, grasshopper."

She screwed up her face. "I remember that show.

My parents used to watch it."

He allowed his lips to curl in amusement and gave her a wink. "Ah, there may be hope for you yet. And no, you are not going on any meditational wanderings right now. Consider this research for one of your travel articles."

A blush of color filled her cheeks again. She almost returned his smile before attempting to hide her mouth by grabbing her cup and downing her last sip of tea.

That pleased him to no end. He'd get through to her yet.

"Um, can we stop somewhere, so I can get something better to wear? I think these clothes are a bit ripe. And I'm cold."

She definitely would need something better to wear. As flattering as the sari was, where they were headed, such a top could get her into severe trouble, to say the least. "I was thinking just that. What do you have in your bag from Saturday's adventure."

"Nothing. Just my skirt and chemise. The thief stole my corset. My very expensive corset. I had the clock wrapped in it."

When she crossed her arms over her chest, he caught himself. He had been staring at her; staring at the tautness of the fabric where her breasts swelled and tugged the cloth open to reveal a delicate expanse of ivory flesh.

She had no vanity. Not once since she had been with him had he seen her look in a mirror. Not that she needed to. No matter how disheveled she became, she was still achingly lovely—as his body's involuntary and repeated response to her made abundantly clear to him.

He cleared his throat. "There's a mall in Truro. It's a couple of hours away. Can you survive that long?"

She nodded. "I don't need much, just some underwear and maybe a pair of long pants and another top." She rose and set the teacup next to her soup from the night before and headed back to the cabin for the shower.

Darius watched her head for the door, admiring the curve of her hips as she sauntered past him. As beautiful as she looked this morning, shorts would never do where he planned to go.

"Mr. Alwin," the receptionist greeted him with a polite smile as he approached the desk to check out. "Someone called late last night, looking for you."

He tensed. Anyone he actually wanted to talk to would have dialed his cell. The tiny brunette behind the counter offered him an envelope. He glanced over his shoulder. Fortunately, Teagan had not followed him into the lobby, but sat on the porch, basking in the sun's warmth.

Unlike modern hotels, part of this inn's charm lay in the fact that there were no modern voice mail devices. Instead, whoever had been on desk duty last night had scribbled the message longhand onto a sheet of stationery, then secured it in an envelope for him to pick up in the morning.

He ripped the seal on the envelope and gingerly pulled the sheaf from within, half expecting a letter bomb.

Sorry I missed the flight. Corrig is enroute. Bonfire at the Miller place. Tick tock. Zahra.

He crumpled the paper in his fist as his skin

prickled with unease. If Zahra knew where he had brought Teagan, then she had probably figured out where they were headed. The bonfire at the Miller place meant Corrig had figured out Teagan had the clock, and he had done exactly as he had warned her. Corrig had burned the place to the ground.

Zahra had the last part right. Time was running out.

Darius strode toward the patio with purpose. At least he had a plan. If it worked, it might solve the current problem for everybody. If Teagan survived the trip.

Through the glass panes of the door, he could see her bent over the railing, no doubt playing with the kittens. *Too tempting.*

For his plan to work, Teagan definitely needed a corset. The fact that the thought of her in a corset made his blood heat was just an added bonus. He smiled in spite of the severity of the situation.

First stop, clothes. Then a trip to the past.

Chapter Thirteen

Chicago, IL

Dana shuffled through the papers on the professor's desk. Bernard Kinsey, besides being an authority on American History, had a passion for obscure legends. He held, as no secret to his students, that he had been working on a book of North American folklore and mysticism. From the piles of papers stacked around the room and the books that cluttered most of the space in his office, he'd been working on it for more than a decade, she guessed.

And the idiot didn't have a clue how accurate his research was.

"Don't leave anything to chance. Make sure every surface is wiped clean. I don't want anyone to suspect anything, or to have a reason to come looking for us," she called to Eric.

She sat down at Kinsey's computer. "Password," she demanded.

Kinsey's arm twitched against the duct tape that held him to the chair. He ignored her, which irked her.

"You know, Dr. Kinsey, the best thing about a boyfriend like Eric is that he knows everything about spiders. So, when I asked him what he would use to do some nasty damage, he immediately knew that a brown recluse would be the perfect arachnid for July. The bite is horrible, but the worst part is how the venom causes necrosis in some people. I hope you aren't one of those people. It can be very painful. I heard of a woman, once, whose scalp gradually peeled away until there was nothing left of her but the skull. They couldn't do anything to save her."

His sharp inhale pleased her. Was that a bead of sweat trailing down the drawn, beard-covered cheek? Fear did motivate.

"Password," she repeated.

"It's just my book," Kinsey burst out. "Why do you want to steal my writing?"

She sighed loudly. "Eric, did you bring your friend?"

Eric, hair straggling over his brow nodded. He slid the backpack off his shoulder and unzipped the main compartment, reached his hand inside, and withdrew a clear plastic container. Inside, sat something dark and dangerous.

"Boys," she said with a smile and a shrug. She transferred her gaze from Eric to Dr. Kinsey. "They do love bugs."

"Spiders aren't bugs," Eric corrected. "They're arachnids. See, insects have six legs and exoskeletons, but arachnids have eight—"

"Eric, that's enough. I'm sure Dr. Kinsey is aware of the difference, and very much as impressed with your knowledge as I am."

Eric smiled at her. *Such a puppy*. When he wasn't trying to pin her down and mate, he could actually be cute.

She stood and moved to where Kinsey sat. She bent over his chair and cocked her head to the side.

"According to Eric here, the necrosis isn't a big problem. It only happens in a diminutive percentage of victims—"

"Yeah," Eric interrupted. "See, mostly, the bite just swells up really big and gets real hard, and hot. Like if somebody stuck a really hot baseball under your skin. Man, that would hurt. Can you imagine if it bit you in the balls?"

Dr. Kinsey uttered an expletive and jerked in his chair, struggling to move away from the boy. "You're insane. Both of you."

"Not insane, professor. Just intent. I need some information that I'm sure you have. Now, once more, what is your password?"

Tiny glistening beads of sweat had broken out across the professor's brow as he shuffled his glance from Eric to her. She could see him trying to make sense, weighing pride against pain.

"Tatiana."

"Tatiana? Hmm, an old student?"

"No."

Dana drummed her nails on the desk expectantly.

"My ex-wife."

Such an attachment promised a truthful answer. "Ex-wife? I had no idea. You seem way too consumed with your work to ever entertain a real relationship."

A grimace tugged at the right corner of his mouth, and he avoided her eyes. "I suppose that's why she is my ex-wife."

"Ah. How sad. Tatiana is a lovely name. Russian?"

"Yes."

"I'm surprised. I'd have figured you for the bookworm type, not the exotic, mysterious Soviet type."

She ignored his response and typed, Tatiana.

The screen flashed and a file popped up. "Ah. Thank you, Professor. This is perfect. Now, one other thing. Which chapter covers North American myths?"

"Wh-what exactly are you wanting?" His eyes darted to the corner where Eric sat, playing with the plastic container.

"Ah. Well, specifically, I need information on a story you told in one of the lectures you gave last year. You were talking about the concept of the dreamcatcher and about astral projection, and you mentioned something about a French tale that came through the indigenous mythologies. It was about a clock. Do you remember?"

He nodded, eyes round with confusion. "But it's archaic. Few people even know of it in this day and time."

"Which is why I'm so interested. I'm thinking of doing my senior thesis on the persistence of mythology in a progressive western society."

No teacher could resist a student's exuberance when it came to academia. Between Kinsey's sexual proclivity for his female students, and a nerd's curiosity, he wouldn't be able to resist her, or her bait.

Kinsey blinked. "And you want to focus on the fractal clock?"

"That's it." She scanned through the files until she uncovered the story he had mentioned, hit print, and waited for the dust covered printer machine to spit out the copy.

She glanced at Kinsey. "Well?"

"There isn't anything to tell. The French who were

driven out of Nova Scotia insisted they would be saved, and that the British would be turned back. But it never happened.

"Why not?"

"No one knows. The one or two references I found were incomplete."

"Indulge me. Tell me what you remember."

He licked his lips, nervously. "Can I…do you have any water?"

Dana nodded to Eric who threw her a bottle of water from the backpack crumpled on the floor at his feet. She opened it and took a long sip, then crossed the room to the professor and held the bottle to his lips. He swallowed a few gulps, then choked, and sputtered. As he pulled away from the bottle, a trickle of water fell onto his lap.

"Now, now, professor. Neatness counts. Let me to wipe that for you." She licked her lips and smiled as she put her hand against his crotch, pressing the water beads into the fabric, and massaging the ever-growing bulge beneath.

He shook his head, embarrassed at her implication. "No. That won't be necessary." He tried to scoot away from her hand. She noticed however, his eyes stayed focused on her breasts, which cleverly pressed against the lace of her top.

"Alright then," she said as she stayed bent over him until his face almost brushed her flesh when she whispered in his ear. "Eric is waiting, Professor. And so am I. Tell us a story."

Kinsey cleared his throat. "The French settled Louisbourg in hopes of laying claim to most of the Maritimes." Professor Kinsey's voice trembled as he began. "Louisbourg had been a thriving port and village for the French. They already had Quebec. They had spent decades forging agreements for trade routes and friendships with the natives, so they had a strong defense for the mainland territories.

He paused, and Dana waved him on impatiently.

He continued. "However, those territories closest to the colonies were of primary concern to the British. King George didn't like competition. There was already unrest in the colonies, and England still used an iron fist when dealing with anyone bent on separation. Scottish prisoners and refugees had filled the lower part of Nova Scotia. The British army and navy intended to seize Cape Breton for the Empire. There had never been any love-loss between the two countries, so between the French and the British, the local tribes didn't stand to gain much."

She yawned deliberately and hitched her eyebrows expectantly at him.

"Yes—well, sorry. Um, there is an entry in a diary I read once. It was something I came across in a museum shop in New Orleans. It talked about a carpenter who lived in Baddock during that era. He was supposedly of French and British heritage, having been the son of an English mother and a French father."

"A mixed marriage—in that day? Tsk, tsk." She waved the water bottle at him, and he shook his head vehemently.

Scaredy cat. Afraid he'd choke, or afraid she'd get too close?

"Ranulf Deschamb was renowned as a master carpenter. Supposedly, the English colonists who lived in Halifax at the time coveted his work; so meticulous was his skill with timepieces.

"Yes, yes, get to the good stuff, Professor," Dana cut in. This was becoming tedious. "Give us the edited version."

"He lived with his daughter. Apparently, his wife had died, and he had raised the girl by himself. Not so unbelievable, but most men remarried if for no other reason than to have a nursemaid and cook. But not Deschamb.

"Despite his French name, he was well-liked by the English, and indeed spoke the king's language like anyone from London. The commander of the navy naturally did not trust him because of his name and his father's alliances, and so he made no secret of his desire to catch Deschamb in an act of treason."

"According to the tale written on the pages, Deschamb played both sides of the fence."

"He didn't want to alienate the French, but also knew that the British could make trouble for him."

"Among his passions was a love for clocks—for time pieces. One of the notes in the margin of the diary I found theorized his obsession with time had everything to do with the loss of his wife. He was obsessed with turning back time so he could save his wife."

She clenched her teeth. "Moving right along, Professor——"

"Whatever relevance that might have, we don't know. However, the journal cited plans had been found in Deschamb's workshop. The plans were detailed in his own handwriting with a blueprint or design for a timepiece that would alter time."

This is what she had come here for. "A time

machine?"

"No, no. Well, not exactly. According to this journal, the clock he had designed held two flaws. Instead of twelve equal sections like you have on a regular clock, this one had thirteen."

Eric looked up from his spider, suddenly interested in the conversation. "Hey, that's like—"

She swiveled and gave Eric a death glare. "Shut up, Eric." She didn't need him giving away anything, yet. "Go on, Professor. You said there were two flaws."

Kinsey glanced sideways at Eric, then back to Dana. She undid another button on her blouse, picked up the water bottle and held it against her chest. Sure enough, he forgot all about Eric again, as he watched her nipples swell from the cold.

Men... such simple, fragile creatures.

He blinked as if to break her enchantment, then continued. "He built it as a cuckoo clock. But there had to be a key."

"So?"

"Well, you see, cuckoo clocks are built sort of on a cog and wheel concept with a pulley. The gravity of the chain kind of primes the clock, keeping it going. It's not like the clocks today which run on batteries."

"And?"

"Well, according to the description, this one had a key. For winding." He stared at her, smiling conspiratorially, clearly enamored with his tale.

"A key."

"Yes, but the key is a mistake. It has to be. Cuckoo clocks don't need a key to wind. They are supposed to be self-winding. I mean, if it really was a cuckoo clock. The author theorized that Deschamb really held a strong loyalty to the Great Pretender, and that as the Stewarts had maintained a close camaraderie with the French. So too had Deschamb."

"Uh-huh. Fascinating." She thought she might have just gained the information she sought. However, in case the old man had another tasty morsel to share, she decided to let him ramble a bit longer.

"I did some fact checking with some of the local tribes a few years back. While no one could tell me of the clock, they did say that the folklore included tales of locals disappearing—being eaten by the spirits that haunted an island off the coast of Halifax. They believed that the island sought revenge for the bloody murders perpetrated there by pirates. Keep in mind, the natives lived in harmony with the earth, so they knew when the earth was out of sorts.

"Regardless of how or why it happened, the locals all agreed that occasionally some part of the island, swallowed people whole."

Her head began to throb. Perhaps she should have shut him up already. "What does that have to do with Deschamb and his time machine?"

"No, no. I told you, not a time machine. Just a clock, so far as anybody knew. But the locals all described Ranolf Deschamb as a man who dared to defy the curse of the island."

"What island is that?"

"Well, it didn't have a name at the time. Or maybe it did by then. Originally, when the British cartographers tried to chart the area, they just assigned it a number. But soon after Deschamb was killed, the king awarded it to a war hero called Smith, and it then became known as Smith's Island."

Rambling. Why did they all ramble? "Wait a minute. Did you say—Deschamb was killed? As in murdered?"

"Oh yes. He was captured by the British with two bags of silver, seized on the road to Louisbourg. The English constabulary insisted he had to have been paid by the French for selling information he had gleaned from his friends in Baddock and Halifax. They didn't even give him a public trial. They treated him as a hostile war prisoner and executed him on the gallows in the garrison. You see, the Brits had just successfully captured the port and taken the fortress and village."

The old man's face glimmered with the fever of enthusiasm as the words tumbled endlessly from his lips. In any other setting, she would have found him utterly boring. Here, in fact, as he droned on about Deschamb, his passionate prattling amused her.

Clearly, he was on a roll. "They accused her, also, of being a French spy, even though there existed little reason to believe she had any involvement with either faction. At sixteen, she was hardly spy material. Not to mention the fact that she was a woman."

Dana bristled at this assertion. *Ass. Why are they all asses?*

Kinsey must have sensed her annoyance, because he stammered, "Not that a woman couldn't be a good spy. It's just that they—Well, back then, men viewed women…differently."

He blushed so furiously, she had to stop herself from rolling her eyes.

"Anyhow, the English had razed Louisbourg, so they decided to take her back to Halifax for trial. However she accomplished it, Deschamb's daughter managed to escape from the English, steal a boat and head for the island."

"And?"

"The local people say she died in a storm or that the island claimed her."

She tried to temper her voice. "What about the clock?"

"Oh. Well, despite the notes about having found the plans for the clock, I never located any evidence that Deschamb ever built a clock, much less a timepiece that would alter time in any way. Remember, it took science another three hundred years before Einstein was born."

"What if he *had* done it, though?"

"Who? Einstein.? Well, if he had built—"

"No. Not Einstein. Deschamb."

"I suppose it would have been the greatest invention of all time." He chortled and looked up at her, grinning. "Forgive the pun. Clock…greatest invention of all time.

She ignored his feeble attempt at humor. *Why do they all try to be cute? Brilliant is enough.*

"What background would Deschamb have needed to create such a device though? No computers, no electricity. What?"

"The local people, and even some of the non-locals, would tell you that such a feat—if it were possible—could only be manipulated through the use of black magic."

"What about DaVinci? Didn't he draw plans for an airplane?" Dana offered.

Kinsey scoffed. "He would have been tried for witchcraft no doubt. The Church would have feared him promoting a man sprout wings and flying like the angels. As it is, DaVinci did invent a whole list of things."

She sighed. Back to the clock. "What kind of magic?"

He looked at her blankly. For all the story he had just related, she needed some theory about where the magic might have originated.

"Perhaps magic is too harsh a word," he finally responded.

She gnashed her teeth again. God this was irritating. She should let Eric have his fun.

She pulled a paper from her back pocket, unfolded it, and put it on his lap. "What kind of markings are those?"

Dr Kinsey studied the rubbings for several seconds. "It's difficult to tell from just the rubbings you present here. I take it the marks are engraved, not embossed?" Fear had turned to interest. He had stopped trying to scoot away from her. Now, he leaned in as closely as his tethered posture would allow.

She tapped the paper. "What difference would that make?"

"A great deal of difference. You see, if this rubbing were taken from something created long after the language upon it might be based, then we might know that from the raised elements. In such a case, the embossed image could be indicative of a fraud. A real craftsmen of that era would engrave, rather that emboss. He would be working from that single piece of wood, and so would carve the symbols into his work. So, which is it?"

She eyed him for more than a couple of seconds,

suspicious of what he said. "Engraved."

He studied the markings a bit longer, then said, "Access the appendix to my manuscript. It's in a separate file. Go to the pre-Sumerian page, print that page and bring it to me."

A moment later, she handed him the printout of the pre-Sumerian languages grid. He eyed it, comparing the two. "This is very interesting, indeed. Did you do it yourself?"

"The rubbing?"

"The carpentry. Did you do it?"

"I did not. That's why I'm here. You can help me by assessing its design and answering some simple questions." She smiled coquettishly at him, tempting him.

He stared at her. She could see in his expression his brain made the connections as he mulled her words. "Then, I'm sorry, my dear. I-I cannot help you anymore."

"Why not?"

"This cannot be real."

His left hand twitched. So did his left eye. He lied.

"Why not?"

"Look for yourself. These markings are Vinca. That would predate most societies by thousands of years. It's not even considered a real alphabet. It's just a series of symbols that predate the Sumerian cuneiform. Most scholars consider it gobbledygook. More importantly, those markings have been mixed with some form of an ogham, and rune symbology. This is a hodgepodge. It really has no significant historical relevance. Whatever you have, it is a fake."

She smiled and loosened the last button on her

brown lace shirt to reveal the red lace bra, beneath. She hiked her skirt a bit and walked over to him, standing so close, his face was even with her abdomen. Straddling him, she lowered herself onto his lap, and slid her hand between his legs, to cup his groin.

"Oh, Professor. Where is your imagination? Not only is it real, but I plan to use it to make history. Unfortunately, your reluctance makes me think you might not be around to witness the magnificence, once I figure out how to work my magic box."

He twitched again, and victory poured over her. "There it is. You have a tell, Professor Kinsey. You don't play poker, do you?"

His gaze told her, as much as the professed ignorance, he knew exactly what she had.

"Hey," she whispered as she stroked him. "What do you know about the key? If this were real, then how exactly would a key work and how could I get my hands on one?"

He struggled against the duct tape, shaking the paper in his hand. The avid attention he had given to her breasts earlier, waned now, as he tried, rather unsuccessfully to ward off her affect on his libido.

"Where did these symbols come from?" he asked, clearly desperate to distract her. "Where did you get this rubbing?"

"Now, now, settle down, Professor. As I said, the rubbing is real enough. The clock sort of fell into my care."

"Clock? You took this from a clock? Where did you find it?"

"Oh, I came across it during a trip recently."

His eyes lit. "It's real? You found a clock like the

one the diary described?"

She ignored his question and asked one of her own. "The key, Dr. Kinsey. How can I get a key?"

"I-I don't know that you could. Most clock makers were very protective of their work, especially the better-known ones. You would probably have to contact the clock maker or the company and have another key cut. Or have them rebuild the whole thing to include a custom designed key."

She didn't like the sound of that. "I don't think that is going to be an option."

"What if you took it back to where you found it? If as the old legends say, it is possessed of some ancient magic, then perhaps whatever is there would yield some answers for you? Perhaps someone there would recognize it for what it is…or is not."

She stood up, and stepped away from the professor, carefully buttoning her blouse as she considered his idea. "Nova Scotia? You said Smith Island?"

"Er—it's Oak Island. Smith Island is what it was called before—"

"Sorry, Professor. I don't have time for any more chitchat. I have promises to keep. At least to myself and to Eric."

A mixture of misery and confusion played across the academic's face. He looked like an errant child, dismissed by a favorite teacher. From across the room, Eric looked up at her and grinned.

Good dog.

"Eric, I'm done with the professor. You can dispose of him however you wish. It doesn't matter much to me, one way or another. Break his neck, feed him to your spider, or scare the piss out of him. He's all yours. Hurry, though. We have to go to the airport."

She scooped the papers from behind her on the desk, gave one last peck on the cheek, then moved toward the door.

"But wait, stop! I gave you what you wanted." His voice came out high-pitched and frantic. "Why can't you let me go?"

She smiled at the old man. "Well, now, consider yourself part of my experiment. If all goes well, maybe I'll be able to show you someday…in the past."

Chapter Fourteen

Truro, Nova Scotia

Darius stood outside the dressing room and tapped his foot, impatiently. "Now."

From behind the wooden slats, she replied, "No. Absolutely not. This is ridiculous!"

"You can either come out now, or I can come in." Then in a lower voice, "Imagine what everyone will think we're doing if I have to step inside there with you."

A brief moment of silence before the door clicked and Teagan swung the door open.

Even he, a master at self-control, nearly lost his composure at the sight of her standing in the doorway. "Hmm. Perhaps I should rethink this plan."

Trying ardently to conceal herself from others in the store, Teagan Miller did justice to the costume in a way that few women could.

The tight black bodice, trimmed with embroidered ribbon, dipped perilously low, barely accommodating her form, exposing not only more of the white chemise, but also a dangerous amount of cleavage.

Flowing from the cinched waist, yards of blue fabric draped over hips broad enough to entice a man.

She'd either be burned at the stake or be married by day's end, dressed as she was.

"I want my old corset back. This one...this one is indecent even by today's standards." She stared at herself in the mirror, shuddered, then glared at him. "You have got to be out of your mind if you think I am going anywhere in this outfit."

"Wait here."

He left her in the dressing room while he stepped into the front showroom to talk to the owner. Within a few moments, the woman had returned arms filled with with a long black lace up corset, embroidered with leaves of burgundy and gold, and a fitted jacket of burgundy and gold.

He accepted the costume in his hands, gingerly, as if the garment were fragile, and returned to the dressing room.

"Try this," he said.

A black over skirt covered the chemise, the corset layered over top. The corset sat high enough in the front to amply conceal any imperfections. The finishing touch was the jacket. Brocade of gold and burgundy buttoned neatly over her curves, offering no more than a peek at cleavage. A gentle ruffle of the silk at the elbows and hem made her face lose its cynical expression.

"It's gorgeous. I'll swelter in it, though. Do you have any idea how many layers there are to this? Not to mention if you're going for inconspicuous, this will make me stick out, don't you think?"

"Not where I'm taking you."

****

Corrig locked the car and walked toward the pier. He had waited most of the day, expecting Darius and the woman to show up. They hadn't. That left one good place they could be—the island. Unless they meant to hide in the national park indefinitely, there was no other place to go. The sun was bright and warm, encouraging crowds of tourists to wander the shops and restaurant near the marina.

He meandered toward the charter, ever watchful for anyone who might be lurking. The captain had stepped up onto the dock and studied his watch.

Corrig approached the man, who looked up at him, a half-smile on his wind-weathered face.

"You must be the man who called about the island, then?"

"Yes. You ready?"

"I am. Are you alone?" Corrig nodded.

"Seems a waste. A lovely afternoon like this. You treasure hunting, eh?"

Corrig didn't reply. Instead, he gestured toward the boat. "Shall we?"

"Ah, right. That'll be forty dollars."

Corrig withdrew a one-hundred-dollar bill and handed the cash to the man.

"I'll get you change."

"No need," Corrig replied. "You can keep it, as long as you keep this excursion confidential."

The man hesitated, rubbing his fingers together over the bill. His glance wavered from the money to Corrig and back again. "Does this make me an accessory to something illegal? I mean, it bein' private and all?"

"No. I can assure you. You are in no way liable or responsible for anything improper. I merely have business with the property holders, and I want to surprise them. That's all. If anyone asks, you only have to deny this trip. You'll see. There's no problem."

He could tell the captain wanted to believe that, and being reasonably weak-willed, at least where money was concerned, he accepted Corrig's explanation, as well as his money.

"Will your friends be needing a ride over to the island?"

"I suspect they've already made arrangements."

The man shrugged. A frown of disappointment tugged the corner of his mouth. He hopped back down to the boat. "Watch yer step—You on vacation?"

"You might call it that."

"And you're American, eh?"

Corrig chose not to reply.

"Where're you visiting from?"

He ignored that question too and posed one of his own. "How long is the ride?"

"About twenty minutes—"

"I think I'll close my eyes and rest." Corrig tilted his head back and heard the captain curse under his breath.

Corrig smiled. End of conversation.

When he opened his eyes again, he met a much different view than the tangled wilderness he had remembered. In three centuries, Oak Island had transformed completely. From this approach, he could see architectural structures jutting up from the scrub of trees that dotted the shore.

Crowds meant complications. If a digging crew were currently hovering, then Darius would wait until dark.

Unless he'd already missed them.

The thought rankled him. Even with a twelve-hour

head start, the two wouldn't have been able to do much yet. Nova Scotia, unlike New York City, did not stay open all night. With any luck, his prey had lost nearly a day, which had allowed him to catch up. He slipped his hand inside his jacket. The hard, cool metal of his gun against his palm reassured him.

"Now there is an inn opened up about 1978 just across the causeway, on the mainland overlooking the western shore. You and your friends interested in the shaft, eh?"

Corrig tried to ignore the man's attempts at conversation.

"You know, there's lots of stories about who might have dug that pit. Some say the Templars did it. I read somewhere they think Sir Francis Bacon helped design it. 'Course, everybody thinks Sir Francis Bacon did something fantastic. If they could connect him to the Mona Lisa or the moon walk, they would. Me, I think Shakespeare wrote his own plays, and that hole was dug by pirates. 'Cause they'd know, wouldn't they, how to keep treasure safe? They're so good at stealing it themselves, you know. I've heard tales that at night, the ghosts of those who died looking for the treasure come back, combing the shores for their share." The old man finally paused. "They made a whole show of it. Who do you think built it?"

"I think, it doesn't really matter who built it. The important thing is that it exists and that no doubt produces revenue for people like you. Doesn't it?"

The captain throttled back and coasted toward the dock. His superfluous, sunny demeanor clouded at Corrig's assessment.

Before the captain could tie off, Corrig jumped up

to the planking.

"What time will you need a ride back?"

"I won't." Corrig turned his back on the man and walked away.

****

"Repeat that, and slowly, please. I missed something the first time," she said as she slid a white macramé sweater over her head. A bell jingled as the dress shop door closed behind them and they headed toward the car.

"We are going back to where it began. If we start over, and manage to fix it, then we satisfy the custodians. Once the error is corrected you shouldn't have to worry about anyone looking for you."

"Just like that. So, we're just going to fly back to Charlotte, go back to Linville, and you'll do the rest?"

His eyes glittered mischievously. In the brightness of the day, they shone with diamond brilliance. How crystal blue could a person's eyes possibly be?

"We're not going back to the Games, Teagan." He stopped at the car, clicked the key control, and the trunk popped open.

Her mouth watered. She could smell cinnamon and sugar from the bakery down the street. She'd bet they just baked cookies. Snickerdoodles? Yum. And coffee.

She forced herself to ignore the delicious scent and focused back on Darius.

"Then where are we going? Isn't that where this all began, with those jerks, and the woman with the binoculars?"

His lips curved in a sentient smile.

She sighed loudly. "Where? Where do we have to go?"

"Smith's Island."

"So, is it a renfest, or a SCA thing?" she asked. "Why did we need costumes?"

"We'll be the only creative anachronists I hope." Darious dropped the bags from the costume shop into the pristine storage unit of the car, then closed the trunk soundly. "You know, for someone whose life is in danger, you seem remarkably calm. I'm impressed. It makes me feel better about the whole plan."

She stared at him. "Well, I'm of a mind that somehow, you've blown this out of proportion and once we get to Smith Island, I can explain that there's been a misunderstanding, and we can hand over the key and let someone else take care of it. And I'll go back to North Carolina, work things out with my uncle and aunt, and try to salvage my article."

His brow furrowed, and he swallowed back whatever he had been ready to say. He gently brushed her elbow as he opened the passenger side door, and she flinched from the tingle that jolted through her.

"That won't be as easy as it sounds."

Teagan shook her head and stopped his effort to herd her into the car. "What am I missing? You said we're going to Smith Island, and we should be able to set things right." Her eyes narrowed. "What aren't you telling me?"

The chill spidering up and down her body had nothing to do with the gentle summer breeze, or the overwhelming scent of sassafras that emanated from him.

Heebie jeebies. Something spooky is in the air.

She put her back against the car and crossed her arms. The memory of the dream—of their first night at the inn settled on her shoulders. She stared up at him. "You are flesh and blood. I am not crazy. You said you walk between the realms of reality and dreams. If this is no dream, then we should be able to fix it."

He inhaled deeply and stepped closer to her. Gently, he placed a hand on either side of the doorframe, near, yet not touching, her shoulders. "I also said that I have a connection to your past as well as the present."

The air crackled all around her. All around *him*.

Teagan reached one hand out and touched his chest. Instant vertigo overwhelmed her so strongly she nearly tumbled to the ground.

Darius grabbed her around the waist and pulled her upright, further complicating her condition.

Her vision wavered again, and nausea slithered through her gut. "Let go! Don't."

"What? What's the matter?" He still had his hands on her.

"You can't," she said as she pushed him away. "Don't you see what it does?"

"See what? What's wrong?"

"When—when you touch me, everything spins and crackles. It's like the flu, and static, and—"

He released her, and her equilibrium returned. She breathed deeply, trying to settle the rolling waves in her stomach, and found his scent too overwhelming. Her head began to spin again. "Tell, me, Darius. Why isn't this going to be easy, other than I nearly faint every time you touch me? What are you hiding from me? What is at Smith Island?"

He stood inches away from her, waves of heat radiating from his body. Concern still marred his expression, drawing his brow and mouth into a frown.

The man of my dreams is literally a man from my dreams.

His eyes twinkled. She knew at once he read her thoughts. "How do you do that?"

Instead of answering her, he looked up and down the street, then moved his head towards her. She turned her face away from him, avoiding his kiss.

Instead, his lips found her ear. His breath against the tender flesh of her earlobe shook her wickedly. His hands were once more on either side of her shoulders, keeping her from escaping.

His lips, so close, muddled her brain, and her breath caught in her throat. She nodded, very much aware that if she moved one hair, she would collide with him. Very much aware that despite the fact they were both fully clothed, on a city street, in broad daylight, not physically joined in any way, her body was beginning to respond in ways it should not.

He hadn't slowed time, again, had he?

She focused on the people walking by. Normal gate, no slow motion. And his scent. Pheromones couldn't touch what this man possessed. Intoxicating. That was it. Like she had inhaled some terrible mind-altering drug. Her body responded as if she were drunk. If he didn't move, soon—

"You really want to know where I'm taking you?"

She held her breath, trying not to breathe him in. Trying to clear her head. Trying to not succumb to this seduction. She nodded.

"1758."

A gentle convulsion flooded through her...from nothing more than his breath against her neck.

She leaned her head against the car, as she turned her face to meet his. Completely against her better judgment, she pressed her lips against his and held on to consciousness as the electricity surged through her body, welling up and exploding as he responded to her lips.

He lifted his head away from hers and looked down at her. "Are you alright?"

She pushed the door open and melted into the passenger's seat. "Yeah. Snickerdoodles and coffee."

He grinned questioningly down at her. "What?"

She closed her eyes. "If we're going that far, I need sustenance.

Chapter Fifteen

Darius grasped the fingers that drummed nervously against the console. "Relax, Teagan."

"I am relaxed."

"As relaxed as a cat in a dog show. Breathe."

"I can't. Well, I can't breathe deeply."

"Why not?"

"Because you smell too good."

He smirked. "What?"

"Besides the whole rhyming thing, I am cursed with a super geek sense of smell. And your scent—your aroma is too powerful."

"Remind me to buy deodorant."

"No. It's not that. It's not a bad scent. It's just…not easy. I-I can't focus if I get overwhelmed. Like the cookies. How far away is that bake shop?"

"The coffee shop? Just a block from the car."

"See? Were we upwind or downwind of the shop?"

Darius paused. "Upwind."

"Upwind, yet I could smell it. Snickerdoodles fresh from the oven, right?"

"Hmm." He lifted one brow. "Cookies, and men. Very interesting. What else can you identify?"

"Ingredients, household cleaners. Any scent I've experienced once, I can recognize again."

"And my scent?"

"Sassafras. And ambergris. It's very heady. And,

sometimes, it fries my brain."

"How so?"

"It's a bit like hallucinating. An olfactory memory, or something. I have this vivid memory of being a teenager, maybe in college, and of being surrounded by that scent."

Darius gripped the steering wheel firmly and waited for the truth to sink in. He concentrated on the road, deliberately not meeting her gaze. Admitting that he'd frequently checked on her, and that he'd infiltrated her dreams, wouldn't make this situation easier.

Several long seconds passed before her telltale sigh escaped as realization dawned. "Does your job description include protection or voyeurism?"

"Which answer would you prefer?" Considering the response he expected, she'd remained uncharacteristically calm.

"Are realm walkers impotent?"

Darius let loose a robust laugh that filled the space between them.

"Is that a 'yes' laugh? Or 'no' laugh?"

This time, he did glance at her, flashing her a lascivious grin. "You tell me."

Teagan's eyes narrowed to slits as she glared at him, apparently trying to discern whether he meant it or not. Good. There were some things she shouldn't know. Yet.

She shifted in the seat, turning her body toward him, bracing her arm to rest on the dashboard. "Okay, how does this happen?"

He instinctively reached down and tugged on her seatbelt, tightening it. He was used to protecting Teagan. Maybe, too much so. "How does what happen?"

"How do you take me back in time? I mean if all this is real, how do we do it?"

He shot her a glance and replied, "Very carefully, of course."

"You know, if you had just taken the clock to begin with, none of this would be happening."

Traffic was thick in town, but a hazard on Mondays. Even in a small town. Everybody had business to conduct. Darius focused on the road ahead again, yet slowly, Teagan's words permeated his brain. He frowned "What are you insinuating now?"

"Isn't that why you saved me? Because of the clock? You said that's what everyone's after. I suspect if you had just taken that, then you wouldn't be here right now. And neither would I."

True. If he had completed his task, and not intervened, then they wouldn't be here now. The other realm walkers wouldn't even know she existed.

"I didn't save your life for a clock. The clock merely serves as a talisman."

"You mean you weren't trying to steal it?"

He paused. "No. I was not trying to steal it. As I said, the clock protects you and your family."

"I thought you did that."

He didn't answer her. What response could he give?

As usual, she wouldn't let the issue drop. "If we're going to go back in time, then why don't we go back and get the clock? We could go back to the airplane and just get it out of the overhead before it gets stolen."

"That's not going to stop the people who are after you."

She let out a frustrated groan. "If someone truly is trying to kill me then why don't we just tell the police?"

"Tell them what?"

"Tell them that someone broke into my aunt and uncle's house and—"

"That you are the person of interest they've been looking for?" he interrupted, his tone purposely curt. Enough with the questions! If she continued to question their every move, she'd get herself killed.

His words apparently did give her pause. When she didn't respond, he continued. "In case you didn't notice, the man who tried to steal your clock was posing as a police officer. You ran from the police, left a crime scene, and without any evidence, you want to traipse off to the police in another country and try to convince them that you are the intended victim of a murder plot. And then there is the arson issue."

"And exactly who is it again? Who is following me?"

"The 'who' isn't necessary for you to know—"

"That's a stupid thing to say. It is necessary. I'm trying to understand this. People stealing from me, someone wanting me dead, kidnapping, time warping. Worm holes and time lords be damned! Why won't you simply give me answers instead of treating me like a child?

"Quite simply, Teagan, you are a child."

She bristled. "Even when I was little, I was never a child. And I have been on my own for quite some time.

Darius guided the car to the curb, and parked, engine still idling. The air inside the car crackled with her anger and her anxiety. What she didn't know might just save her life. "Teagan, I have existed for centuries.

You have existed, only a few lifetimes. Don't forget, dredging up old memories means dredging up old hurts. Is that really what you want?"

She cringed ever so slightly. "That didn't seem to be an issue for you last night, or the night before. You might as well tell me. That way, I'll be prepared. 'Better the devil you know'…"

"There is a reason most mortals do not remember past lives."

"Why?"

"Memories fade with death, flowing from the body as does the pain of the memories left behind."

"But not all memories we have in a lifetime are bad."

"True. Yet most mortals tend to hold onto the tragic memories much longer than they cling to the good memories."

"I'm not most mortals."

He didn't dare reply. She had no idea how much truth hid in her words.

"Darius, if everything that has happened in the past forty-eight hours is real, then I need to know as much as you can give me. It may be *your* mission, but as you keep reminding me, it's *my* life we're tossing around."

"Sit back and rest. Close your eyes."

Her eyes widened in surprise. She shook her head vehemently. "I will not—"

"Do you want answers, or not?"

"Yes."

"Then you need to be able to concentrate. Close your eyes and clear your mind."

"You want to do this now? Here? In broad daylight, in the car?"

"Right now, you are far safer inside this car, than outside. On several different levels." He deliberately flashed her a lustful smile, which deflated her anger.

"How about you concentrate on getting us where we need to be?" she quipped. He noticed, however, the way her lips tilted slightly.

"I am impervious to the world you know."

"But this world is not impervious to you. I saw what effect you had on the people at the festival."

He smiled, in spite of the seriousness of the situation. "Right you are. It is a good thing we will be where we need to be before nightfall. So that all mortals are safe, lest I be distracted by your beauty."

That achieved him a torrid silence for nearly ten seconds.

"Why?" she finally asked.

"Why what?"

"Why are you distracted?"

"That isn't a legitimate question."

"Yes, it is. You are immortal. Or something other than mortal, so you say."

"And so you have witnessed."

"What I have witnessed is a master at hypnosis who has me wondering if he is a protector or a predator."

"You still doubt me?"

"I don't doubt, exactly. Though maybe I should. But something's…" She harumphed and frowned at him. "Something is missing. It's like a jigsaw puzzle. Let's say you bought a jigsaw puzzle and had seen it complete, then you tossed the box away, putting the pieces in a bag, but you left out a few pieces. Then you gave it to me."

"Beware of presents from strangers."

"You know what the puzzle looks like, Darius. You know how the pieces fit together, and what's missing...I don't know."

****

The aroma of jet fuel, mixed with the acrid scent of fresh asphalt, only made the heat of the day more oppressive. Dana finished wiping off the passenger's door and handle, then ran the antiseptic wipe over the top of the car. She followed every curve of the vehicle, wiping away fingerprints, dirt, anything that could help police in any way.

She locked the car, then repeated her ritual cleaning the keys thoroughly with the bleach wipe before tossing them onto the thick plastic wrapped bundle in the trunk. Shame. *Such a handsome body.* And a pretty good fuck. For an instant she wondered if the opened eyes, barely discernible beneath the layers of clear vinyl, could actually see her looking back.

That's the sad thing about pricks. Other than their anatomy, so few of them have anything else going for them.

Well, Eric didn't have to worry about his next meal or his next lay, did he?

She retrieved her carry-on bag from the parking garage floor and started toward the elevator. She tugged her hair into a tight bun at the base of her skull. She tossed the container of wipes into the trash, making sure not to discard the used ones. Those she would flush, once inside the terminal.

A blast of cooler air hit her as she stepped into the elevator and punched the button. She retrieved the silk scarf from the back pocket of her jeans, neatly wrapped it around her neck, then slipped into the linen jacket. Simple, bland, boring. In other words, completely inconspicuous.

She still had two hours before flight time, just like any good, conscientious passenger. No rush, no pressure, no notice.

With any luck, she'd be miles from the border before anyone asked any questions. Maybe even years away.

Chapter Sixteen

Chester, Nova Scotia

Darius dropped the shopping bags on the bed before securing the door of the room. He stretched tight muscles, glad to be free of the confines of the car after several hours scrunched behind the steering wheel.

From the window of the hotel room, he could just discern the shoreline of the island in the mist. The fast-moving clouds gathering over the bay were sadly reminiscent of another such day on this same stretch of coastline.

"Why are we here if where we want to be is there?" Teagan's breath fogged the window as she spoke.

She stood with her hands on her hips, her shoulders and back straight, emphasizing her curves. Her breath caressed the glass, and a menacing lust surged through him. He thought how easy it would be to forget what they both had at stake. How easy it would be to lie beside her and move into her dreams, taking every pleasure with her, casting aside any thoughts she held while the thread of time she clung to unraveled, leaving her forever on the precipice of euphoria for a mortal's concept of forever.

He had almost done it before. He'd even tried it once on her. How susceptible she had been that time. How open her mind had been to the swirling vortex of voices that moved through the night. But she had sensed him, and he had hesitated, wondering if she recognized him. She could have been anyone. If only he had not known the truth. Momentarily, he regretted everything since Deschamb had died.

Teagan shifted her gaze from the coast to him and dragged him from his thoughts "Oh wizardly one—"

He blinked and took in the sight of her again. He regretted *nearly* everything. "How is your swimming?"

"Why?"

"Because, right now, you would have to swim out to the island, under threat of a storm."

"Guess we'll take a boat?"

"For a worldly woman, you seem to be having a difficult time with simple logic today."

He watched her eyes flare as she turned and hit him in the chest. "What's that supposed to mean?"

She hadn't flinched when she touched him. And her voice held a teasing lilt. She was warming to him. He shouldn't care, but he did. "Boats don't go out in stormy weather," he told her.

"Don't you have a way to make the storm stop? I mean, you did it at the faire."

Darius tensed at her accusation.

If only it were as simple as she thought. Or as safe. "Do you have any idea how much power it takes to halt an ocean current?"

"No." Her expression morphed from intemperate smirk to contemplative scowl.

"Even if I could stop it so you and I could—what?—walk on water to the other side, what about anyone out there who might be waiting for us?"

Teagan stood before him, mouth open, with no

retort. For once. She blinked, scowled harder, and shook her head weakly. She glanced once more out the window, then walked over to the bed and sat down.

"Good God," she exclaimed on an exhausted sigh.

He turned away from the view of the beach below and leaned against the wall. "What's wrong?"

"I've dreamt up a character straight out of some sci-fi movie who can walk through walls, through time, who knows intimate details of my life, of my dreams, and who whisks me off to some mysterious place on a treasure hunt."

"Are we back to puzzles, again?"

Teagan nodded. Her lip did not quiver, nor her eyes well with tears, yet her aura wavered.

Darius breathed deeply, willing her to do the same. Eyes wide and doubtful, her lips parted and she inhaled, slowly, deeply, her abdomen expanding ever so slightly as she drew the air into her lungs.

He exhaled, slowing the movement in the room, stretching time, making minutes linger.

"Relax," he whispered. "There is nothing wrong with your grasp of reality, as mortals choose to comprehend it. You are merely overwhelmed."

Darius withdrew from the window, meandered to the table, and poured two glasses of wine from the bottle. Though they had dined downstairs, he had ordered a bottle of wine and dessert for the room.

Teagan breathed out, her muscles releasing some of their tension.

He handed her one glass and stood guard ensuring she drank as did he. Did she revel in the scent of the oak cask which lingered in the richness of the draught? More importantly, did the magic of the grapes, pressed to make the burgundy elixir, penetrate her blood stream to create a hypnotic effect on weary limbs and ironclad will?

He held his own willpower in check. Her effect on him was too dangerous. Especially when she stood so close to him.

"Lie back and listen," he coaxed as he planted himself on the voluptuous velvet chaise.

"Listen to what?"

"Teagan—"

She downed the remainder of her wine, set the glass on the nightstand, and flopped back against the comforter, knees and feet still dangling over the edge of the bed. He coaxed a few more breaths from her, cautiously staying on his side of the room.

If he dared to cross to the bed, he wouldn't be able to protect her from…anything, including his own desires.

He drew in a deep breath. "In the time before our people were written of, we walked the continents. Some sought the lands to the east, others traveled westward toward Britain.

"Where did you come from?" Her voice, softer than usual, echoed in the space between them.

"We had evolved over centuries into sentient beings—creatures with human form, yet minds that could transcend the confines of our flesh. The earth spoke then, and humans worshipped her. She bestowed upon us the wisdom."

"Wisdom? What do you mean?"

"She gave us the tools to help her."

Teagan's brow crinkled. "I don't get it."

"All life is energy. All existence, energy. All

matter is form, created from the power of molecular cohesion. A rock appears dead, lifeless, yet the molecules that make up the rock are frenetic at a subatomic level. A good example is limestone.

Her eyes lit. "I know that one. It's oolite. Any species of limestone. I learned it playing Balderdash. The crystals form from gathering of lime in the water, right? And crystallization is the change in the molecular energy and structure. When the liquid cools down the molecules slow down and cling together. Right?"

"Sort of. Limestone demonstrates how matter, regardless of its origin, possesses the power to change, or shift.

"Like you. You shift from tangible physical being to someone who can walk through walls."

Perhaps this wouldn't be as difficult to explain as he thought. "Walls are just molecules we perceive to be cemented together."

"You're messing with my mind, now. Way too *ooh-wee-egoooh* for me."

He allowed himself a small smile. "Right. Digressing. So, thousands of years ago—"

Teagan lifted her head from the mattress and turned curious eyes in his direction. "You're thousands of years old? Not just a few hundred?"

He winked at her and continued. "—the earth spoke to her children and warned us of the imbalance that plagues all existence."

"Explain imbalance."

He considered this for a moment. "What happens to dough when it sits out?"

"If it's a yeast dough, it rises."

Darius nodded. "And is malleable. Imagine if the

energies, the earth's magnetic fields turned upon themselves—"

Exasperated, Teagan relaxed once more against the mattress, her limbs slack with defeat.

"Well, that's not possible," she grumbled.

"Because?"

"Because…well, I don't know why. It just isn't. If it were, we'd be in some black hole or something, I think. I don't know. English major. Not a physicist. And besides, what does this have to do with what's going on in present day North Carolina and Nova Scotia? In my own egocentric universe?"

"Nothing. And everything. Tell me, Teagan, who built the pyramids?"

"The Egyptians, of course."

"Who built Stonehenge?"

"The—the Celts?"

"Much too old for the Celts."

"The Druids?"

"Stonehenge had already settled and showed signs of erosion the first time they emerged as a religious movement."

"Then…who?"

"We did."

****

She sat up and stared at him. "You?"

"Well, not me, exactly. I think I was still wandering around what you know as Kazakhstan. However, that circle of standing stones is our work."

She shook her head. "You've lost me."

"In this beginning, when we learned of the energies, we were given tools to help us keep the earth safe. The stones draw energy out of the lay lines and keep it from building up. Too much electromagnetic energy and the earth begins to contract. It's like a cramp."

Teagan ran one hand through her thick hair in frustration. She frowned at the strands that stuck to her fingers.

"Stress induced hair loss?"

To Darius she tossed, "Ha ha. Very funny. You got me. What is this, let's see how gullible the blonde is?"

"You asked for answers. This is no joke. Like lightning rods, the structures we devised around the world, are meant to channel the energy."

"What for?"

"To perpetuate the earth, and her children."

"Ridiculous."

"Why do you find this ridiculous?"

"Because it's just something that crazy burned-out hippies spout."

"It's much more than that, Teagan. Think of pyramid power. The ancient city of Ankgor, The Tower of Babel, Avebury, the Easter Island, Chitzen Ictza…all of them are tools for redirecting the energy, for completing the grid. Imagine a computer-generated circle. When asked to transform that circle into a ball, the program will reconfigure the design and create a grid of lines to form a sphere."

"You're saying that the reason the earth is round is because the pyramids and other tourist sights are making a grid."

"No. I'm saying that the reason that the earth stays that way is because the grid continues to pull the electromagnetic waves outward, perpetuating the sphere."

"So where do I fit in? What am I to the great and mysterious universe?" *What am I to you?* She bit back the question.

Darius sat for several seconds. struggling with the words that played upon his tongue. "You, Teagan, are an anomaly."

"I don't get it. Why am I an anomaly?"

"Because—" he paused, clearly weighing his words. "You aren't supposed to be here. You, as the daughter of a clockmaker in Nova Scotia in 1756, were not supposed to be saved from drowning. That's why the other realm walkers are searching for you."

At his words, her stomach clenched. *Not supposed to be here.* "But, you said they're looking for the clock. And I don't have it anymore. So, the whole taking-back-the-clock-that-doesn't-work thing is moot."

"Not exactly." He tipped his glass and swallowed the last of his wine, then moved to stand next to the bed where she lay.

She fisted her hands against the comforter and forced herself to remain calm. At least until she finally had all the information and knew whether or not to reignite panic.

"Why not? Exactly?"

"Corrig, the one we know was hunting you doesn't know we no longer have the clock. Does he?"

****

Corrig settled himself on the floor of the cabin. The owner's absence was convenient enough—no need to immobilize or eliminate unnecessarily.

Fog had crept over the dune that separated the shoreline from the cabin. No bother. Even if Darius could make it to the island tonight, the woman could not. Not with a storm threatening.

They were such weak creatures, mortals.

A millennium had honed his cynicism where humans were concerned. They were slothful creatures with little real insight about the world or its wonders. They cared only for what they could possess.

What did Darius see in this particular human? Why would he risk everything for her?

Corrig pondered his own question for a moment. He supposed she could offer some distraction, sexually. He had often found that women did serve a purpose in that regard. And yet, besides the primal urges he could draw upon to sate a realm walker's appetite, mortals seemed little more than a shell.

He closed his eyes and allowed the silence to settle on him. The incident in North Carolina would not be repeated. He definitely could not allow such a heinous creature to thwart him again. Averal had gifted him with powers once more just for this purpose. He did not intend to fail this time.

Nearly three hundred years ago, he had failed to find the damned thing before Darius had set this chaos into motion. If Darius had not meddled, then clock, its builder, and girl would have been history that no one remembered.

Why had Darius intervened? Lust? Friendship? Greed? Surely not an overinflated sense of duty? Corrig tossed these options around and settled on friendship. After all, they had all been comrades once, hadn't they?

But that was ancient history. That was before another walker succumbed to the temptress...and plummeted to the hell of humanity.

"Darius—" Corrig sent the call out into the evening

air, certain that his nemesis would hear his call. "Take care. Your impertinence could forfeit all you hoped to preserve. I will not fail again."

****

The heat was nearly unbearable, churning into a roiling hunger. Thus far, Darius had been able to stave off his desire for her. However, he had never been so close for such a long period of time.

He watched the rise and fall of her chest as she slept in the cool night air. He glided his hand over her form, careful not to make contact with her flesh, yet let the warmth of her lap at his palm.

Since their first night, in Cape Breton, he had been careful not to coax her. He needed his strength. So did she.

As she lay sleeping, she inhaled more deeply. He wondered if she was dreaming of him? How easy it would be to steal into those dreams.

Not now. Not yet.

As if her body had heard him, she tensed, her nipples thickening, teasing him. She stretched an arm above her head, reaching toward the bed frame and her back arched seductively toward him.

Temptress.

His groin tightened and swelled in response to her movements. In the dark, she shimmered beneath him. Her skin sparkled, silver and white, her aura flared blue and red with her body's heat. A golden, molten, vibrant red radiated from between her thighs, and he did not need to invade her dreams to know that she wanted him.

As he had always wanted her.

If he lunged into her, if he took her, consumed her,

165

she could surely lose her mind. Or seduce him to lose his.

Lust was one thing. A kiss, a fondle. But to vent his sexual desire with a human woman was, indeed, madness.

"Darius—"

Corrig's voice echoed in his ear. Hollow, yet threatening. "Take care. Your impertinence could forfeit all you hoped to preserve. I will not fail again."

As if to protect her, he moved his own body to float above Teagan's. He concentrated his thoughts, his energy, on establishing a barrier that would keep Corrig from seeking her as she slept. If he could hear Corrig's warning, then Corrig might be near enough to sense her.

As close as their bodies were—his nearly grazed her flesh—he willed his own lust to cool, aided by the discovery that this most dire threat to Teagan's life waited. Nearby. Watching. Listening. Waiting.

Tomorrow they would set things right. Regardless of the outcome, tomorrow, he would make amends for the sin he had committed.

Chapter Seventeen

Wood. Earth. Something sweet. Overripe fruit? The aromas swirled around Teagan, teasing her until the dark fog cleared and she could see. Evergreen trees surrounded her like soldiers marshaled to protect their charge. Beneath her the dampened ground chilled her bare feet.

It had rained. Her clothes were drenched. No wonder she was cold. Despite the rain, the scent of stale fruit clung to her. She had to find it. Teagan searched the ground, gently testing the fallen leaves splayed upon the earth.

It must be here. Where else could it be?

Teagan glanced down and saw a stain upon her shirt. Dark, and glistening against the muslin fabric. Newly made. Fermented grapes and plums. Like stale wine.

She cursed under her breath. As she studied it, the stain began to spread, growing upon the whiteness of the cloth. Dark. Wet. Putrid.

Not wine.

Blood soaked the cloth now, and the scent altered. Her spine tingled with fear. Intense fear. Similarly, this sweet rancor tinged with the tart coppery aroma saturated her senses.

Stop it. Stop! Stop it!

As if commanded by her words, the scene around

her melted. Trees and earth faded to fog, evermore dense, until she could not see her hand before her face. Her body swayed with the movement of the air that surrounded her. Rocking up and down, like waves, rocking her back and forth.

Salt. The astringent air stung her eyes, and she blinked against the fog, trying to relax upon the waves until someone could find her.

No. No one must find her. She must make it to the island before they found it.

What? Found what? She couldn't remember. She tried to stroke a hand through the fog and met with the resistance of the water. Not fog, but water supported her weight, tempting her to sink into its depths. Another roll pushed her forward. This time the wave swept over her and dragged her beneath the surface.

She tried to breathe, only to find her nose and mouth filling with cold seawater. She kicked and struck against the swirl that clawed at her, trying to drag her down.

No! Up! She pushed herself toward what should be the surface, only to meet another swell of the current. She broke through, spitting and gasping, flailing to grab something. Anything.

Where did it go?

Her hand swung out against the impenetrable fog and smashed against the side of the rowboat she had been in.

When? Where had she been in a rowboat? Hope flooded her limbs, warming away the chill of the water.

She grabbed at the wooden frame of the craft, desperate to hold on. A more determined wave crashed upon her back, smashing her against the boat as it swallowed her.

Again, she struck against the water, clawing toward—

Something grabbed her wrist and yanked hard, pulling her through the sea toward the blinding whiteness.

"Breathe."

That single word reverberated through her brain. Air filled her lungs, and Teagan sank into the darkness beyond dreams.

****

Dana tugged the seat back tray down and retrieved the stack of papers from her bag and splayed the documents on the empty seat next to her. Photocopies of documents so old the manuscript teased her brain. Handwritten ledgers, records of land deals, journal entries, some neat, some scrawled phonetically. Ironically, technology really *had* ruined her generation. Hell, nobody wrote things by hand nowadays.

If Kinsey had been right about this clock, and the lore around it, then perhaps she could make some changes herself.

I could change history.

She suppressed a tingle of vanity at the thought of creating a rift in the timeline of the world by introducing technology a few decades early and reaping the rewards. After all, the difference between Alexander Graham Bell and the other scientist working on telephone communication was only an afternoon's visit to the patent office. Imagine what concepts she could take advantage of if the lore were true.

One name glowed on the page before her. Alexander. In the margin of one of the pages, fine dark lines of new cursive script, presumably in Kinsey's, referenced the name Alexander. Smith's Island, clock. Pad—something. Handwriting scrawled. North Carolina.

She'd seen that name before. But where?

Dana closed her eyes and thought back over the past couple of days. The visit to Kinsey's office, their ill-fated trip to Vegas, the plane ride home.

Plane ride. That was it.

The woman sitting in front of her had gotten up after conversing with the flight attendant. As she stood, the woman had braced herself by holding on to the back of her seat, boarding envelope in hand. That was it. The name on the boarding card flashed in Dana's memory.

Alexander/T.

The plane she was currently on dipped, and Dana heard the familiar chiming signal before the flight attendant started blathering about tray tables and electronic devices and re-stowing personal items.

Personal items. Her own penchant for procuring any item that appeared particularly interesting and expensive had landed her the clock that rested in the overhead cubby.

Kinsey's note made it clear to her just what a treasure she had found.

She had scored the antique of a lifetime. And she intended to use that to its full financial advantage. If it turned out to be magical, like Professor Kinsey's lore indicated, well…she couldn't pass that up, could she?

Time in bottle be damned. She had time in a clock. If the stories were real, she'd have all the time in the world to make good use of it. If nothing more than bedtime tales, she could put a profitable spin on that, too. Either way, she might have to look up T. Alexander some day and thank her. So far, she had handled both Kinsey and Eric satisfactorily. That snit of a woman who would let such a clock out of her sight and protection could not possibly offer any real trouble.

The plane banked to the right and Dana glanced out the window at the sliver of an island that represented Nova Scotia.

How could something so small hold the possibility of something so great? Greed combined with superstition surged through her fingertips at the thought of the wooden box overhead. She'd been a thief of one sort or another most of her life. Hearts, ideas, secrets, she'd purloined them all out of boredom over the years. A clever thief always managed to stay one step ahead in the game.

Now, she intended to make the killing of a lifetime.

First, she needed to find the island that Kinsey had spoken about.

She chuckled to herself. Smith, Oak, or Fantasy. Regardless of the name it went by, to Dana it equaled Treasure Island.

****

Teagan awoke to the chime of a bicycle bell. The sound broke through the dream in which she had been racing through a house to answer a doorbell.

Within the four walls of the hotel room, silence. She looked at the clock. Digital. No noise. No tick-tock, or gentle electronic purr. Just a red blur denoting 9:30 a.m.

She rolled over, and found the bed, and the floor beneath it vacant. Likewise, the bathroom door stood open, the room beyond quietly dark.

Where was Darius?

Sunshine spattered the carpet with splotches of light, piercing her eyes rousing her to wakefulness.

He must be at breakfast. She inhaled deeply. No sassafras or ambergris. Somewhere nearby, however, pancakes or waffles were sizzling, and coffee was brewing. The aromas were faint, but then, doors and windows were closed.

She headed toward the bathroom, did a quick wash, and twisted her hair into a knot before throwing on her clothes and sliding into her sneakers.

She didn't remember getting into bed last night.

For that matter, how had she gotten undressed? Again? She bristled at the thought of not remembering Darius putting her to bed. If he could hypnotize her so effectively, what else could he do?

She slid the room key into her back pocket and exited the room, intent on finding the origin of the java wave that had wafted through the cracks in the door. Down the stairs, to the dining room.

No Darius.

She waved off the attendant. She'd be back as soon as she found her mad hypnotist.

Despite the fact the calendar indicated it was July, the Nova Scotia coastal breeze this morning was brisk. She shivered and wished she had long pants. The air, as if to slow her by sheer chill, whipped around her legs like a cat as she wandered along the boardwalk toward the marina.

Sea air and wood smoke swirled in the wind. The heady mixture soaked her senses. Comfort. Like home. Only she had never lived by the sea. And she seldom had occasion to build fires. No matter. The sun's rays were a welcome adversary against the breeze. She allowed herself to bask in the magic of the morning.

She stopped along the stone path through the courtyard and shaded her eyes against the brash sunlight. Gazing onto the water, the morning haze made her view fuzzy, but she thought she could see something in the distance. The island?

She blinked and turned away. *After breakfast and coffee.* After she found Darius.

The marina was viewable from where she stood. She could see the outline of masts and ropes, and people milling about on the pier. One tall dark figure grabbed her attention, and she squinted to focus.

Darius. And a woman.

Teagan's feet stayed rooted as she watched the lithe brunette talking to Darius. The woman reached a hand outward and stroked his arm, with obvious familiarity.

Somewhere deep inside, jealousy twinged. Her gut clenched, and her cheeks grew warm. She gritted her teeth. *Don't be stupid. He's nothing to me, and I mean nothing more to him than a way to a clock.*

Fine words of reason did not assuage the irritation she felt at seeing Darius's hand slide across the woman's back. He pointed to something in the distance. The woman followed his lead and stared toward the same point.

Her stomach muscles knotted. Not jealousy, she assured herself. Just hunger. Dinner had been more than fourteen hours ago. Her head pounded an order for caffeine of some sort—tea, coffee, chocolate, migraine medicine.

Whatever her body tried to convey, jealousy was

not part of the message.

The two separated. Darius moved toward the end of the dock, as the mysterious woman headed toward the parking lot.

Despite her body's protestations, Teagan took a step in the same direction the woman followed. Then another. And another, until her sneakers scuffed the asphalt of the parking lot, bringing her deftly to a halt, breathing hurriedly.

She knelt to tie her shoe and conceal herself as she watched the woman click something in her hand. A small convertible chirped, and the woman lifted the door of the trunk.

Teagan shifted to tie her other shoe, never taking her eyes off the brunette, who reached to pull something from the bowels of the trunk.

What was the woman retrieving? Shopping?

Pain stabbed behind Teagan's left eye, and she clenched both eyes closed for an instant, willing the annoyance away. When she opened them again, she caught a glimpse of something familiar peeking out of the bag the woman set carefully on the ground. The woman turned to close the trunk of the car and Teagen squinted in effort to eye the object more closely.

Wood and brass? Shadowbox? Birdhouse?

Clock.

A wave of nausea rolled from her abdomen toward her head, dragging in its wake guilt, anger, and fear.

The image floated like a mirage before her. *The damned clock!*

Teagan straightened and shot a glance toward the end of the dock where Darius had been headed.

Bells, whistles, sirens sounded in her brain. The

clock, the touch, the car to die for. Darius had an accomplice. And now he had the clock. Then why had he kidnapped her? He didn't need her if all he wanted to do was destroy the clock.

"The clock needs a key."

Like the hammer striking the bell, realization hit her resonated through her body, shook her to the soles of her shoes.

I still have the key.

Everything he had told her had been a lie. The clock hadn't just been stolen from her. Darius had made sure his accomplice walked off the plane with it firmly in hand, planning all along to meet here once he gained Teagan's trust.

Why? All he had to do was ask, and she would have given him the key.

No. That wasn't true. She would never have allowed him to steal an heirloom from her aunt's house.

He could have stolen it.

Teagan slid her hand in her back pocket. Her fingers brushed against the cold butterflied metal of the hilt and stroked the shaft of the key. Still there. At least there was that.

The woman Tegan identified as Darius's accomplice now sauntered back down the dock toward him, bag slung over her shoulder.

Damn. Arson, theft, murder, mind control, abduction, fraud. Darius had managed to break all the major rules in his quest for a stupid antique clock, which surely possessed no true mystical powers this morning. Otherwise, she would have used it to send herself far away from this searing bit of reality.

She had trusted him.

She swallowed hard against the fury and hysteria rising in her throat. She'd been set up, played for the fool. Now that her hero had the clock, he'd come looking for the key. Then, he'd only need to do one more thing to complete his mission.

Eliminate the witness.

Chapter Eighteen

The morning haze hadn't yet burned off, leaving a trickle of mist hovering in the distance, clinging to the island's coastline. Darius sensed the woman before her car door slammed shut. A prickling sensation raised his hackles, and he cocked his head enough to see a petite leggy brunette striding toward the dock.

Dangerous. Deceptive. Delinquent. In every sense of the word. High heels and white jeans were the trademarks of someone who did know her way around a marina. And she maintained the rhythmic breathing of a panther. A predator.

Not a realm-walker.

Inwardly, he smiled. In another moment she would be near enough for him to hear her pulse. Near enough to glean the misdeeds that she hid behind those sunglasses.

"Excuse me." Her drawl, while not completely affected, was exaggerated as she maneuvered closer to him. "I wonder if you can tell me if there's somewhere around here where I can rent a boat?"

"You don't look dressed for a day on the water."

She unfurled one hand and stroked his arm coquettishly.

Liar. Thief. Murderer…Sexually promiscuous.

"Of course, I'm not. At least not yet. I just want to talk to someone about the rates and availability.

Speaking of availability—what is yours? For that matter what's *your* rate? I would love to rent a few hours of your time, handsome."

Interesting. *A thief. Hungry. But not for food. For power.* What did she dream of at night?

He smiled. "Presently, I am not for sale, or rent." He motioned toward a boat moored near the end of the dock. "The gentleman down there, second boat from the end should be able to give you some information. Or you can check with the resort. I'm sure they can make arrangements for whatever you need."

He used the opportunity to slide his hand across her back and something black surged in his brain. Whoever she was, this woman had a vicious mind...and an evil sense of self.

Odd. Women seldom possessed such sociopathic tendencies. Occasionally, he would run across one that needed a few nightmares to temper some bad behaviors before a murder rampage ensued. This woman, however, very cleverly planned every lie that came out of her mouth. Not pathological. Just extremely cautious, and wily.

As if she sensed his appraisal, she pulled away. "That's magnificent. I'll try the resort. Thank you." She paused and flashed a flirtatious smile at him. "Now, if you change your mind, I'm sure we could negotiate some type of deal."

"Another time, perhaps."

She pursed her mouth into a pout, turned, and sashayed back up the walkway toward the parking lot.

He watched her gait quicken. She no more intended to go on a luxury tour of Mahone bay than he did. What was she lying to protect, though? She had her guard up and he couldn't quite penetrate her thoughts.

Not his problem. Not this day.

He followed his own advice and headed toward the man he had pointed out to the brunette. He needed to secure the boat and get back to Teagan. That she had slept through the night meant she'd be better prepared for the task ahead of them.

As if someone had thrown an egg and struck him in the head, the blackness splattered against the back of his brain, again, and he wheeled around. At the top of the landing stood the brunette, a large soft handbag struggling against her shoulder.

Tick. Tock.

She descended the boardwalk once more, heading in his direction, and he realized with some remote satisfaction what she carried.

Was it a trick? Or a trap?

"I thought I'd try your guy after all," she shouted to him.

"I'm afraid you're too late. I just booked his last available rental." He focused on slowing her steps. If he could stall her advance, he could stop her, and everything else, long enough to reclaim the clock she had somehow stolen.

Stolen. Damn. If Teagan and her bloodline were no longer in possession of the clock, that meant…

The time keeper's tock proves safe haven by clock

that no harm shall come there to the creature made fair

By the will of his vow when he fell from their grace.

The clock protects those with the key to its face.

Deschamb's clock rested in the bag concealed

beneath her arm. Her hand toyed with the folds of paper that strongly resembled a map.

He had forgotten the inscription's warning. Without the clock, Teagan became more vulnerable to an attack. She had no forcefield, and at this very moment, no realm-walker guarding her.

"Perhaps we could work something out," he ventured. "If you really need the boat today, perhaps we could share a ride. Or, if you're looking for some place in particular—" He cast a glance around at the dock. Water meant difficulty. He could manipulate minds and slow time, yet water was always tricky to work with. Especially when his attention was divided.

She batted her eyelashes at him, as if it were scripted, then extended her hand toward him. "Dana's mine. What's yours?"

"Darius. So, are we a team?" He needed to secure the clock, and he needed to secure Teagan, before anyone else arrived. Corrig's words trickled over him. Teagan was alone in the hotel with no protection against the one realm walker who most wanted her, and the clock was gone.

"Darius. That sounds positively dangerous. Should I be scared?"

He recognized the flirtatiousness in her question and wondered how many men she had seduced or scared in her limited lifetime. Luckily, she bore little threat to him, in either way.

Opportunity, need, and timing were everything this day. He allowed an evil smile to curve his lips as he wrapped his hand over hers. "Petrified, my dear. You should be petrified."

****

Teagan shoved the door open with her shoulder with the finesse of football player and charged into her hotel room. She had no time to waste being quiet or subtle. Darius and his accomplice conspiring by the boats meant she had one quick chance to steal away.

She had only what she wore, and her bag. She certainly didn't need any costume now.

Passport. She grabbed her purse and rifled through the folds of fabric from the skirt and scarf she had stuffed inside. No passport. The few dollars crumpled at the bottom wouldn't even get her a taxi into town. What about the hotel courtesy van? No. She could be identified if...no...when Darius and his accomplice came looking for her.

Well, she could always walk, if she found her passport.

She checked the dresser and bedside table. Nothing. Where had she left the damned thing?

"Sonofabitch!" She hadn't *left* it anywhere.

Darius had stolen her passport.

****

Darius guided Dana toward the hotel room. Complacent, calm in fact, the woman appeared willful as she allowed him to guide her down the corridor.

The small flashes indicating her mind fought against his control impressed him. He seldom used this strength. He seldom needed to. However, this thief had a sharp mind and a disciplined ego that made it nearly impossible to play any other way. Both he and Teagan needed the clock, and they needed no witnesses identifying them to anyone.

With little effort, he could flood the woman's brain with too much blood, or he could just stall the blood flow. Stroke. Aneurism. Either would be termed a natural death.

Realm walkers, though, were charged with the task of maintaining a balance. He wouldn't kill the woman for stealing. His choices had placed the clock within her grasp.

Her breath was ragged and slow. As much as her mind struggled against his, her body's neurological system behaved as if she were meditating, sending messages to her heart and lungs and autonomic system to relax. He had, effectively, drugged her with thought.

He unlocked the room door and ushered his guest across the threshold.

"Teagan?"

The empty bed, and silent reply caught him off guard long enough for Dana to regain some of her strength. She gasped and flailed at him. Mid-swing, though, he stopped her. He also halted everything in the room.

Bathroom empty. Apparently, his charge had gone to breakfast.

He hoped. The energy in the room had been disturbed recently. He could feel it. Frenetic. Angry.

The outfit they had purchased the day before still hung in the closet. Glasses untouched on the table. The bedside table drawer stood ajar.

Such a small thing. And yet, something was wrong.

He seized Dana and moved her to the bed. Having placed her on top of the sheets and crumpled duvet, he stood over her and moved into her mind.

He had suspended her body and her mind, albeit, momentarily and now had to do something to keep her sleeping, and out of the way.

No dreams lingered. Dark shadows hid her thoughts. When this woman did dream, her fantasies and memories were usually violent.

"Dana."

"Who are you? Let me go. Why can't I move?" She struggled to wake herself, to open her eyes, her mouth.

"Dana, stop fighting. No harm will come to you if you follow my lead."

"Follow your lead? I'll cut your heart out and feed it to the seagulls if you don't—"

"That is not following directions." He jolted her with a burst of light energy, and her thoughts faltered, words stuttering to a halt. He could feel her body writhing against the jolt of a seizure. *"Fighting it will only hurt you in the long run. If you relax, I'll help you forget about all of this, and you can take a wonderfully decadent nap. I promise the dreams will be worth the sacrifice."*

She resisted him still, until he shocked her a second time.

This time she lapsed into a vacant state. Temporary but necessary if he didn't mean to kill her. He stroked her libido, and her subconscious began to writhe to life. Her brain synapsis glittered, and he could see the nerves sending messages to the different parts of her body to respond to the emergence. Heat enveloped him, as the image of her hand stroked against him. *"That's it, Dana. Hold on to that image. Pleasure. Pain. Ecstasy. Sleep. Sleep."*

Darius withdrew from her mind and sucked in the stale air of time suspended. His own body writhed against the caress she had delivered in her dream. As he exhaled, he blew time into swirling again. The change between time moving and standing still would be imperceptible to a mortal, yet electrons and protons shimmered against his skin as air and light began to move.

Only an instant.

He hung the "privacy please" sign on door and moved for the stairs in pursuit of Teagan. At least she was mortal. Mostly. Which meant he could track her. That he moved faster than she did meant he could catch up with her before any harm came to her.

He moved through the restaurant and found exactly what he had expected. Nothing.

Had Corrig found her? Or had Zahra sent others to claim her?

He spied the movement from across the parking lot. Teagan was by their car. He slipped his hand into the pocket of his jacket and wrapped his fingers around the rental car key ring. Whatever she hoped to accomplish, she would need the keys. He started in her direction, pleased with the newest development in his plan. The clock had come to them. Teagan had the key. Now all they had to do was manage to avoid Corrig and slip down the rabbit hole.

Teagan's head popped up from behind the car. Like a wary hare, her eyes widened as she saw him, and she ducked once more out of sight, even as he waved to her.

Teagan. What is it?

No response.

He searched the parking lot but saw no sign of a realm walker or anyone suspicious. However, her wariness, and expression told him something was not right. Even if he had not been able to sense her thoughts, he would have guessed from the fact she was hiding behind the car.

He thought the question a second time. *Teagan!* He dared not call her name out loud.

Scattered frenetic bits of emotion flew to his mind, fragments, like shattered glass.

A second later, she threw a brick through the car's passenger window. Glass shattered at the same time something exploded behind him. Something struck him in the back. His body tilted and he slammed against the asphalt.

Teagan—

The parking lot, the sky, the distant car all melted to darkness. The echo of the shot ricocheted as the impact scurried up his spine to his brain, followed by the hollow click of high-heeled shoes.

Chapter Nineteen

Teagan ducked her head as she released the brick and waited for the resounding crash of stone against glass.

"Shit. Son-of-a-bitch." Darius had seen her. She couldn't outrun him if he halted time. "Please, God. Please, God." She reached into the shattered window, threw the lock, and opened the door. She ignored the shrapnel and reached to open the glove compartment.

"Sonofabitch!" The damned thing was locked. Teagan opened the console between the seats. Nothing. "Damn it."

Run. That's all she could hope to do.

She clambered out of the car, scrambling to brush away broken glass and move forward at the same time. *Don't look back. Run. Before he—*

"Tea—"

The voice in her head, died away, cut off. A pop, like a car backfiring echoed.

She lunged away from the car. As her muscles flexed to sprint, Teagan glanced over her shoulder. Darius was gone.

Not gone. She spotted the lump, a collapsed body on the ground. From the corner of her eye, she saw a flash in the sunlight. She turned toward it and met the barrel of a gun aimed at her head.

She knew perilously little about guns, other than

the bang frequently preceded somebody on the ground, and lots of blood. She yelped at the sight of the woman standing not ten feet away, threatening her with a piece of metal.

Brunette, long legs, with a bulky bag slung over her shoulder.

"That's quite a thing you and your boyfriend have going on there," she said motioning toward Darius's limp figure sprawled on the asphalt. "He's pretty good with the hypnotism. What's your part in it?"

Teagan stared beyond the woman at the body on the ground. She straightened her shoulders as if in slow motion, and replied, coldly, "I could ask you the same question."

The woman advanced, scouting the parking lot for onlookers. Teagan retreated a step.

"Uh-uh-uh…I think we should go this way." The woman flicked her wrist, and the gun barrel pointed toward the dock.

"Why? If you plan to shoot me anyway, why not here and now?"

The woman closed the gap between them, grabbing Teagan's arm with one hand, as she slid the other hand up under Teagan's sweater, gun resting against the curve of her back. "Because your boyfriend wanted what I have badly enough to try to catch me. Only I don't follow orders as well as some people would like, so his soothing voice and parlor tricks didn't stop me in my tracks.

Teagan shuffled along distractedly, trying to make sense of the woman's words.

She had seen them both on the dock earlier which meant they had both known where the clock was the whole time. Only, the deceitful duo was down by one.

She had little doubt that the woman would shoot twice. She tried to stall. "But why are we going down toward the boats? Just shoot me here. I'm tired of this. All of it."

She *was* tired of all of this. But the longer she stayed in the parking lot, the greater likelihood someone would notice the crumpled body in the parking lot and call the police.

She turned to stare at Darius's form on the ground, and something churned inside her. However angry she might be, she didn't want him dead.

Her captor snorted. "When I do pull the trigger, it won't matter where we are. First things first. Right now, you are going to take me to the island, and show me how to use the clock."

****

Darius floated on an ebony lake.

"Hey, mister, are you alright?"

The voice called from far away, beckoning him to consciousness. Someone shook him, and he groaned, partially from the annoying backache, partially from the taste of rock, and tar, and carbon that had filled his mouth as he lay face down on the blacktop.

"Crap! Hey, man," the voice said, "Stay still. D-don't move, we got somebody comin', okay? Just, just don't move." The voice faded a bit. "Go tell somebody, down there. Call the police. He's bleedin' bad."

Darius's mind sprang open as his eyes did the same. Bleeding? Realm walkers didn't bleed. Then again, when had a mortal last pinned a realm walker?

The young man nearly fell onto his back when Darius, lifted himself onto his knees to evaluate what *bleeding bad* meant.

A soreness on his left side, distinctly below the heart. Hmmm. A good shot. Meant to incapacitate. Not meant to kill.

He flashed a jolt of current through the immediate area and everything halted. Just as it should.

Where was Teagan?

He looked toward the car, noted the broken glass, and the open passenger door. No girl.

Little wonder. Whoever had shot him, had no doubt taken Teagan.

Corrig?

Simple but not likely. Corrig didn't need bullets.

That left Dana. He had pegged the woman for dangerous. She had proven him right.

He looked toward the figure still kneeling beside him. He was definitely on Santa's good list this year, unless the cops fined him for making a fraudulent call.

He moved the guy off the asphalt and onto the grass, then walked over to the guy's friend and turned the phone off, before sliding it into the kid's pocket. No call, no cops, and hopefully no Corrig. The illusory puddle of blood had vanished. When time resumed, he would be halfway down the pier which meant no blood, no body, and no bother.

Next item to tackle. Where were Dana and Teagan? The woman's car still sat where it had been earlier, in the parking lot. She must be close.

Not the room. If she had just escaped from there, she wouldn't go back.

"The water it is, then."

Before his feet hit the boards of the dock, he heard the whirrrr of the small motor as the boat he had rented pulled away from its mooring.

Damn. Didn't either of them realize how difficult it was to stop water?

****

A little knowledge does a lot of damage, Teagan rationalized as she maneuvered the boat into the cove and toward the rocky shore.

If the woman holding the gun hadn't known just enough about the clock to feed some ill-fated sense of greed, neither one of them would here now.

"If you had the clock this whole time, why make Darius continue the game? Why not just have him dump me in Chicago? It would have saved both of us a lot of trouble. You could have killed him without a witness. I'd have been no wiser."

"Right now, T. Alexander, I don't give a rat's ass about anything but the magic this device can give me."

"Stop calling me T. Alexander. Or does that impersonalize all this for you?"

"Ms. Alexander, you have no idea who I am. I am all about personalizing it. You and your boyfriend tried to kidnap me to get the clock back. A clock that you left sitting on a plane so you could go sit together on that airplane. Finders, keepers."

They had maneuvered to the most shallow part of the waterway. "Alright, out. Move gently, or this," she nodded to the gun, "might just go off again." She smirked. "Then you'd be in the same boat, as it were, as your boyfriend back there in the parking lot."

Teagan slid over the railing and trudged through the water up to the shore, followed closely by her captor. Even by summer standards, the water was too cold. Her feet were numb by the time she squished onto the sand.

"Keep moving, T."

"It is Teagan. And you didn't have to shoot him. And, he wasn't my boyfriend. I know you two were in this together. I saw you. Believe me, I meant nothing to him. It's just a stupid clock. If you had just stolen it from my aunt's house, then none of this would be necessary. It still isn't."

"Yeah? Well, it's still missing something. Something your non-boyfriend didn't seem to have in his pocket. I am particularly good with pockets. Especially men's pockets."

Teagan slid her hands into her own back pocket. Still there.

"It's easy to pick a man's pocket," the brunette continued. "If he balks, you just bat your eyelashes, and tell him you're admiring his ass or that you're horny. He'll practically hand over his wallet if he thinks you're trying to squeeze his ass, or his balls."

Grass rustled in the wind, ever so slightly, setting her even more on edge. The faint scent of pine and oak washed away the scent of the bay and the musk-scented perfume that had overwhelmed Teagan since they'd gotten into the boat.

No cave. No neon sign screaming "this way to the exit." No other tourists lined up to sight-see. Just grass and scrub. A small copse of trees ahead in the distance did not look promising. It did however, look like a great place to hide a body.

"We might be in the wrong place." She hoped they were. Stalling, good.

"That's what maps are for. Nope. This is Smith's cove. We're at the far end of the island. We have to walk a bit to get to the pit.

"The fact is, you had this first. That means you must have a good idea how it works. And so, for now, you are very important to me."

"I only had it because Darius told me to take it. And if you're going to kill me anyway, don't you think I should know your name? Since you already know mine?"

"No. I don't think. But I suppose it can't hurt. Call me Dana. I'd shake your hand, but that would just be too congenial for the situation don't you think?" She prodded Teagan to keep moving.

They had made it beyond the first ridge of scrub. The woman had ditched her high heels in the boat, for a slim pair of drug store tennis shoes she had pulled out of her shoulder bag once they landed.

Shorter than Teagan, she seemed to be more mouth than muscle. However, the tennis sneaker clad seductress was still holding a life-threatening piece of metal. If they wandered up toward the trees, Teagan might be able to run, or at least find a stick.

"That's the sad thing about men. They are great for sex. But the moment you trust one, you're sunk. I learned that long before I could even drive."

"But you trusted Darius to get me here."

"Look, I trust no one. What you saw this morning turned out to be an opportune coincidence. Son-of-a-bitch happened to be there on the pier when I showed up to ask about a boat. He tried a bit of charm, himself, I might add. He's good. Really good. He had me back to the hotel in no time at all. Nearly got me into bed, with whatever mojo he works. Damn fine specimen. He'd be a great lay. Like I said, though, never trust anyone."

Coincidence. The word struck her like a lead balloon. "You mean you and Darius weren't in on this together?"

"Like I said, he'd be a great diversion, but I don't know him from Adam. I take it from the little jealousy thing, you've got going on, you two did."

"We did not. I am not jealous."

"Uh-huh. Well, then, what was he renting the boat for?"

Teagan lied. "I-I didn't know he had. I woke up and went out to find him." Not a lie, exactly.

"And you just happened to be at the resort when I showed up with the clock."

A breeze fluttered, and the scent of the trees grew stronger. "How much farther?"

"I figured you might know. It's your clock. At least it was your clock."

"I know nothing. That's what I'm trying to tell you."

"Lying is such an ugly trait. Useful, but ugly."

"I'm not lying. I just don't know. You said you needed me for something. Why don't you explain it to me. Maybe, I can help."

Stall. "Why are we even here?"

"Teagan Alexander. Your name was in the margin of a manuscript I came across the other day."

"Mine? What for?"

"Well, it seems you have something to do with this non-existent, folklore clock that may or may not have magical properties."

"Well, it's been hanging on the wall in my uncle's cabin for as long as I can remember, and the only magic

I've seen it do this week is make people crazy."

"Yeah, crazy with the notion of its value. Stories like this one don't surface and hold on for years without some thread of truth. The man who wrote your name down had a decent handle on reality, and on this story. And when I showed him the clock, he recognized it."

"What man?"

"Just a professor I had taken some classes with once. He's dead now."

Teagan caught the expression on the woman's face and did not bother to offer condolences or wonder how the man met his end.

They reached the trees. A slight grove of oak and evergreen, the trees did little to offer any significant veil, or sense of security. Beyond the trees, sat a clearing, well defined. Definitely manmade.

Support rigging marked what Teagan supposed must be the pit. *Yeah, much better place to bury a body than a grove of trees.*

Earth. Soft and moist. Despite the sun overhead, she could smell the dampness of the ground that had been so recently excavated.

"Is this it? Somebody's been here already."

"Somebody is always here. You really should read up on your travel destinations, Teagan. This is one of the best kept secrets in the western world. There's even a show about it. Supposedly, some kids stumbled across the spot about two hundred years ago, and everybody's been trying to get to the bottom of the pit, ever since. King's ransom, pirates' booty, Knight's templar treasure. Everybody has a theory."

"And yours?"

"Mine? Mine is that you are going to help me get

to the other side of the world and time according to what the doctor said. Just think about what someone with my brain and my looks could accomplish. Opportunity abounds for someone who recognizes it."

Dana's last sentence faded as Teagan nearly choked on the heavy scent of oak and…tobacco.

She hadn't seen him drop from the tree, or step from behind it. The odor of burning leaves heralded the materialization of the one person more threatening than the gun toting thief.

She turned to see the figure wrap his hand around Dana's throat, as he disarmed her, tugging her upward until she tottered on her toes.

"Ffffu—" The expletive died on Dana's lips, as she struggled against her assailant.

Corrig removed the gun from her hand, dropped the woman to the ground, and turned to his attention to Teagan. "My, my, Miss Alexander. Where does the time go?"

Chapter Twenty

For the second time today, Teagan stood facing the barrel of a gun. Without so much as a cup of coffee. "Out of your jurisdiction, aren't you?" she asked.

Through the sunglasses, Corrig's eyes burned cold with intent.

"On the contrary. Wherever *that* is," he said motioning to the bag that sat at Dana's feet, "And wherever you are is my jurisdiction. Especially as you are a person of interest in an arson investigation."

Dana rubbed a hand over her neck and cleared her throat.

Both of them. And me. And the damned clock. Teagan crossed her arms and hiked herself up to her full height. "You want the clock, take it. I don't need it."

"Indeed, you might not. Permission isn't necessary, now, as you don't seem to be the one holding it." He glanced around. "We are missing our fourth for this game. My patience is beginning to waver. Once your bodyguard arrives, we can begin."

"Bodyguard? What bodyguard?"

"Darius."

Dana coughed and scrambled to her feet. "That guy on the dock? If you're waiting for him, then we're gonna be here a long time, then. I killed that bastard this morning."

"Doubtful."

"Why doubtful? Because I'm a woman? Because you sneaked up behind me?"

"Because you, while a bit of a harpie, are a mortal. Darius is not."

"Right. Well, your friend the hypnotist might be a lot of things, but impervious to bullets he is not. Her bodyguard bled red this morning."

"I'm sure he did, Miss—?"

"None of your business."

"Dana," Teagan answered. "Her name is Dana. And she doesn't have a clue about you or Darius, or any of the so-called others." She tried not to focus on the gun in his hand. "What do you mean about Darius not being dead? I saw the pool of blood. There's no way he could have survived. Is there?"

"Damaged is not the same as dead. As realm walkers, we can only be killed by one of our own. I suspect he would be touched by your outpouring of emotion over his demise."

Dana interrupted. "You called him a 'realm walker'. And what would that be, exactly?"

Teagan's temper flared. "Killers. Liars. A lot like you."

"Judicial beings," Corrig countered.

"Judicial?" Teagan asked. "Is that what you call it? Stalking innocent people? Threatening me? Breaking and entering? Stealing? Invading people's minds? Where is your justice in that?"

"And I take it, tough guy, that you're one of these realm walkers? What, exactly, does that have to do with a clock that shifts time?" Whether wariness or interest, Teagan detected the change in Dana's voice.

"Everything," Corrig assured her.

"A clock that really shifts time?" Interest. Avarice. As if the sun had warmed her like butter, Dana's frigid demeanor melted. "Now how does an antique piece of wood and some screws manage to do all that? If you don't mind my asking."

While her two captors were posturing for a sparring match, Teagan edged her way toward the construction site.

"A clock that defies the laws of gravity, space, time, and the American way," Dana's drawl thickened. As if she were drunk. "Now that is a story worth hearing, don't you think, Teagan?"

She bristled at the familiarity with which Dana used her name, as if they were pals. Still, she'd thought the same thing about the clock. Stalling of any kind, had to be a good alternative to being killed instantly by a metaphysical bounty hunter.

"Fascinating. Perhaps Mr. Corrig can elaborate on the subject."

Corrig relaxed his stance, as if he had all the time in the world. "Teagan. An interesting name. Poet, I believe. Are you a poet?"

"No. I prefer to deal in facts. Tangible, versus intangible."

"I don't think I believe you. You certainly didn't have any trouble with intangibles in North Carolina, now did you?"

"Apparently, the only trouble I had was you. A crooked cop. A thief. And, I take it, an arsonist?"

"Unfortunate that we couldn't conclude our business at your family's place. Could have saved us both some time. Pardon the pun."

"Look, I know that you have orders to get rid of the

clock. But why do you have to kill me, too? I could just walk away, never return to Nova Scotia. Never mention the clock."

"Ah, yes. The clock. The magical box that protects you. Sort of like that blue police box on television. Larger on the inside than meets the eye. This one protects you and your family. Keeps you hidden and protected. Like a forcefield. Except, now that we have it, and you, in close proximity, we can prove that it doesn't work as well as Deschamb had hoped."

"Deschamb? You know about him?"

"And I see that you do, too."

"Darius said he was a clockmaker. An inventor. I can see why you would want to destroy the clock, but Darius said we could set things right if we brought it back here. That's why I came. All we have to do is bury it or destroy it and this can all be over."

"A poetic sentiment. But the fact is, it won't be over until both the clock and the catalyst are destroyed."

"Catalyst? You mean the key?"

Contempt poured over her as he glared at her. "The key, and the clock are merely a conduit. How could they possibly have been worried about a mortal threatening their world?"

"What?"

Corrig's expression altered slightly. "How much did Darius tell you?"

"He told me about saving Deschamb's daughter."

"And?"

"And that the realm walkers wanted her—I mean me—dead because of some rule about stealing a death, and imbalances, and setting things right."

"And he never mentioned *where* Deschamb came from?"

"He said his mother was British, and his father was French. That he had lived in Louisburg at one time."

Corrig's smile broadened. "Are you telling me you don't know?"

"Know what?"

"Oh, this will be much better than I had hoped. It's almost worth the time stolen, just to see the look on his face, and yours, when he realizes. When you realize." He stopped. A bellowing laugh rumbled up from the depths of his chest.

"Know what? What don't I know?"

"Did it not occur to you to ask why a being so superior would bother to save Deschamb's daughter?"

Teagan's arms goose fleshed. She hesitated in answering. What did his question imply? Why had Darius broken the rules?

Dana picked up the clock and hugged it to her body, causing Corrig to *tsk* reprovingly at her. "Not your toy, little girl. If you break it, you'll have to pay with your life. Might still have to, whether you break it or not."

"He…Darius saved her because it was the right thing to do at the time."

"Not quite. The right thing would have been to destroy the abomination. She should never have been born. Much less, left to wander into the world, to roam the streets. To mate."

The stench of his anger filled Teagan's mind. His anger, his scent, the tobacco, all nearly overwhelmed her. What was he saying?

"You, poet, as your name indicates, were once the

fair one. Teagan Deschamb, was her father's daughter, after all."

"I still don't get it."

"You were the hybrid. The dangerous half-breed."

"The what...?"

Ranulf Deschamb was a realm walker. He forfeited his immortality for a vile human lust. And you were the spawn. He gave up everything and got you. Teagan Deschamb. Half human, half disengaged realm walker. Half human, half not-quite. Of course, the realm walkers wanted you gone. We couldn't have such a questionable creature running around the globe. And then he built a device that not only protected you but allowed you to meander in and out of the realms."

"I don't—"

"Of course, he didn't tell you. He would have to admit to knowing the vulgar truth of it to himself. If he admitted it, he would have had to admit what an abomination you are...or were."

"And just what is that?"

"You, Teagan Alexander, nee Teagan Deschamb, are one of us. As I said back in North Carolina, we always recognize one of our own. And soon, I'll return you to the dust whence you came. When I've finished, I'll mete the same justice on the one who defied our rules by saving you. By keeping you hidden away for these two centuries. I failed two hundred and fifty years ago. I won't fail again."

****

Corrig motioned toward the pit. "This is the final act, ladies."

They stood in the clearing, two women, the man with a gun, and the clock. Teagan looked at the infamous pit. Barely a hole. The small crevice had been secured with a frame of wood and enough metal work to have built a skyscraper.

Dana flashed a seductive smile at Corrig. "You're clever. I like that in a man. And I am really good at everything I do. Why waste that? I suspect you and I could have a lot of fun—"

"Toss it in," Corrig said to Teagan, ignoring Dana. "I'll make sure you join it. I'll even make it look like you were trying to trespass and died in an unfortunate accident."

Small, confined, and booby-trapped. How could anyone move down that? Teagan didn't contemplate the physical probabilities anymore. She slipped her hand into her back pocket, withdrew the key, turned her back to him, grabbed the clock from Dana as if she were going to toss it into the hole... and inserted the key into the slot on the clock and twisted it to the right.

Nothing happened.

She heard a click as Corrig cocked the pistol.

She twisted the key to the left. The ground beneath her shifted and rumbled ever so slightly as Dana grabbed for the clock in her hands. Not before the mechanism within began to crank to life, propelling the hands as if by magic. Wind whipped around them, moving them both toward the rabbit hole, each tugging to gain control of the time-peace.

A flash of lighting in the mid-morning sent tendrils of electricity spiraling through Teagan as if something hard rammed her, knocking both women off balance and pitched them over the edge of the shaft...and down the rabbit hole.

Chapter Twenty-One

Cold. Damp. Earth and sea. The scent of brine irritated her sinuses, and Teagan covered her nose and mouth with her hand. She opened her eyes and found only perverse blackness surrounding her. The wind howled somewhere in the distance, drifting, wavelike, to chill the air.

Blind. She tamped down the panic that rose in her throat and attempted to sit up. Had Corrig fired the gun? *If this is death, it sucks.*

A careful evaluation of mobility and various body parts determined that no blood had been lost. Hair and extremities were intact. The only thing currently missing was her ability to see.

The vision of Corrig and the gun flashed through her brain. The shaft. She had fallen down the shaft with the other woman. And the clock. Where were they?

She ran her hands gingerly over the ground around her. Earth. Firm, yet dank. And stone. Smooth, as if polished by years of erosion. Smooth stones meant no traction.

"Dana?" She didn't know why she whispered instead of calling out loudly. However, she did know that she couldn't see what, or who, else might be in the shaft. Stories of skeletal remains and booby traps, mingled with the very practical realization of animals— possum, raccoon, snakes—Teagan yanked her feet and her hands back to her body, eagerly tucking all appendages beneath her. Just in case.

"Dana," she called again. The woman had to be here. Not that she relished the thought of bonding with the madwoman. Between insane thieves, and insane non-corporeal creatures, she preferred things that could halt time to things that walked with guns.

Ambergris and sassafras struck an olfactory memory, and Teagan's breath caught in her throat. Dana had shot him. Killed him most likely, regardless of what Corrig had said.

Corrig. Up at the top, most likely. Still wielding his pistol as well. Waiting to see, or hear, if either of them survived the fall.

Good. Let him wait. Her body trembled, and she closed her eyes against the impenetrable darkness.

Why? How? How had she ended up here? What turn of fate had marked her for this hyperbolic exercise in fantasy that carried her so far away from everything she knew so no one would ever find her body in this hole?

She should have trusted Darius.

Again, she scented ambergris and sassafras. An olfactory memory. This time she buried her head against her knees. In a few minutes the memory would fade. She would be more aware, and she could try to climb out.

The rustling and muffled groan nearly sent her up the slick wall by sheer fright. Teagan gasped and fought to quiet the scream that billowed inside her chest. But when the back of her head struck the wall, both the scream and her patience escaped.

"Alright, damn it. If you're in here, you fucking

sociopath, say something, or kill me, or help me. Just don't stand there staring at me."

Almost as firmly as her head had met the wall, two hands grabbed her and pulled her into an embrace. She struck out and hit.

Ambergris and sassafras saturated her senses as one arm wrapped around her body, hugging her close, while the other hand cradled her head as his mouth closed over hers.

…not Corrig. Not Dana. Darius. Not dead.

Fear, fury, and aggravation melted against the heat of him, replaced by a fiery swell of lust and electricity that blazed through her. She clawed at the fabric of his shirt, and he tightened his hold. She had never been so glad of anything, of anyone, in her life.

She answered his kiss, rising up to meet him, plastering her body against the warmth of his, raking her hands over his torso, his hips, hugging him close. Clinging for dear life.

Shhh. Not spoken but thought. His lips would not release her. She wouldn't let them. *Quiet, my love. Breathe. You are safe. I am here.*

Her body quaked at the comfort of him. And at his words.

"Is this real or am I dead?" she asked when he finally broke the kiss.

His chest rumbled with amusement, and he whispered against her ear, "You must be alive. There are definite rules about seducing corpses." His mouth trickled down the line of her jaw, until it found her mouth again.

"Why?" The question burst in her mind as she stood locked in the embrace. "Why did you let me think you were dead?"

Again, he released her mouth, never lessening his hold on her body. "Dead?"

"Yes, as in, Bang! Fall-to-the-ground-blood-seeping-out-crazy-woman-pointing-the-same-gun-at-me-dead. Dead!"

"Keep your voice down."

"Why? All you have to do is make everything stop."

"Not quite."

"Why not?"

"I can make most things stop. But if Corrig is up there."

"What do you mean 'if'? He's got to be standing at the edge. He nearly—"

"That was before."

"Before what?"

"Before the clock opened the vortex. And you and Dana and I rushed through."

"You? What vortex?"

"Remember what happened when you turned the key in the clock?"

"What? You mean the tremor?"

"There is no fault line beneath the island. To you, it felt like a tremor, but in truth, a portal opened. That's when I rushed you."

"You?" Something hard had hit her just as she fell. "You hit me? You were there?"

"Just long enough to see Corrig aim the gun at you before I pushed you both into the rift."

"Pushed me? You pushed me down this shaft? You son-of-a-bitch!"

"I had to. It is what we were trying for anyway.

Just not quite the way I had hoped."

"I can't see. You hit me so hard, I can't see anything. I'm blind, Darius!"

"Blind? Why do you think you're blind?"

"I don't think. I know. I can't see a damned thing."

"Teagan, think about it for a moment. You are in a shaft that descends for more than two hundred feet. If Deschamb's clock did its job, then you are two hundred feet and two hundred and fifty years from when you turned that key. You are not blind, young one. You are standing in a very dark, somewhat unstable hole in the ground."

The seconds ticked by in her head as his words sank into her consciousness dripping like molasses. Impossible, her brain argued. Yet, some part of her recognized that, so far, every impossible word he had uttered since she met him, proved not only possible, but true.

Her muscles spasmed throughout her body, wrenching her involuntarily. Whether cold, or something she could not explain with physics, Teagan's body convulsed as if being yanked from all sides.

"Darius!"

"Shhh! Relax, I have you."

"I ca-can't re-relax!"

"Your body is in shock. It will pass."

"Pass? What do I—oh, it hurts. Everything is cramp...ing. Agghh!"

Her body contracted in painful coils, charlie-horse spasms, limbs seizing, muscles swelling, battling against her flesh. Teagan heard her scream but could not recognize it as her own.

Darius lowered her to the bedrock floor of the

cavern and pressed his body on top of hers. Spreading her arms to her sides, he laced his fingers through hers, tackling her body's protestations with his own weight.

Lightning flashed. Teagan found herself standing, peering down at their prostrate forms on the ground. She tried to yell out, unsuccessfully. Silence buzzed in her ears, as she tried to move her arm to jostle Darius's form.

Heat trickled over her shoulder, and she turned to find his hand shimmering and not at all opaque, brushing her own translucent form.

"What's this?"

"Ah. This is you, out of your body."

"That's impossi—"

"Apparently, like most of your misconceptions, it is not."

"How?"

"I am a realm walker."

"So, you did this?"

"No. You did this. With my help. In times of physiological pain or stress, the human mind frequently has great capabilities. Your body is dealing internally with the transition using a shock response. That's why my body warms yours. Your brain allowed much of your energy to project away from the corporeal form."

"Out of body."

"That's it."

Teagan watched her body writhe beneath his. Lust welled. How could that be? Her mind and body were not at the moment connected. She could see! How could she see in the dark?

Out of body. Not confined to it.

As if the thought were a spring, Teagan's body

snapped her back into the confinement of her skin. And sore muscles. And a burning sexual hunger that arched her back as she rocked against the warmth and firmness of the body atop her own.

In reply, he shifted his weight, and thrust against her, the bulge between his thighs growing hard as he rubbed touching her.

Both fully clothed, she lay pinned beneath him, slaking her body beside his form. Her nipples swelled in protest against the binding of her bra. Heat pooled, hot and wet beneath the silken fabric of her panties.

The grinding of his hips increased as did the ministrations of his mouth upon her neck, all the while his hands held her arms captive. Harder and quicker, she rubbed against the fabric of his jeans. Steadily thrusting friction. Molten, enraged lust, building, roiling, seething, until her body and mind combined in an orgasm that exploded throughout every fiber. Muscle, nerve, flesh, all bucking in revelation at the sensual glory of the cataclysm that delivered her body from the ravaging effects of the journey through the rift.

Time, space, reality, all need ceased as Teagan floated, suspended. Nothing more than synapses and electrons firing simultaneously. Frenetic.

Pure energy.

****

Darius held her beneath him and allowed his lust to seethe within his own skin. Lust meant heat, a commodity she needed now…badly. Thank the heavens, they were both fully clothed. Otherwise, he would not have been able to control his desire.

She writhed against him, and he hardened in anticipation. He could take her. Her flesh was willing.

As was his. Once he claimed her physically, she'd be lost forever. Condemned to his caress. Never another's. He dared not. He'd waited for almost three centuries, and nearly as many of her lifetimes. He could wait longer.

He felt the lunge as her spirit leapt from the shell of her body, and he could not stop the wicked chortle from escaping as he consumed the groan that pressed against her lips.

Intensity. A certain catalyst for astral projection. Fight or flight. Wise to flee from him now.

He moved his hips against hers, seductively, and her body replied in kind.

Still holding onto her, rocking against her, massaging her form with his own, he left his body, and found her essence hovering near the wall.

"What's this?" she asked as he stroked her luminescence.

"Ah. This is you, out of your body."

"That's impossi—"

"Apparently, like most of your misconceptions, not."

"How?"

"I am a realm walker."

"So you did this?"

"No. You did this…"

He explained the basics to her, all the while, monitoring his own body's tension. He wouldn't take her like this, easy as it would be to tear through the fabric and part her, taking her regardless of the consequence. Shattering her, pounding her, branding her as his.

Realm walkers knew no mercy in their pleasure.

Only gluttonous, dark, primal hunger.

An orgasm ricocheted through her body, sucking her back into herself. Darius focused on calming his own loins, grinding his hips feverishly against hers until his body exploded in a spasm against hers, frantically pumping against the fabric that protected them both from her destruction.

Her body fell limp beneath him, saturated and sparkling with the orgasm that would heal wounded muscles. His own body began to relax, and he allowed her to sleep, cloaking her with his own body's warmth.

How ironic that what could save her body from the shock of the trip through time, could, if not guarded, rip her mind apart, plunging her into madness.

Frail creatures. Humans.

Chapter Twenty-Two

Gradually, sensation returned. First to her fingers, her legs, her head. As if waking from a long sleep, her brain began to sort out the wheres, whens, and whats related to her being.

Her body welcomed the chill of the earth beneath them. Somewhere in the darkness, she expected to find Dana's body. She hadn't heard anything to indicate the woman had survived.

"She's gone," Darius murmured against her ear.

"How…?"

"When we are this close, I can read your thoughts. Dana's not here."

"Not here? How can that be? She had hold of the clock. Wait, where's the clock?"

"Gone."

"What do you mean gone?"

"Not here. Along with our thief. She came through, as far as I can tell. Or at least part of her did. I found a shoe near the shaft opening."

"If she came through and escaped, then that means that it's safe. We should be able to do the same."

"I think we'll take another route."

"What other route?"

"Well, it wasn't built with only one access point, now, was it? There's a tunnel."

"A tunnel? You never said anything about a tunnel.

I never read anything about a tunnel."

"That's because in the future, which is where we were, when you turned the key, the tunnel no longer exists."

"But it does now? Wait, where are we? Or rather, when are we? What year is it?"

"That depends on you and the clock. With luck, we are in 1758. And yes, right now, a tunnel does exist. Although if we are as much as twenty years off, the tunnel might be gone."

"What does that mean?"

"Time, erosion, sinkholes. By the time the British were concentrating their efforts on the lower thirteen colonies, time and nature had sealed the passage between this one and the next island over."

"There's another island?"

"There are lots of them around here. That's why Descamb chose it."

"Off," she said.

He obliged her, moving away from her, and pulling her to a sitting position.

"Darius?" She pulled her knees into a crisscross position.

"Yes?"

"I'm sorry. If I had trusted you to begin with, then…"

"It's alright. Neither of us expected her to show up with the clock just when we needed it the most. I couldn't read your thoughts. I had no idea what you were thinking, because you were so far away. You could easily have been seriously injured, you know."

"But not killed, right? I mean, I had the clock."

"If the clock had been destroyed, you would have

been as susceptible to death as any other human."

"I don't understand. If this device has protected me for three centuries, then why have I died? I remember my childhood. I've seen pictures of myself as a baby."

"Your host has died. Natural aging. As your bodies died, over the centuries, your spirit, your energy moved on to a new shell. Sometimes an infant, sometimes an adult."

"And what about the other thing?"

"What other thing?"

"Remember the missing puzzle piece?"

"Yes?"

"I know what it is now."

The air inside the shaft changed ever so slightly, and she heard him draw a breath across his lips.

His silence told her Corrig had spoken the truth. "Ranulf Deschamb was no ordinary clock maker."

"No?"

"No," she said with conviction. "You didn't tell me that he had been a realm walker at one point. If that is so, then I am part realm walker, too. Aren't I?"

Silence.

"Darius?"

"I am here." In the dark, his hand found her and tugged her to stand. "We need to start walking."

"You can't just stop a conversation like that, Darius. This is important. I don't know what I believe anymore, but there is somebody out there who thinks I am one of you. Or some threat to whatever you and Corrig are. That's why they want me dead, isn't it?"

"Yes."

"Then, I am not safe anywhere. With or without the clock."

Her body ached. The dampness of the pit saturated her bones, and her head still pounded, but she managed to stay on her feet.

"Come."

"No. Not until you are truthful with me."

Heat surged out of his body. It radiated as if he were a space heater. As if he were an infrared creature. He yanked her by the arm.

"Stop it," she hissed.

This time his grip spared no politeness as he clamped down on her mouth. "Silence. We will talk of it once we are out of the tunnel. Do not make me force you."

Not bloody likely.

"Do not test me, Teagan,"

He could read her mind. And he thrust his own thoughts into hers now. "*I have guarded you for more than two hundred and fifty years. I would destroy you myself before I would let Corrig do it.*"

Teagan shuddered at the ferocity of his thoughts. Her headache increased, and so did the nausea that surfaced as she stepped carefully, following Darius's lead.

The mountain. The garden. The airport. Corrig. Everything flooded her brain with triggers, and her adrenal gland kicked into high gear. Fear. Not trust. Abject fear filled her veins, her muscles, her bones. More than anything, right now, she feared the creature that had just threatened her.

Whatever they had shared in those brief moments just now on the pit floor, dissipated like fog.

She heard the promise in his threat. He would kill her before he would allow another realm walker to claim her life.

She wanted to trust him.

Instead, she believed him.

****

Corrig.

Darius closed his thoughts to her.

Corrig had told the girl her origins. How much easier it would have been if she had not known of Ranulf's true nature. For it was that nature that inevitably destroyed everything the man had touched.

He moved delicately through the tunnel, virtually dragging her after him. Well, he couldn't hope to save her or solve any of the problems, with her in the pit, could he?

Had Zahra instructed Corrig to reveal the truth to Teagan before he killed her? Had she meant it as some torture for whatever remnant of realm walker remained in Teagan's mind? Corrig had long been Zahra's best hunter, who was sent to clean up messes. He moved easily among people, assuming local dialects to fit in, managing to assume social positions that allowed him to do his job. Without potential for discovery.

The tunnel sloped to nothing more than a crawl space, barely broad enough for his shoulders.

Behind him, Teagan's breathing had become ragged and heavy. "I can't," she whispered.

"Yes, you can. I am here, remember? The tunnel is safe. We're nearly clear."

She started backing up, scurrying, unable to turn around in the small, confined space. Her pulse beat so loudly, he could hear it drumming. He had to do something before she hurt herself.

Flash.

She never quite stopped as those around her had. Neither did she question him about why everything else had stopped when she didn't.

Here, at least, he could control her somewhat. He slid through the final hundred yards of earth and slate, found the opening, then turned around, and slid back into the hole before making his way back to Teagan. She'd moved ever backward, fighting against the threatening claustrophobia.

"Stop," he whispered. "Give me your hand, Teagan. I'll pull you to the end."

Fear halted her senses. She couldn't have heard him even if he had shouted at her. The pressure of the water overhead, combined with her own thoughts, gave her a false sense of deafness.

"You'll kill me. They'll kill me. I cannot go out there. The spider waits upon its web—its prey sits at the fair."

"Reach out your hand," he conveyed.

She brushed something furry, immobile in the crawlspace, and yelped, drawing farther away.

"The lion and the unicorn fought for the crown..."

Darius grabbed her hand and tugged her gently. Damn it. If she were totally human, he'd not have this problem. So much easier to coerce a human.

The dark irony of that thought startled him. He grabbed both arms now and flipped her onto her back. She kicked against his efforts.

Seventy feet.

"All about the town."

Sixty feet.

If she were totally human, he'd not have been in a position to save her. He'd have left her to the others.

Fifty feet.

He pulled more ardently, whisking her along the root filled shaft, toward the first grey light of dawn. The wind whipped against his backside, reminding him that time shifted, had landed them not in the summer's warmth of present day, but in the same year when Ranulf had died.

The tide was out now, but not for long.

The opening flared briefly, and Darius pulled them both through the last few yards of rock and soil.

Night still clung to the edges of the small cave, offering little respite from the dark beneath the round. Slivers of grey fell in tendrils, heralding morning.

****

Teagan landed in the grass beneath the cave's entrance, moving lethargically, until Darius ended the enchantment. At once, the world around them, as well as the woman in it moved at will, once more.

She blinked against the dove grey of pre-dawn. "Are we here?"

"Yes. We are here."

"I was rhyming again, wasn't I?"

"As you do. It is not a horrible thing. There are much worse things you could do when stressed."

"I'm scared."

"I know. You would be a fool not to be."

"What do we do now?"

"Well, first we set a fire to warm you and to ward off the damp. Then, we'll have to set about making our way to the coast."

"I didn't see any treasure."

"Treasure?"

"You know, the treasure that everyone is looking

for. The Oak Island treasure."

"What did you expect to find?"

"I don't know. Coins. Maybe some jewels or at least a map, or something."

"Abandoned untouched for two hundred years?" Amusement trickled into his voice, and she blushed at his teasing.

"I don't know. I just thought that if so many people were willing to die searching for it, there might be something to it."

"Ah. Well, there you have got a point. Few tales survive the centuries without some bit of truth in their telling."

"So, is there a treasure?"

His heart caught in his throat at her query.

"There was. There is still."

"Where is it?"

"Do you covet it?"

She felt her cheeks heat again and shook her head. Was she actually embarrassed?

"I just wondered, that's all."

She sat cross-legged on the grass, having not moved since she emerged from the burrow in the earthen mound. Darius collected a few sticks and some dried weeds, and stacked them into a pyre, which he ignited with two stones.

"How does that work? Realm walker magic?"

"Flint. Very popular before matches and lighters. Admittedly, a realm walker can no doubt make it spark quicker, with less work. Yet it works for everyone about the same way."

"Don't make fun of me. I'm only asking."

"I'm not making fun. Much. Here, feed the fire. I'll

go and get some more wood."

He handed her the sticks he had gathered. He made his way toward the two closest trees, and picked up the dead branches and bark that littered the ground. Not much to work with, but better than nothing. He bent beneath the larger tree and brushed the dirt from a stone tangled in the roots. He lifted the marker, and reached beneath, searching for the mossy cloth stashed there. Beneath the moss lay a small burlap bag. He pulled it away from its hiding place, unfolded it, reached in and counted the pouches within. Three left. Then, retrieving two of the pouches, he folded the returned the last one, inside the burlap, to its hiding place, replaced the moss and stone, and made his way back to Teagan.

"This should help." He set the largest of the branch and bark bits into the fire, and he watched the flames lick at the smoldering edges.

Teagan's eyelids were heavy. Darius sat down and pulled her into his lap. "Curl up and rest in the heat. When the sun is high enough, we'll make our way across."

"Thank you," she said, yawning into his arm. The lightweight fabric of her sweater did little to provide warmth, or coverage. Darius could feel the curves of her breasts as she hugged his arm and sidled up against him. Once she slumbered, he moved so as not to have her body touching his.

Her breathing had settled to a steady deep hum. He placed the two small pouches on the ground near her head. No pot of gold or rainbows. Just something set aside for a rainy day.

The day had barely broken, yet he could feel the storm brewing.

Chapter Twenty-Three

Darius sat for several minutes struggling with the words that could put things in perspective for her. "It is true. Your father was one of us."

"My father was not. I remember my father very well and he had none of that going on."

"The father you knew in your most recent life might not have been, however Ranulf Deschamb was."

Teagan stared at him, dumbfounded. "A realm walker. Like Corrig said?"

"Probably not quite like Corrig described him, but yes, Ranulf Deschamb was a realm walker. He had existed since our beginning."

"But I am not."

"Well, not exactly. You are half realm walker, but mostly mortal."

"Not that I believe you, but how does that work?"

"What blood type are you?"

"I have no idea."

"Exactly. Have you ever been hospitalized?"

She paused, considering the question. "No, I don't think so."

"Have you ever had any major injuries?"

"No. Why?"

"Barring the goons at the festival, have you ever been in a situation you couldn't handle?"

"I am self-reliant. I don't get into things I can't

handle."

"Exactly. How many kids, teenagers, young women on their own can say that?"

"More than half, I would think. Besides, to hear you tell it, you have always watched out for me."

"Ah. And yet, you would be wrong. I have only intervened when someone who could do you significant harm hunted you," he said, not wanting to implicate his own kind. "You are completely in control of things, like never being in a wrong place at the wrong time, always walking away just in time, or being able to make every deadline."

"Every deadline? I'm constantly late. I'm the biggest procrastinator I know."

"You can afford to be when time bends to your will."

"What?"

"It is ever so subtle, Teagan. Yet you are your father's daughter. The once or twice you've been near something tragic, you've walked away unscathed, or you've managed to avoid it completely."

She drew her knees up to her chin. "I don't believe you."

"As it should be, then. If you don't have any ill-conceived notions of grandeur, then you won't do something stupid."

"Like what?"

"Like tangling with men who want to break your neck."

"Well, I seem to be making up for all I've missed with this past week. Thugs, cops, arson, theft, and guns aimed at me. So much for your avoidance theory."

"The thugs were employed by Zahra."

"And she is, again?"

"One of us. She is, for lack of a better term, an enforcer. An auditor, of sorts. She makes sure that rules are followed."

"And what rule do I break?"

"You were born."

"And that breaks what realm walker regulation?"

"There is no regulation. Realm walkers aren't born or conceived. We just are."

"Well, apparently not. Not if Ranulf Deschamb had a kid and that kid grew up to be me."

"Ranulf Deschamb broke the rules."

"How so?"

There was no delicate way to say it. "Realm walkers tread carefully between reality and dreams. As such we enjoy the pleasure of those we visit."

A blush rose in her cheeks as she grasped his meaning. "You have sex with mortals? Like an incubus?"

"Not quite. We can pleasure those we visit, and enjoy their ecstasy, but we do not engage in intercourse, the way an incubus would."

"Oh. So, you are impotent."

He smiled at the note of disappointment in her voice. "No. Impotence is not the problem. Rather, when we do engage in intercourse, the passion is too fierce. The mortal does not handle it well. Frequently, sex with a realm walker results in sexual addiction, or drives the mortal insane."

"Insane?"

"Varying degrees, but yes. Seldom do people recover from the experience well enough to have what you would term normal relationships, afterwards. It's almost as if a bonding happens in the human's brain."

"But not for the realm walker."

He tried to hide the lascivious truth from his eyes and avoided looking at her. "No. Realm walkers do not bond…with humans. We are free to take pleasure where we want, but in our wake, we leave souls that cannot find solace, or appeasement."

She laughed outright. "God, you sound so conceited. 'Free to take pleasure…cannot find solace or appeasement.' Do you know how ridiculous you sound?"

Frustration flared in him and tempted him to prove his words to her. The image of her spread beneath him, crying out in ecstasy flashed through his mind, and he nearly lunged across the space between them.

His thoughts, unguarded, permeated hers, and her laughter faltered. She unfolded her body and sat straight, shoulders square, breasts prominently displayed beneath the drape of her sweater. She stared at him for several seconds, lifting her chin in defiance, daring him to act upon his fantasy.

A dare he would not answer.

"You were a fool to sleep as you did on the blanket so that others could watch you, at the festival."

A slap would not have sobered her more. "You are an ass."

"Better an ass than a rapist."

The air was rife with unspoken words between them. He deliberately held his thoughts to himself, to protect her. And himself. If she encouraged or challenged him in the slightest, he might lose all control.

After a time, she asked, "Is that the rule Ranulf

broke? Did he drive someone insane?"

"Most realm walkers care little about the sanity of humans. No. Ranulf Deschamb gave up his immortality. He became human."

"How?"

"By the grace of the gods. He took Reagan to bed, allowed himself to bond with her, and transcended into a mortal being."

"How is that possible?"

"Sheer will. But in doing so, he forfeited his abilities to walk between the realms. Those who made us, gave us free will. Thus, we police ourselves. Ranulf became mortal, knowing that he would no longer know our way of life. He forfeited up his true form for your— for Teagan's mother."

"How is that even possible? You said they have no conscience about sex with humans."

"He did not want to outlive Reagan."

"So Ranulf just gave up realm walking and settled down to have kids."

"Something like that. It had never happened with our kind before. Many were not pleased that he turned away from us."

"Were you one of them? Did you resent him for giving up what you are?"

"Ranulf and I had known one another for centuries. When he left us, I thought him a fool. And yet I could not argue at his happiness. He truly loved the temporal realm. He marveled at the novelty of changes as his body aged. He relished sleeping in the arms of another whom he dearly loved, and of waking to have her each morning. I thought he had gone mad at first. I was wrong. And then you were born."

"Me?"

"Well, as Teagan, that is. I visited him occasionally and saw how he marveled at your very existence. No realm walker had ever sired a child. You shone like a fiery opal. In the dark of night, you shimmered with a luminescence that he recognized as a part of him. When your mother died in childbirth, with their second child, he knew he must build the clock. He did not want to lose you too. He had accepted mortality for Reagan. With that bond broken, he could not guarantee your safe keeping. She had died and abandoned him. Might you not do the same? He knew that your uniqueness marked you as a target for other realm walkers. Those who would abuse you, toy with you, just to punish him. And that is why he built the clock."

"Is that why he let himself be captured? So he could die, as Reagan had?"

"He never meant to leave you, Teagan. He was merely living as normal a life as he could."

"And because he had become mortal, it took one small band of British soldiers and a rope to kill him? But when Reagan died, you said he wasn't bound to mortality anymore. Couldn't he just have switched back? Corrig said that realm walkers couldn't die except by another realm walker's hand. That's how he could have protected Teagan. Wouldn't she have wanted that?"

"He never told her. Never told her mother. As far as both women knew, he had always been a mortal. He built Oak Island as another portal once he discovered the truth about his daughter. He never had the opportunity to finish it, which is why so many have died. It will not work for mortals. Not without protection. It is unstable."

"And that's why he built the clock?"

"He initially built the clock to protect you, to protect her, like a force field."

"He should have told her."

"And risk her anonymity? Remember the time he lived in. People were killed for being witches. They were hanged for speaking their opinion against a king. He couldn't burden her with the knowledge that she was something more than those around her."

"So, he just left her to be captured by the British, risk torture, and who knows what else, all so that other realm walkers would leave her alone and stop being jealous of a dead man's portal-building skills?"

"That and because of what he begat. He had sired a human with non-human traits. That and the fact that the clock can alter energy and thereby alter time, infuriated them. It created an artificial realm walker vortex. Ranulf had given a gift of the gods to creatures who had no sense of its power. Barely a sense of right and wrong."

"Like so many of the realm walkers understand that." Her sarcasm was not lost on him.

"Ranulf Deschamb became corporeal, lived a human life, loved Teagan's mother, became a father, and made a life among the mortals. Yet he used his knowledge of his immortal existence. He knew the importance of time and how malleable it could be. The clock he designed could do for him, for you, and your descendants, what he could no longer do."

"Which is?"

Her hands tensed in frustration, and Darius lowered his voice.

"Protect you from *untimely* death. Allow you to move across the threshold when necessary."

"If it protected Teagan, then why don't I have her memories?"

"I took them from you. I couldn't let you remember any of it."

"You? What do you have to do with it?"

"Once I knew that Zahra and the others intended to destroy the clock and take Teagan, I tried to warn Ranulf. I had been dispatched, as had we all, to destroy the clock. I did not get to him in time, however. Once he was gone, I turned my task to saving you, on his behalf. For a friend. You, as Teagan had been taken prisoner at Lunenbeurg. Your fate, if not execution, would have been a prison. You escaped, however…stole the skiff, and tried to make it to the island. When your boat capsized, you sank into the sea, drowning. I intervened in what would have been your natural death. The death of a semi-mortal. I pulled you from the water, swept the memories you held from your mind, and made sure that no one, mortal or immortal knew of your survival. A woman with amnesia, left in a safe haven to live a quiet life."

"You saved me?"

"I delivered you to a convent in the colonies. If you were cloistered, few realm walkers would recognize you."

"Recognize me? What do you mean, recognize me?"

"That is the problem, Teagan. You are luminescent. Realm walkers would know you as one of their own."

"Oh my God! How many times have I heard that

phrase? That's what it means? That I am one of you?"

"Enough to spark curiosity. You are part of our lore. Enough so, that our elders wish to see you dead, lest other realm walkers entertain notions of bonding with humans to create a new race."

This time she snorted at him. "Create a new race? Like realm walker evolution?"

"Keep in mind, realm walkers are purveyors of balance. If we wantonly impregnated every female we came across, just to create hybrids, imagine the devastation we would reap."

Teagan opened her mouth to speak, and a venomous rage poured out. "Always did well in school. Always avoided trouble. Often knew what others were thinking. Could see things others could not. Dreamed things, other kids had no knowledge of. Things that would come to pass. Had my own mother questioning my sanity!"

"You danced in between the realms, unwittingly. And I sought to protect you, as best I could."

Anger simmered in her, bubbling up like lava. She bolted to her feet. Her aura flashed red with passion and fury. "Why? Why would you even care? It was not your job. According to you, realm walkers don't bother with emotions, they just observe the balance. Why did you ever bother with me? I am an outcast. A hybrid. An abomination."

He dared not admit it. How could he? From the moment he had set eyes on her, lying in a cradle, still swathed in a blanket, some part of him had been claimed by her? That he had been sent to take her life, and that had instead, threatened his own existence to save her? That he, in a moment of weakness, had chosen to ignore the very nature, the absolute balance of the universe?

"It is my penance."

"For what, Darius? Why wouldn't you tell me? Why would you keep all this a secret from me? You knew all along what I was? How could you steal those memories, and keep me locked away, and let me think I'm just some freak? Why would you visit me in dreams, and torment me? Making me think I was crazy? Never able to hold onto anything long enough to build a world of my own? I am a grown woman. Teagan was a grown woman. We deserved to know what we were…what we are."

Darius covered the ashes of their fire with sand and dirt, then rose. He stepped in her path to stay her steps. She swung at him, her hand striking him hard across his jaw. He grabbed her and held her at arm's length. Rage flowed freely from her, sparking the charge between them.

Because I wanted you for myself. Because I envied Ranulf.

He fought to shield the confession from her. Otherwise, she would sense the darkness, the madness of his desire for her that he had held for more than two centuries. Born of a human, she existed like no other creature, an ethereal being in the corporeal, and-all-too-fragile, shell.

He lusted for her like no other creature he had ever known. He wanted to consume her.

His own greed shamed him, and he lied. "Ranulf was my friend, and so I took you to charge."

"That was not your right."

"As I said, you became my penance for my own

sin. The others did not know I had intervened. I would not let the one glorious thing that a realm walker had created die so quickly. For that I am condemned to the service of protecting you. For my friend."

Not all of it was false. He had kept Ranulf as a brother. And he did hold the memory of their friendship dear.

Rage deferred to reason, and the tension eased within her just enough for him to release his hold. Teagan crossed her arms defiantly and stared at him. "And so now, we find ourselves back where it all began. You, me, and the clock, running around a barren blackhole, trying somehow to set it right? And how do we do that?"

"You have to live it again."

"That's impossi—"

"Destroy the clock, save Teagan from capture, and Deschamb if we can, and we might reset both her future, and yours."

She paced back and forth, as she had in the cottage, that first night. The sun had burned off the fog and hovered halfway between the horizon and its peak. They would have to move soon, to make it to shore during the busiest part of the day, to fade into the crowd.

Anything to be rid of you, of all of this. Her thought stung him more than her blow had. "How do we do this?" she asked.

"We make for Lunenburg and try to save Teagan's father. If we have arrived in time."

She glared up at him, mistrust in her eyes. "If the clock was so powerful, why didn't Ranulf use it when the British captured him? Why didn't he save himself, and her, the first time?"

"Because the British weren't the problem."

"Who was?"

"Zahra's henchman. Corrig."

Chapter Twenty-Four

Lunenburg, Nova Scotia, August, 1758

Darius found the raft where Ranulf always kept it, on the far side of the isle, so as to not be seen by mainlanders. Hidden by reeds and swamp grass, it waited, like a soldier set to sentry, until needed.

Their crossing was uneventful. A command of the raft, and a talent for controlling the elements gave him an advantage. A necessary one for the look on Teagan's face. Her rage had faded. At the moment, the pallor of her complexion combined with the misery on her face, reminded him she had not eaten for more than a day, and that her body still trembled, weakened by her travel through the portal.

For an odd minute he wondered what had happened to the woman who had stolen the clock. With any luck, Dana had not made it through, with them. Inanimate objects like a shoe or a clock might be able to withstand such a transition. Darius doubted however, that normal flesh and bone, could.

They met the shore along a brake of large rocks. The outline of a few scarce buildings marked the village in the distance.

"Stay here, stay still. If anyone comes near, hide. I'll be back."

She obeyed him. He returned with a horse, and a

cloak for each of them. She did not bother to speak to him.

He had used a few coins from the bag to procure a room at the public house. The German woman who accepted his money, doted on them once she saw he traveled with a wife. Before he could usher Teagan up the stairs, Frau Koehler had set a table for them—fish and mussel soup with cream, fresh bread, and beer.

He thanked their hostess and closed the door grateful that the woman had thought to build a fire for the weary travelers.

If he had thought she would need prodding, Teagan proved him wrong, as she fell upon the table and seized the food like a ravenous animal.

Without even shucking the pilfered cloak from her shoulders, Tegan emptied the mug of ale, and poured more from the pitcher on the table before dipping a choice piece of the newly baked loaf into the soup and slurping it hungrily.

"I take it you and your appetite have been rejoined since we made land?"

In reply, she scooped a mussel from the bowl, and plucked the savory meat from its shell.

He managed to steal a bit of bread and a mug of the ale for himself before she polished it off completely. No coffee, however. The presence of English troops in the town meant that the innkeeper did keep tea in stock. A rap on the door brought Darius to his feet. He accepted the second tray, shooing her away, proclaiming his wife "too tired for visitors". Not until he poured the dark aromatic liquid, and finished it with a drop of honey, did Teagan speak.

"I forgive you," she said at long last. She teased,

but he was grateful for what benevolent absolution she sought to offer him.

"For the price of a cup of tea?"

"No. For the price of the cloak, the meal, and the pot of tea." She motioned to the teapot. "You shouldn't need caffeine, right?"

He laughed outright at her. "Right."

He sipped his ale, as she finished the entire pot of tea, never once complaining about the loose leaves that trickled into her cup.

"What next?" Her eyes were brighter now, for the sustenance and tea.

Even in the daylight, she shone. Very much like an opal, rare and fiery. All fire and ice beneath the creamy flesh.

He sucked in air and tried to clear his head and his libido. "We must find Deschamb. I asked below when I made our arrangements, explaining we had lost our way, and our party. Herr Koehler says the date is August 26, the year is 1758.

"Then Deschamb is on his way from Louisbourg," she said.

"How do you know? I don't even know."

"I had a dream. A couple of days ago. She watched him hang you know."

"Who?"

"His daughter…me. I watched them hang him. I crawled under the scaffolding after everyone else left and stayed there with him…so he wouldn't be alone. So I wouldn't be alone."

"How do you know he was on his way from Louisbourg?"

"In the dream, he was trying to stop me from

meeting him there. He had been acting as a spy for the British. That's how it all began. Someone accused him of acting as an agent for the French because he traveled from the north, toward Lunenburg."

"And you are sure of this?"

Teagan nodded. "As sure as I can be. Should we go now?"

"Not yet. Not dressed as we are. We need to fit in."

"I'm sorry I don't have the outfit you bought me."

"Well, life happens. Sometimes, it gets in the way of the plans we make."

A ruckus outside the window caught their attention. Shouting and bellowing. Several wagons ran through the narrow street, fleeing from whatever was headed their way.

They could hear the hammering of the feet before they could see the mass of English soldiers, dressed in faded, thread-worn red jackets, marching in formation, hats intact for the most part, rifles at their sides.

"The British are coming," he quipped.

Teagan giggled at the reference. "Not for a few more years. Looks like they've already landed in Canada, and like they've been fighting. If it's late August, it could be Ticonderoga or Louisbourg."

"A fan of British history?"

"A teacher. Remember? Besides, the magazine I was reading on the plane had an article about Nova Scotia."

"Good girl."

A skirmish broke out between a couple of boys spouting French insults at the officer leading the group. One of the boys threw a rock at the officer, striking the horse, causing it to rear. In kind, two soldiers seized the boy, while another applied the butt of a rifle to the teen's head. The boy fell to the ground, limp, as the rest of the crowd dispersed.

"Stay here."

"I don't want to. I'm awake now. I'm better, really. The quicker we move—"

"Teagan, right now with those soldiers out there, locking yourself in this room and the chair against the door is the safest place for you to be. There is only one place in this town where they can quarter lodgings and food, other than ransacking the villagers' homes, which I have no doubt they will do. Here, though, they'll find ale. Drink, food, and a fire. In about ten minutes, the whole of Lunenburg will be rife with hungry, English soldiers ready for whatever they can find to quench their hungers. The last thing you need is for them to see you in slacks and a sweater. Stay here. Stay quiet. Stay safe."

Without waiting for her to argue, he downed his own drink, and strode through the door, slamming it shut behind him.

Chapter Twenty-Five

Corrig sipped the wine offered him by the lieutenant and eyed the serving girl appreciatively. Even in a room filled with people, he could hear her pulse race as she moved from table to table tending the guests.

Not the normal staff one expected at a dinner party. War with France had rid most of Halifax of its males, to fight for control of Canada. Still, the Judge offered a decent port and a better than decent distraction with the servants.

Of course, the normal dinner conversation had waned as well.

"What does he do?" the man asked. "How does he conceal his dealings?"

"He apparently is a most accomplished clock maker," Corrig replied, adapting his accent to match the lieutenant's. "As such, he can travel the countryside as it pleases him, like a tinker traveling on the pretext of plying his trade. He is French. That alone should be enough to arrest him."

"Why has no one done so?"

"He serves a purpose to the British commander, or so it would seem. He has convinced Boscawen that he is loyal to the British—by his birth, rather than his name—and that he serves only King George. I have heard it said that Wolfe prefers not to associate with the man."

"Boscawen?"

"No, Deschamb. Ranulf Deschamb. Wolf fears such an alliance could damage his career. Lawrence, however, views him an instrument."

"What if this Deschamb really is a British agent?"

"I do not doubt that he has provided information to the English. I do suspect, however, it is information he has been told to feed to them."

"By whom?"

"He does wear his name upon his cuff, does he not? Louisbourg has fallen. Would it not be a good time to sever the straggling sinews of her spies, before they can infiltrate England's ports to the south?" The mere suggestion would serve to fuel the officer's ambitions. Corrig smiled knowingly at his companion.

The lieutenant nodded in agreement. At Corrig's bidding, the man would surely enjoy a healthy career fighting for King and country.

A movement caught his attention. The serving girl again. "Tell me, who is the girl attending the table tonight?"

"Some chit the Creighton's wife took in. With so many of the able-bodied men engaged, we find ourselves depending on rabble for table service. Only women to serve the meal, as though it were nothing more than a public house."

"She is skilled. And quite ripe to the eye. She has a polish about her that I've not seen in a while." In fact, he had not seen it in a decade or more among mortals.

She glared at him, as if she recognized him.

A rapacious hunger welled in him. "Seldom, in fact, have I seen her kind on this side of the ocean. She has the look of the continent about her. Polished. I think I might have her for my dessert."

The lieutenant smirked and lifted his glass in praise of Corrig's candor. "Bed her well. She spilled sauce on my coat sleeve earlier tonight. I'd rather see her flogged. She did not so much as apologize for her sloppiness."

Corrig tuned out his pompous companion's blathering. He had delivered his message. He had planted the seed that would ferret Deschamb and his daughter. While he waited, he would see his own entertainment.

****

The only sounds in the blackness of the night were the rustling sounds from the stables. Hours had passed since the tables had emptied of gamesmen. Even the scullery was quiet, now.

Corrig had little difficulty sniffing her out. The table wench had a scent unlike the other women in the room. He couldn't quite define her, and that intrigued him. He slipped into the room she shared with two other servants and found the other two deeply tethered to their dreams. In the corner closest to the door, one snored so loudly, he could barely fathom that the other two could find enough peace to sleep at all. Yet, her cot sat empty. Clever girl. Why waste time in a cot, if you could warm the down-filled mattress of a gentleman, or gentlewoman, in the main house?

Corrig discovered her outside the judge's office, still in her day clothes, pocketing something beneath the cotton layers of her skirt. Fine, delicate hands played at the edges of the fabric. No servant, this one. Her hands were far too soft for the work he'd seen

240

others do. A spy perhaps? How delightful.

Corrig followed her as she slipped through the door into the governor's private library. He moved to cloak himself in the shadows, content to watch her mill through the stack of correspondence on the desk.

A lover? Had she penned a letter she regretted, and now sought to retrieve it? Even better.

As if she sensed him, the woman's posture changed. She stood up, listening to the silence of the room, waiting for some telltale sign in the air around her.

"I knew it was you. Here to finish me off?"

"You have me at a disadvantage. Have we met?"

She turned to look at him and tilted her head as she studied him.

Even in the evening shadows, he could see her a cleverness in her gaze. She was not afraid of him. Somehow, she knew him.

Her pursed lips curled into an inviting smile. "You remind me of someone I met recently."

"Ah. I must apologize for interrupting your—late night tryst."

She chuckled. "A slap and tickle. No more. At least not with this one," she waved her hand and scrunched her nose, as if the owner did not impress her.

She leaned back against the desk and raked her gaze over him. "You, however, are a different cut from most of the others who dined here tonight."

Such a tempting morsel of a mortal. "I assure you, I am not like the others."

She licked her lower lip, as she contemplated his words.

Wickedness radiated from her. This one was quite

a handful, morally. Definitely naughty.

Had they met?

He moved toward her, and her smile broadened as her gaze combed his torso settling on his hips. "It could enhance my evening."

"What could?"

She tugged her bodice and adjusted her cleavage invitingly. "A bit of tit for tat."

Fascinating character. "You are not like the other girls in the house."

"I'll take that as a compliment." She closed the space between them. She reached a hand toward his face, then trailed a finger along his jaw, and down his chest, his abdomen, until she found the laces of his trousers. She plucked the laces gingerly, before gently clawing at the bulge beneath the fabric. "Hmm. Definitely a cut above the rest. I do like a challenge."

Such an invitation.

He could smell deceit on her. Her mind played at all manner of things. She had a knack, this one. She also possessed an insatiable carnal appetite.

"I promise, I'll be discreet," she teased. She tugged on his waistband and drew him toward her as she moved back toward the desk.

He trailed his hand over the swelling curve of her breast, and she groaned seductively. What was she playing at?

Corrig waved his hand, and everything slowed. This private room would serve much better for his intent than the crowded closet of a room she shared with the other girls.

He caught her with her arms outstretched, one at him, the other reaching for the desk. A desirable position, with a bit of maneuvering.

He stepped behind her and wrapped an arm around her waist, thumbing the fabric of her stays beneath her gown. She wore perfume. Definitely newly arrived then. What in the world brought her to this forsaken rat hole?

She liked shiny, expensive things. And she was sharp. Much smarter than the others in the house. He pulled the note from her skirt and unfolded the missive.

A few items on one side—coin, linseed oil, linen, boots, along with a list of dates and towns. On the other side, however, she had written the names of several officers at tonight's dinner. By their names, she had scrawled notes about them or their homes. Atop the desk was a note in her handwriting with the words, *Midnight toil and mischief maid.*

An interesting pun. The list impressed him. Thief or spy, she was thorough.

He brushed aside her hair and pressed his mouth to the soft flesh of her nape, drawing her back against him. Something stirred within her. This one had a *rendezvous* with Judge Creighton, himself.

Voracious wench.

The right drawer pull on the governor's desk was ajar. Inside, lay a pistol. The thief intended to take a weapon. Clever woman. The judge would never admit the gun's theft, by so-doing admit his folly with a maid. Apparently, she liked to play all sorts of dangerous games. He could smell a distant hint of death on her. A thief and…a murderer. And such lascivious desires. Quite the triple threat.

He could not manage the suspension for any great length of time, but then he had other tricks. He whispered a few words in her ear and set her hands firmly upon the desk, loosening her gown so he could release the orbs of her breasts and fondle them. The scent of her made him hard, as did the firmness of her nipples as he drew first one, then the other away from the gown and pommeled them.

She stood virtually immobile, entranced. Her pulse raced as he fondled her. Her body's response suggested pleasure from his touch.

He slid a hand beneath her skirts, searching for her entry. Soft, and warm. She shuddered against his touch, and he stroked her, fervently whispering words to seduce her. "Does it please you?"

Her eyes fluttered and her body moved ever so slightly toward him.

When she was slick, he unsheathed himself and slipped inside, even as he fondled her, until the slightest of whimpers escaped her lips.

"Yes," her mind whispered.

Standing, she rode him until he came inside her. He then stroked her until she spasmed against him. A treat indeed, as she tightened around his member, begging for the sexual release.

Had she been abed with the others upstairs, he might have merely teased her in her dreams, pleasuring her and her roommates until he sated his lust, and theirs. This, however, pleased him so much more. The scent of her, the sound of her as she writhed against him.

She enjoyed sex and was experienced enough to not weep at the dreaming of it. He could have such fun if she had any memory of him once morning called.

He withdrew from her and helped her to the settee.

Once she awoke, she would no doubt wonder at the seizure that caused her to fall into such hallucinations. If she did not wake, then the scandal at her discovery in the governor's office, in her present state of dishabille would surely shake the local gentry with its decadence.

He grasped her hand in his own and studied it for a moment. A thief. Of course. She did enjoy the moment, her thoughts raced with a carnal desire and his own blood thrummed in his ears. He hardened at the sight of her swollen nipples displayed for all to see. How befitting. The thief would have stolen what few women ever freely gave. Pleasure.

He turned her chin so he could stare into her eyes. Her eyes shifted to meet his glance, and something flickered deep within them once more. Recognition.

How did she know him?

He slid her hand along his shaft, rudely, burning the memory of his flesh into her mind before taking his leave. As he moved away from her, something fell from her gown onto the floor. Even by the moon's shallow light, it glistened against the rug.

He bent and retrieved the object. The metal burned against his palm as he stared in disbelief.

A key winked in the moonlight at him.

****

Stroke.

The thought penetrated Dana's consciousness. Yes, she must be having a stroke. Otherwise, why couldn't she move, or talk, or remember what she had been doing?

Someone hovered near her, pressing her for information. Asking questions. Dana didn't want to think about that question. Not yet. The dream. She'd been having a terrific dream. A decadent dream.

"Where did you find it?" Her inquisitor's voice poured over her like velvet, laced with sandpaper. Her pulse quickened. She blinked and fought the urge to rouse herself from the trance.

"Where?" The question had lost its novelty. Reluctantly, Dana allowed her eyes to focus on the form lingering in the shadows.

He sat across from her on the settee. Yet, how could that be? She had entered the judge's library alone. Hadn't she?

Impatient man. Couldn't he see she couldn't talk?

"You don't need to talk to tell me how you procured such a key."

This time, Dana was certain his lips had not moved.

"Who are you? How did you come by such a remarkable item, my dear?"

She knew him. Didn't she? She was not dear to him. Oh, such a dream it had been. Her breasts tingled from the memory of it.

"I could please you again. All you have to do, is tell me where it is," he said out loud.

Please me? She ached between her thighs. *"Did you please me? I can't remember."* Dana could see him better now. Yes. He had been in her dream. Touching her, stroking her, entering her.

A menace lurked in his offer. Some part of her was intrigued.

She tried to move, to get up, to kick at him. In a flash, he vanished from in front of her, only to reappear, hovering behind her, leaning down to whisper in her ear. His hands settled on her shoulders, gently pressing against her flesh as they moved downward toward her chest.

"When they come in here and find you sprawled so, upon the settee, they'll know you for the trollop you are. And a thief. Or is it a spy? Or a murderer?"

Stolen clothes. Stolen identity. Panic prickled her as he stroked the exposed areola. How did she get undressed? For that matter, how did she get here? In this position?

Recognition flared in her mind. *"I know who you are!"*

For an instant, he paused. He caught an image of her falling. As if this surprised him.

He didn't remember the fall.

"What fall?" This time the question was real. His words brushed against her ear, his breath cold. "Tell me how you know me."

She tried to open her mouth, but still could not. What had he done to her?

"You don't have to speak. You can't, really. It is much more convenient if you just let me sift through your thoughts. I found some very naughty ones before."

Naughty. Before. *What happened before?*

Another flare of memory, and her body convulsed from the aftershock of the orgasm. Her heart began to throb in her ears, louder and louder.

"Such improper thoughts, and language, from a lady. But then, you aren't a lady of breeding, are you?"

His teeth grazed her earlobe. "I could keep you here, until the maid comes to stoke the fire and finds you. I could play with you, and fuck you until your mind shatters completely, and they would find only little pieces of a madwoman remaining in the guise of a whore. You'll be lucky if they don't dip you in hot oil, or sear your flesh with a branding iron for your wantonness. You are not the docile creature you portrayed at supper. Tell me how you know of me and how you came by this lovely key, and I can give you whatever you want, I can make all your troubles go away."

A shuffling outside halted his threats. Someone was at the door.

Lightning quickly he vanished into the shadows, as the hinges creaked, and the door gave way.

"Here, puss, puss. I trust you have not been left too long on your own, my dear."

Her hand twitched. Thank God. Her muscles flexed at the pins-and-needles sensation of the blood flow returning to her extremities. She peered into the shadows, searching for the man who had aimed a gun at her several days ago on the island.

Gone.

"Not to worry. If you are chilled, I can soon warm your bones, and set you to purr."

The glow of a single candle breaking the darkness framed Lord Amherst's face. Wearing nothing more than his nightshirt, and a salacious smile, he quickly stole across the threshold, closing the door behind him.

Having captured Louisbourg, the general's appearance in Halifax had been most serendipitous. Dana had made sure he noticed her as she tended his room. She needed a man of power until she got her bearings. Neither ugly, nor abhorrent, she would easily separate him from his gold.

"What a strumpet you are. You are vaguely attired."

She gathered her courage and her voice. Damned if she'd let some phantom undo her. She had made it out of the hole, made it off the island. Where there were soldiers—she had learned as a teen—there was usually money and a willingness to share.

She cleared her throat, surprised to hear the sound of her own voice. "I was to clear away, so I sent the other girls to bed, so as to have an excuse should anyone see me." She traced a hand delicately across one exposed breast, invitingly. With her other hand she retrieved the key from her lap, found the fold of her skirt, and plunged it into the cloth, lest he question her about it, as the man from the shadows had done.

"You should have found my bedchamber, and not dispatched me to find you."

"If found in your bed, your Lordship, the Governor's wife would turn me out. Then where would I be? Homeless, penniless, in a savage warring land, with no one to protect me." Though she cast her gaze in the nobleman's direction, her sights were set on the shadows beyond him. As were her words.

She knew her prey well. Men preferred a vulnerable woman.

The general moved into the room, setting the candle down upon the desk, then moving to stand before her. "You would not be without comfort for long, I suspect." His eyes combed the exposed flesh. "You do not seem the wench to work in another woman's house. How come you to be here, in such service?"

Dana's hand moved up the length of his leg to his thigh until she found his interest. She cupped his balls and lied. "I am widowed. A woman without a husband

249

has needs. Financial and...otherwise."

He flexed in her hand, and gasped satisfactorily as he brushed a tendril of her hair and urged her face closer to his anxious member. "In times of war," he whispered, "negotiation can be a treasured asset.

Dana pushed away thoughts of the creature who had tampered with her, however entertaining he might be. She would deal with him later. She smiled invitingly at Amherst, then set her mind to the task at hand.

Survival.

Chapter Twenty-Six

"It's no use, I can't breathe," Teagan gasped.

Darius slipped his arms into his jacket. "Nor can any other woman who is appropriately dressed to walk in public."

"Seriously. I know what the number one cause of death is. Collapsed lungs." She turned around to reveal the cause of her distress. Pale cream cotton peaked out from beneath the burnished russet silk of the corseted bodice. Beneath the peplum fell layers of golden linen, cinched to ruffle near her ankles.

I don't know what I look like, but I feel ridiculous. You can't really expect me to be able to do anything dressed like this. The whale bones are skewering me."

"Acceptable as long as the stays keep those in place." Darius eyed the mounds of flesh cresting the lace, and a wicked smile lit his face.

"Stop that."

"Trust me. That is exactly what we need if we are to glean information about Ranulf's whereabouts. One look at you, and the British will hand over the coffers, artillery, and all their military secrets."

"Why, Mr. Alwin. I have not heard such unmitigated drivel in all the time I have known you."

The flash of amusement faded, and he stared speculatively at her. "Do you have a weapon of any sort on you?"

She snorted, in spite of herself. "I thought I was the weapon. Seriously, no one could get at me through all the fabric and whale bone, and hooks, and laces. I'm trussed better than a Thanksgiving turkey."

"He handed her a dagger. Strap it to your leg."

"And wait for it to slice through my thigh? No thank you.

I'll just tuck it in...in my..." she tried slipping it beneath the sleeve of her jacket, unsuccessfully. "My—waist." She slipped the point beneath the peplum to try to hide it beneath the corset. "Ouch. Why the hell don't these things have proper pockets?"

"A soldier might search your pockets. But he's not likely to search beneath your skirts. At least, not in polite company. Tie it to your leg, high enough so no one will see it as you sit a horse."

"Easy for you to say. You've got proper boots on. Where did you get these from, anyway?"

"There is a captured cargo ship from France in the bay just south of here. The English plan to use it to deport people from Louisbourg. I merely lightened its inbound cargo."

"A cargo ship? To move the residents of Louisbourg?"

"That's what the talk is."

"Hmm."

"Hmm, what?"

"Just filing away pieces of information as they come to me. Never know what I might need later."

She had managed to shift her leg onto the bed but could not manage to circumnavigate the layers of cloth or the stays-of-death, to reach her own thigh. "Okay, magic-man, how do you expect me to get to the dagger to save myself if I can't even find my legs?"

The wicked smile retraced itself across his mouth, and he dragged the chair over to the bed. He removed the ribbon and the blade from her hands, as he slid his free hand up the length of her leg.

"No. No. Don't you dare."

"My goal is to see you safe."

"Uh-huh. I think your goal is to see me. Period. Be careful what you do with that thing."

"Are you referring to the dagger or some other thing?"

His touch shocked her as it always did, sending currents of electricity up through her body to her ears, momentarily stunning her. Her breath caught in her chest, and she plopped onto the mattress. His fingers deftly circled the flesh above her knee, urging the ribbon higher, until he found the spot he wanted. He splayed the dagger against the front of her thigh.

"Don't move," he commanded.

She dared not. The metal felt so cold it stung her skin, his hands so hot they did the same. She couldn't think rationally or talk, and prayed she could stay still against the temptation of his fingers playing to knot the fabric.

She flinched at the tightness of the tether. Once he had tied it high, he crisscrossed the ends of the ribbon around the thigh, lacing them twice more around the blade of the dagger, so it rested securely against her leg, its hilt barely brushing the top of her thigh.

"Lie back."

"Why?"

The tremor in her voice made him smirk. "Just trust me."

Not likely. She did as he asked, however, and held her breath as he reached for the bottom of her corset. The sounds of bones crunching and cracking echoed in her ears, and she jumped away from him.

"What are you doing?"

"Sit up."

She did. This time with ease. She ran her hand over the front of her gown and found he had broken the boning less than two inches from the bottom of the stays, so that while it offered her support, she could now bend at the waist. And she could reach her own thighs.

"Thank heavens. I was worried I wouldn't be able to use the restroom ever again." As it was, the concept of a chamber pot paled in comparison to the practical application of skill it took to properly utilize one. "Why couldn't Deschamb have lived after the invention of the toilet?"

"Privy. Remember you're in the eighteenth century, not the twenty-first."

For the first time since she had dressed, Teagan paused and studied his attire. The waistcoat of brown wool, cut away revealing a brocade vest. His shirt and stock, like her chemise, were cream-colored. Unlike the current fashion of pale trousers, his matched his coat. The form fitting slacks and riding boots accentuated the long lean lines of his body, and she wavered in her resolve not to succumb to her own sexual fantasies.

Of course, he'd be gorgeous. Like a cover of a novel. The man of her dreams was nothing more than that. A dream.

The fragrance of him mingled with the scent of bread baking in the kitchen. She wished she had eaten more. Last night's sleep had been fretful. She had jumped at every sound on the stairs, heeding the warning of a raucous camp within the town, in search of entertainment. At one point the noise from below had been so loud, she wondered if they were tearing the place apart.

Twice last night someone had tried to breach the door and, finding it barred, had given up. When she finally fell into a stupor, she did so alone.

This morning, however, Darius had arranged for a sitting bath, and hot water, along with tea and bread. A long way from the inn's breakfast he had first shared with her, this morning's treats were no less welcome. Especially the small washtub of hot water that soothed cold, tired muscles.

Never would she wish for simpler times, once she made it back to her own.

A bell sounded.

"What is that?"

"A call to Church." He stood and moved toward the window.

"To church? Why? What's happened?"

He shook his head. "Nothing out of the ordinary. It is Sunday. People here gather to give thanks and praise."

Heat rose in her cheeks. "I'll have you know I've spent my fair share of Sundays inside similar walls, doing the same."

"Good. Then, shall we?" He extended his arm in invitation.

"What? We're going to church, too?"

"How better to mingle with the locals?"

"Can you do that?"

"Mingle with the locals?"

"No. Go inside a church."

"Why wouldn't I be able to go inside a church? Granted, I will have to lower my head to make it through the doorframe, but I should be alright, once inside."

"You won't vanish into thin air, or burn, or something?"

He stared blankly at her.

"Not like a vampire, then?"

He cocked an eyebrow in contemplation of her supposition. "Not in the least. I can offer you no entertainment in the brimstone of Bram Stoker's hell."

"Ah. Sorry."

"As am I. Apparently your concept of my existence is built upon the notion that I am some demon." His features remained calm, yet his words were sharp.

Teagan did not answer, choosing instead to grab her skirts and move across the room toward the door.

"Your cloak."

"Good grief! I don't need a cloak. I'll pass out if I have to wear that on top of all this. It's August."

He grabbed her arm and stopped her from passing through the door.

"Teagan. You must follow my lead. There are no fewer than twenty soldiers, downstairs. You will wear the cloak. Play your part. And for both our sakes, keep your mouth closed."

She wanted desperately to argue with him. However, last night's revelry roared in her head, and she thought better of it, allowing him to drape the cloak over her shoulders, before leading her onto the landing and down the stairs.

Twenty turned out to be an understatement. Stepping through the rubble, over the sprawled bodies, and around the furniture and gear reminded her of playing hopscotch.

Having traversed the minefield of redcoats, they had no trouble making it through the rest of town to St. Andrews Presbyterian Church.

As feared, the August weather made it impossible for her to cover herself for long. Darius graciously carried her cloak as they entered the church. He did have to bow to keep from leaving a dent in the door frame.

Most of the pews belonged to families who had long held a traditional seat in the congregation. She and Darius found seats along the side and joined the other inhabitants in the ritual of the service. The novelty of singing hymns *a cappella* reminded her of lazy summer days spent crammed into revival tent services, where everyone sang uniformly off-key.

Following the service, as they departed, Darius introduced himself to the minister, referencing Teagan as his new wife.

"Ah, honeymooners. I daresay this is an odd place to find yourself enjoying your first days of matrimony." A wink and nod to Darius ruffled Teagan's feathers, but she bit her tongue.

"We find ourselves separated from our guide. We were traveling from Halifax to Louisbourg.

"Louisbourg, say you? That is a questionable place for a new bride, is it not?"

"As much I fear, Reverend. However, I seek a watchmaker, an old friend of my wife's family who is known by his trade, and I had heard we might meet him there."

"A watchmaker, say you. By what name does his shingle hang?"

"Deschamb. Ranulf Deschamb."

The minister, who had been shaking hands as Darius spoke, faltered. A move which neither Darius nor Teagan missed.

The reverend recognized Deschamb's name. Their use of it unnerved him.

Several young soldiers bowed and nodded to Teagan as she stepped from the church yard. For a brief moment, she appreciated the effect the fashion had upon her admirers. Until the dust made her sneeze, and she remembered her fear of a punctured lung.

She accepted the seat offered by one of the local men, as she sought shade. No doubt, the man also found comfort standing beneath the shade tree, enjoying the view of her ample cleavage as she tried to breathe.

"And what aid of advice did the kind reverend offer, Mr. Alwin?"

Darius nodded to the man who stood leaning against the tree. He raised her gloved hand to his lips, an obvious display of intimate affection which caused her admirer's ears to go red. He pushed away from the tree, scarcely bothering to look over his shoulder as he hurried away from Darius's threatening stare. Once they were alone, Darius took the seat next to her.

She yanked her hand away. "Stop that and tell me what he said." Just what she didn't need. Distraction.

He said that Ranulf Deschamb left two days ago for Louisbourg, with a package. Alone.

"If he is alone, then where is his daughter?"

"She is attending friends. A family north of the

town. The woman has delivered a new baby, and Teagan—the other Teagan—has gone to assist with the housework, while the mother recuperates."

"For now, then, she's safe."

"So it would seem."

"But you are not convinced?"

"By these dates, we only have five days to reach Ranulf and warn him. Ranulf Deschamb was arrested on September 2."

"That should be plenty of time."

"If we had a computer, or e-mail, or a cell phone, or any twenty-first century convenience. But not for this."

"Darius, you are a realm walker. Walk into a dream or something."

"Teagan, this requires more. Somewhere nearby, there is at least one other realm walker hell-bent on destroying Ranulf, his daughter, and the clock."

"How can you be so sure?"

"Because, the last time I was here, that was my assignment, as well."

His confession hit her like a lead weight. His assignment. Darius Alwin had not come to save them the first time. He had come to destroy Ranulf and his...

She swallowed her doubts and kept her mind on the task at hand. "Then we need to talk to the daughter. If someone has already reached Ranulf, then it's too late to help him. Chances are, however, the daughter knows where the clock is."

"Unless he has it with him."

"Darius?"

"Yes?"

"What if we do find her? I mean, is there a problem

if we do? You know that whole, no-two-things-can-occupy-the-same-space that they always use in movies, is that real?"

"You'll be fine."

"Will I?" She wanted assurance. "You said last time—"

"If I were here to kill anyone, I wouldn't have wasted time with this façade. Teagan Deschamb, the creature you were held another body, then. She will not recognize you. Neither will you in your current vessel present any risk to her. The universe is a great and wondrous place. Stranger things happen all the time."

She sighed as much as she could, given her attire. "I don't think it can get any stranger than this."

"Excuse me—"

They looked up to see the minister walking briskly toward them.

"Yes, Reverend?"

"I've just had a thought. Since our friend Deschamb is unavailable, I wondered if you might break bread with us this day. My wife was eager to meet you when I told her you are recently wed. It is a humble meal, but it satisfies the palate. And, of course, news from Halifax would no doubt satisfy the mind. Will you join us?"

Girl, clock, Deschamb. Teagan shook her head, ready to blame the heat when Darius stood and offered his hand to the man.

"We would be most grateful, Reverend."

"Excellent. We will expect you for Sunday dinner, then. The minister nodded to them. Sir, Mrs. Alwin, good morning to you both."

He turned on his heel and hurried back through the

churchyard gate.

Morning's breeze faded, along with Teagan's patience. "Darius, why in the world would you say yes, since you are hoping to depart town on the fastest horse we can find?"

"Because, Mrs. Alwin, the most reverent minister, is lying."

Chapter Twenty-Seven

The evening spent in the company of the reverend and his wife had been advantageous on two accounts. Firstly, the meal, while not sumptuous, made the inn's food seem like slop in comparison. Elizabeth, Mrs. Reverend Morreau, had roasted a fine duck, and served with it a blueberry and oat pudding upon which she had poured brandy. The duck, a gift from one of the townspeople, had been stuffed with barley, onions, and potatoes.

Teagan's mouth watered for the savoriness of the feast.

"Prithee, will you take a glass of port, Mrs. Alwin?" Elizabeth asked.

Teagan's hesitation in answering prompted Mrs. Morreau to insist. "We hold no tendency toward gluttony, I assure you. 'Tis only that we are bound by that which our neighbors afford us. There being many Germans, and now an ample number of French from the north, and troops from the south, we find that much barter is in wine. If you would rather not, we be not offended."

"I thought the French were being expelled."

"Aye, they are. But a few have made their way south, trying to escape to New England to make their way to New France. Poor dears. Imagine being cast out with nothing, save the clothes on your back."

How in the world had this woman, so gentile, come to this place, Teagan wondered. In the modern world, no woman would have assumed such gentility. Especially with the surplus of English troops littering the two streets that marked the town.

Teagan cleared her throat and tried, as best she could, to imitate the woman's style of speech. While not Shakespearean in its lyrical quality, the style of a mid-eighteenth-century woman's speech far exceed the flourish of a twenty-first century American's dialect.

"I would be grateful for such generous libation." There. Simple. *Keep it simple, stupid.*

As if he had heard her thoughts, Darius chuckled, though he and the reverend seemed engaged in serious conversation.

"How long since you and Mr. Alwin were wed?"

Uh-oh. She had no idea how to field such a question. "Um, we are newly married. Only a few weeks."

"And what news bring you from Halifax? We hear so little that is not of the friction between the English and the French, or of the incursions by the natives."

"Truth be told, Mrs. Morreau, I am of the Colonies. I can give you no news from Halifax."

The woman's face wilted a bit, then recovered. "I see. Well, I have heard there is much movement in the Colonies to petition for self-government. Do you find any truth to such rumors?"

Teagan chose her words carefully. "There is often talk among educated men to facilitate growth. Whether such ideas of independence will meet with fruition is not for me to speculate."

Regardless of which king Elizabeth Morreau paid

allegiance to, Teagan intended to remain on neutral ground. Until told otherwise. In celebration of circumnavigating a question she knew could get her in trouble, she lifted the glass to her lips and sipped the dark wine.

"Do not think me crass to speak of notions political. It is only that I seldom have much opportunity to speak of anything other than my husband's business. We serve the Church of England, as is our trust. We have lost so many either to disease, or to violence these two years hence, I am comforted by the opportunity to speak of anything that does not bring mournful memories."

"Oh. I am sorry. I had no idea. I—"

The reverend's wife smiled jovially. "Your attire is most becoming. Is it the new style in the colonies, then? The lower decolletage?

"I—um, it is part of my—rather, the gown was a gift for my trousseau. I could never afford such a dress."

Not for the first time since they had entered the cottage, did the man's wife look covetous. And why not? Stuck in a town with little to offer, other than the assurance that someone would always be knocking at her door, in need of something.

"Do you aid your husband in his ministry?"

"I would hope I aid him in all things," she joked.

Teagan looked up to see her smiling, genuinely. "He is a most learned man who finds himself challenged in his work as schoolmaster."

"He teaches as well?"

"He serves the community with prayer and penmanship. His prowess at languages makes him a popular guide and mediator. Often, he is called to help negotiate between two farmers in their land disputes."

"A skilled man."

"He serves those within our community as best he may." He hid something, as had her words of sympathy for the French exiles. "And your husband? What is his business?"

For an instant Teagan panicked. What possible business could she reveal? Time lord? Realm walker? Assassin? She remembered the booth he maintained at the festival.

"My husband works with silver. He is a jeweler."

Her eyes sparkled with interest. "Ah, and yet you wear no band about your finger."

Sugar-honey-ice-tea! "It is an embarrassment to admit that he has asked me not to wear it in public, for fear that we would be set upon by deserters or thieves."

"Indeed. He is a wise man. Wolfe's troops would surely melt it down to make shot for their muskets. I heard he has raided the whole of Cape Breton to turn out the French and to loot what he can for his soldiers, regardless of the carnage he leaves in his wake."

"Then I am fortunate we will soon be away from here."

Mrs. Morreau glanced sideways toward her husband, then whispered as she set to clear the table, "Be well away. I fear we will all be murdered in our beds before long."

The day had melted into a soft pink dusk by the time Darius and Teagan nodded farewells to Reverend Morreau and his wife.

Tucking Teagan's hand into the crook of his elbow, they stepped through the courtyard and away from the cottage.

Teagan couldn't wait to get back to the inn, to lose some layers. And to hear what Darius had learned from the jack-of-all-trades, Morreau.

The earthen road still radiated the warmth of the day's sun as they walked arm in arm in the summer's twilight. While no one hovered or followed them, Teagan couldn't keep herself from whispering. "What did he tell you? Where is Deschamb?"

"Deschamb's package was not as small as we thought."

"What was it? The clock?"

"A family."

"A family of what?"

"He is trying to get a family on one of the ships bound for the Colonies. It seems that the French sympathies do not rest only upon Deschamb's shoulders, but upon most of the townspeople here. There are tales that Wolfe and his men are sweeping Cape Breton, marching westward toward St. Lawrence, with the French people in an exodus to rival the Jews in Egypt. A family who made their way into town last week, told Morreau that the English were burning homes, killing livestock. I gleaned from his thoughts that several other families weren't lucky enough to escape."

"They're killing them? I thought they were supposed to put them on ships and evacuate Louisbourg."

"Some are leaving. Some are killed. For a select few, though, it seems the English are not so merciful."

The vision of a woman and her daughters being hunted through the woods, set upon by a pack of soldiers, flooded Teagan's mind. She could see the man's hands clawing at the girl's skirt, dragging her to the ground as she tripped on a tree root.

Where was the realm walkers' balance for them?

They had nearly reached the inn. As they passed a house above which a sundries shingle swung, Teagan noticed two soldiers lurked. Watching them, it must be close to midnight. Even from the distance of twenty feet the air swelled with the evidence of their time on the march. Urine, sweat and a scent that made her tremble in revulsion smothered her. She stumbled on a rock, nearly falling. Darius clutched her by the waist, pulling her to him, to steady her. In reply, one of the soldiers cleared his throat and spit in their direction.

"Get me out of here, now. Please, Darius."

Her unease grew as they made their way back to Mrs. Koehler's. From the raucous sound spilling across the threshold, Mr. Kohler had his hands full with a tap room full of drunken men, all of whom had left their manners and any sense of hygiene back in England. Mrs. Koehler had her hands raised, threatening one with a large ladle when they stepped through the doorway. At the sight of Darius, she paused, blushed briefly as her glance met Teagan's, then swung out at the man who attempted to reach across her workbench to pilfer a loaf of bread, as well as a bit of Mrs. Koehler, herself.

Someone reached out and grabbed at Teagan, latching on to her bottom. She screamed and swung out so hard and fast that her fist sent the man reeling backwards, head over heels off his stool, like a hedgehog, to his friends' enthusiastic laughter.

She turned to continue her assault, a *bean sidhe* howl emanating from her as she lunged at the man.

Flash.

Thick as molasses, her movements slowed, while the cacophony of the soldiers' revelry ceased, and the men fell immobile.

Darius passed by her, heaved the man up, with one hand to the man's collar, as if he were no more than a kitten, and tossed him through the still open door, out to the yard in front. He closed the entrance door, up-righted the stool, retrieved the bread from Mrs. Koehler's pest, and grabbed two mugs and a pitcher from the sideboard.

"Darius!" she tried to cry out again. Unable to physically do more than whisper, she moved through the invisible quicksand, hanging precariously on the lower landing to the stairs, waiting for some reprieve.

He disappeared momentarily, out of sight, then reappeared, at her side. "As much entertainment as the promised wrestling match might provide, my love, I cannot have you garnering any more attention from the troops, or our hostess. Out of sight, out of mind, though cliché, is accurate."

Without releasing her from the sorcery, he scooped her up, slung her over his shoulder and bounded up the stairs.

All she could see from her vantage point were his boots and the stair rail.

She heard the door close and latch. The world turned upside down as he flipped her from his shoulder to the bed, then carefully set about unlacing the front of her stays.

Darius.

He stared her in the eyes and smiled wickedly at her. "There are such advantages for a realm walker at times," he said as he tugged on the laces.

His fingers played upon the fabric and whalebone, loosening the bodice until his hand found the sheerness of the gown beneath.

The air crackled around her as she lay prone, staring at him, waiting. What would his hands feel like, stroking her flesh, she wondered.

While her body had not moved, her pulse did flutter, racing until she wondered if she might have a stroke from the anticipation.

Darius moved his hands over her legs until he found her boots and removed each. He slid his hands beneath the layers of petticoat up her thigh until he found the dagger he had tied earlier. Deftly, he released the tether and removed the weapon. Her limbs tingled as the cool evening air met her skin. She longed for him to continue.

Good grief, don't stop there. I am too hot.

He peered down at her. From where she lay, she could see the fine outline of his body, taut in the fitted pants. He removed his own jacket and vest and untied the cravat and stock about his neck. His hair curled just beyond the cut of his collar. He looked utterly menacing, like a figure from a romance novel cover. And of course, she lay in repose, half undressed herself.

Forget clocks. Forget soldiers. She could lie here and just watch him for a very long time.

His head snapped up, and he peered at her.

Please.

"Please what, Teagan?"

A crash and the sound of voices raised in argument downstairs told her that time had resumed for the patrons in the public brewhouse below. As the noise broke the atmosphere, so too did Darius release her from the spell that slowed her movement and silenced her voice.

"Sonofabitch. What was that for? Stop playing tricks."

Something smoldered just below the surface of his expression. "Be careful what you ask for."

Inwardly, she trembled at his question. She resented the embarrassment that crept over her at his warning. *Yes, what, Teagan?* she asked herself. What did she plead for?

****

He turned his back to her, keeping himself and his thoughts to the open window. Teagan gratefully chose the opportunity to discard the embroidered overskirt, and the layers of skirts that still clung to her legs, until the only layer that covered her body was the lightweight cotton shift.

"Why are you mad at me? It's not my fault that idiot got grabby. What did you expect me to do, let him grope me?"

"I am not angry with you. You did what you believed necessary. I followed suit."

"But you are angry, now. I can feel it."

"Not angry." He turned to face her, his expression held hostage by the shadow of the candlelight behind him. "Focused."

"On what? Dressing me, undressing me, teasing me? Embarrassing me? Besides your parlor tricks, what are you focused on, Darius Alwin?"

As if her utterance of his name invoked the demon that lurked behind his facade, his eyes glittered, and he moved away from the window's ledge.

Instinctively, she backed up also, finding the bed and curling up in the middle of it.

As if that could protect her.

He prowled toward the bedframe, placed his fisted hands on the mattress and said in a low guttural tone, "I am concentrating on keeping you in one piece, whether you want me to or not." He leaned across the quilt until his face nearly touched hers. "Even if that includes keeping a room's length from you, so that you don't invite me to do something that you might later regret."

"How do you know what I would regret?"

"Besides keeping an eye on you in each of your incarnations over the past two-hundred-fifty years?"

He backed away from her, and the air inside the room cooled. "Celibate sanity is preferable to sexually sated lunacy. And neither of us can afford to be off our game anymore. If Deschamb has moved the family safely and is on his way, as you believe, then he cannot be more than a day's ride from Lunenburg, now."

"Do you think he plans to meet his daughter?"

"I suspect if he is concerned with moving the people who are being shoved out by the soldiers, that he might be trying to move her as well."

"And that is how he gets nabbed by the lobster-backs. So, all we have to do is catch up with him before he gets caught."

"Not so easily done."

"Why not?"

"We don't know where she is hiding. We don't know what circuitous route he is following. And we don't know who else is looking for either of them."

"What do you mean 'who else'?"

"I told you before, I was not the only one sent to

find and destroy the clock."

"You mean…Corrig could be here as well?"

"Among others."

"Well, can't you use your powers to tell him to back off?"

"That hasn't seemed to work in more recent adventures, has it?"

"I'm sorry I ran at the marina. I should have trusted you. I do trust you."

A sigh so deep it shook the timbers of the room escaped him. "Get some rest. The soldiers downstairs are moving tomorrow. If they move south, then we are free to move north toward Mahone Bay."

She lay back against the bumpiness of the unmilled cotton mattress, willing herself to sleep, yet could not escape the image of Corrig aiming the gun at her. She knew he didn't need a weapon to kill.

Corrig was one.

Chapter Twenty-Eight

Smoke still curled from the rubble that just a few days ago provided shelter for families. The bay was otherwise untouched. Fishing boats anchored, rocked gently on the water. The air however, shivered with the malignancy of murder.

Retaliation for Louisbourg.

Three days ago, eight Mi'kmaq had attacked two families, as agents for the French. Scattered attacks had put everyone on edge, waiting for the blaze of vengeance.

Darius didn't want to bring her here. He dared not leave her in Lunenburg. She was infinitely safer with him than away from him. A chance clue that led them here, something he had overheard one of the soldiers say yesterday morning.

"If they could get the old man to turn on his own, tinker-turned-spy, they could win the war," the lieutenant had said.

His drinking buddy replied, "I heard he stopped 'em from killin' more. Mumbled somethin' in French and made 'em run away."

An hour later, he paid for two saddled horses at the livery, and helped Teagan onto her mount.

"Where would you be going to, sir?"

Darius ignored the hungover soldier as he led the two horses through the yard.

"Sir, I asked you a question. Do you not understand English? Are you perhaps, a Frenchie? Let's see your papers, then? We could confiscate these horses and arrest you both—"

Darius turned and punched the man solidly in the nose, laying him out cold.

"You could have just answered him or done that time halt thing."

"You told me to stop doing that."

"I meant on me."

He knelt near the man's body, whispered a few words, then straightened, and climbed into the saddle of his own horse. He winked at her. "Sometimes, it just feels good to make contact. Don't worry, he won't remember how he got there. Only how much he drank."

A precarious day's ride later, they found the clockmaker in a fisherman's croft, drinking wine, and reading a weathered copy of Homer's *Odyssey.*

"Mon ami! Come in." The old man welcomed them in, and invited them to sit, as he rummaged for two more cups.

"I did not expect to see you for a few more days, Darius. What brings you north.

"A warning, and a favor. You, my friend are in trouble. You have been set up. Trust me, you have no idea just how far we have traveled."

Ranulf winked at Teagan. "He should entertain you with something more fitting than a fisherman's cove side inn. Tell him you want to go to Halifax. He can take you on an adventure, you know."

"She knows all about me."

Surprise glimmered in the old man's face, briefly, before he masked his features again with amusement.

"Darius and I have been friends for more than a lifetime, no?"

"Where is your daughter now?"

"My daughter? Do not worry, my friend. She is safe." He thumbed the book on the table. "Homer holds up you know. Such trials he suffered. And yet, he never gave up on his family."

"She won't be for long, if you do not listen to me."

"I have taken precautions to protect Teagan. Do not worry. Whatever befalls me, she will be provided for. She need have no fear of the tragedies that surround us, now. Eventually, the war will end, and we will return home." He leaned back in his chair and eyed them cautiously. "What are you playing at?"

Teagan reached across the table and placed a hand on his. "Trust me when I tell you that Odysseus had no stranger an adventure than we have. We have traveled more than two centuries to find you and make sure you are both safe."

He stared at her for a moment, digesting her words. "I must admit, you are lovely, but I do not believe we have met. What did you say your name was?"

"My name is Teagan. I am, or was, or will be your daughter," Teagan said.

Ranulf Deschamb swallowed and shook his head. "She speaks of stranger things than you and I, old friend."

Darius accepted the glass of wine his friend passed to him and emptied it. "She speaks the truth, Ranulf."

"What mean you, Darius, to play me for such a fool? Look at her coloring, it is nothing like her mother's. She looks nothing like my Teagan? What ruse are you conspiring?"

"If your daughter finds you, in these days to come, it will surely mean her death."

Ranulf's face, ashen from the stress of the past few days, paled even more. "No. I have seen to it, that cannot happen." He laughed at a private joke. "Darius you are a wit at games but must keep at mind that I no longer walk between the realms. That is why…" His words trailed off.

Darius knew Ranulf feared telling anyone else what he had crafted. "I know about the clock. I discovered it. As one who lived between the realms for so many millennia, can you not see how this is set to end? You cannot play with time so frivolously, and not expect Zahra's wrath for forsaking that knowledge which the gods bestowed upon our kind."

"I assure you, there is no frivolity, friend Darius." He peered at Teagan, as if trying to find something in her face.

"Look at her, Ranulf. Her hair and clothes might be different, yet she is your daughter, reborn. She is your Teagan three centuries from now."

Teagan blinked at him, shyly.

Interesting. Teagan had never done anything shyly, for as many lifetimes as Darius had observed her. Yet in this, she appeared awed.

Worry creased the old man's brow. "And you say you used the clock to travel here?"

She nodded and sipped from her cup, as if to hide her face from his perusal.

Darius pressed on. "Zahra knows about the clock. Watchers everywhere, my friend. You and I were to meet in Halifax. But Corrig and I were sent to destroy the clock."

"No. You mustn't."

"I know." He motioned to her. "It has served her well for more than two centuries. That is part of my crime. I must confess, I have committed a sin as heinous as yours, Ranulf."

"Pray, tell. What is your crime, that you have come so far from this child's time to confess to me?"

"You know for as many years as I visited you and your wife, I was bound by the friendship that you and I had long before."

"I do."

"And yet when I looked upon your daughter's face, I was consumed with a yearning more powerful than I had ever known."

"Darius—"

"Hear me out, Ranulf, to know my crime. Therein lies your understanding of why we arrived here, now. Even in her infancy, Teagan sang to me."

"I will not hear this. You are a realm walker."

"You must hear it."

Pallor exploded into rage upon Ranulf's expression. He rose from his chair and slammed his hand upon the table. "You would defile my daughter?"

"No."

"Yet you say she sang to you. That she cast upon you a yearning. You are a realm walker. You are possessed of a power and a lust that would move you to madness if you did not seek a release either in the pleasure of passion or of pain. She is a mortal."

"And thus, I did not act upon your daughter's virtue. I only ensured her safety." From the corner of his eye, Darius could see that Teagan sat with her lips open, speechless.

"Then what is your crime against my daughter and my family that brings you to account for, here, now?"

"I hope to save you and your daughter. Corrig has set a trap. If you are caught in Lunenburg, English troops will arrest you, and execute you for treason. Four days after your death, your daughter—while trying to escape a similar fate—will try to make it to the island and to the clock. Without success."

"What?"

"I will rescue her from her natural death."

Silence settled between them as his words settled.

"To stop a natural death is forbidden, Darius. It goes against—"

"I know. I did not do this frivolously. The death of one so rare, and so prematurely, could surely not be meant as fate. I could not help myself. I dredged her from the depths of the water and purged the water from her body."

"That means you told her what you are?"

"No. Not until recently." He nodded at Teagan and found her still sitting quite calmly, as if that she were watching a scene from a play. "The clock must be destroyed. That is why we are here."

"They all know of its existence, then?"

"Zahra knows of the clock. That is why Corrig has set a trap."

"You mustn't destroy it! It is all that protects her. My Teagan. No. Leave me to what death may await me, Darius, but I will not desert my daughter to the evil I see that would touch her, once I am gone. She will have need of its protection."

"Don't you see? That is why we *are* here. She will have you."

"I am no longer of that ilk. I cannot protect her."

"Your daughter will have you until she has need of me. I have protected her these many centuries, minding her safety. Do you not trust that I remain vigilant in that duty?"

"I trust that your weakness might set you upon her."

"As you set upon Reagan?"

If Darius had hit the man, it could not have struck a harder blow. Ranulf Deschamb's face reddened, whether in fury or in shame, and he fell still.

As soon as the words escaped his lips, Darius regretted them. He knew the accusation was not true. Yet he had to make his friend understand. For all their sakes.

"I did not. I loved Reagan beyond all compare. In a millennium there had never been a creature that so tamed my nature, so enflamed by heart. How dare you insinuate that I seduced her. 'Twas I who was seduced by her perfection."

"As was I, by your daughter's. I heard her singing in her dreams as a child. I tended her in dreams, comforting her after your death, and shielding her when necessary, as best I could. I ensured she passed from one mortal shell to the next in ample years, peacefully, with no harmful memories to bear."

Teagan's head snapped up at his last comment, her eyes glistening as she met his stare. Damn the woman, how could she look so vulnerable now?

Ranulf's shoulders slumped a little, as if Darius's words weighed heavy on his reason.

"Ranulf, she is spectacular. You must know that I have kept her safe for nearly 300 years. I would and have risked everything for her safety."

Deschamb nodded toward Teagan, "Do they hunt you both now as well? In the future?"

"It has begun. But I believe all can be set right. If we can find the clock."

"How is that?"

"If the clock is with us in the future, when it is destroyed, then nothing from the past would be affected."

"What of...my daughter?" Ranulf shifted for the first time to stare at the woman sitting in the corner of the room. "You do have her eyes. Do you remember me? Or am I a ghost to you?"

"I feel connected to you, but the memories are like a dream."

"What I did in the past would still come to pass, yet in her future, she would have my protection. If we stop your unnatural death, then we might be able to alter the events that facilitate the moment when her boat capsizes."

"And if you are cast out? What if you have no power to protect her?"

"You forfeited your mortality, not your power. Teagan, ever was and still is your daughter. The blood of a realm walker runs through her. It has taken many mortal lifetimes for her power to grow, but her strength continues. I believe she will one day have the capabilities of a realm walker, herself."

"And will Zahra not kill her for this?"

"I do not believe so. I think Zahra would find her an anomaly, not an abomination. Imagine a realm walker who comprises both mortal and immortal traits. I think she would recognize once your device no longer exists that your intent was pure, but that device is dangerous. For mortals to play with time artificially, imperils all reality. Surely, you must see this."

"I had to do something!"

"And you did what only you could do. You used your knowledge and your skill to protect that which you loved most. But it is at an end now. It must be."

Ranulf rose and walked to the window.

Teagan had not been so quiet in a lifetime as she had been here, sitting before the man who literally gave her life. The room breathed with energy.

When Ranulf turned around, Darius lifted Teagan's hand and touched his fingertips to hers. A blue thread wove between their hands, crackling, like electricity. "See? No mere mortal."

"It was the same with Reagan and me. She shimmered in the darkness." He grabbed the book from the table. "You must help us get away, then, my friend. You must help us escape. I cannot let Corrig or Zahra take that which I hold most precious." He put a hand on Teagan's shoulder. "Mortals live many lives, seldom remembering their previous incarnations. It is the best way to forget the pain of living. I trust your lives have been better for the forgetting."

"Tell me where she is, and I will find safe passage for you both, to wherever you wish. Then you may have it, the clock."

"Is it on the island?"

"No. That would be too easy a target."

"Where then?"

"There is a church not too far from here."

Darius and Teagan smiled at one another, as they asked simultaneously, "Reverend Morreau?"

****

Teagan shared a hug with Mrs. Morreau, before she joined Darius. Morning, still some time away, would bring an English curiosity that neither couple wanted to entertain.

Ranulf had left the clock with the Reverend Morreau and his wife. The original clock was much more beautiful than the aged three-hundred-sixty-year-old version she had taken from her aunt's house. The wood polished until it glistened served as an appropriate case for the dazzling engraved metal of the face, and the intricate mechanism that kept time, as it were. There, amid the numbered inserts lay the thirteenth sliver that housed the keyhole. Nearly imperceivable except to those who were looking.

She traded her russet gown for a simple one of grey from Mrs. Morreau. The minister's wife was glad to help with the plan once she realized their shared friendship with the clockmaker. She and Darius would meet with Ranulf halfway between Mahone Bay and Lunenburg. A clockmaker with a clock would not be as suspicious as a newly married couple traveling along the war-torn roads.

A grain sack had been partially filled, to accommodate the clock, and still hold enough grain to disguise the fact until they met him. After all, a sack of barley in a town with a brewmaster offered little subject for suspicion.

Darius secured the sack behind the saddle of Teagan's horse, then lifted her up into the saddle. As a precaution, he had brought a nearly empty one, on the premise it had been emptied as they traveled, using the grain to barter for services.

Three miles out of town, they encountered a group of soldiers posted as a roadblock.

Darius guided both horses into a copse of trees.

"Stay here. I'll be back in a moment."

"Darius—"

"Shh."

The vision of the men chasing the family through the woods floated to mind. She had heard stories of people killed along the road, robbed of their belongings, some of them by cutthroats, some by soldiers for sport.

"Wait here. Our mission will fail if they seize us here. I'll go ahead and deal with them. "I'll come back when it is safe. You sit hidden under that tree."

She listened to the reason in his voice, which calmed her more than anything had in days.

The two horses snorted gently to one another, as they grazed in the shadows of trees. Tired and more aware of the passage of time than her current realm-walker-in-charge, she spread her cloak on the grass, plopped down in a root-free spot, and allowed her mind to drift. In the dim moonlight, clouds clung to the breeze that rustled the leaves overhead. She lay back and listened to the night, expecting to hear the footfall as Darius approached.

Exhaustion nearly overcame her, dragging her toward sleep, until she realized she was staring at something in the tree limbs above her. Teagan glimpsed a pair of eyes watching her.

Before she could scream, a hand clamped over her mouth.

****

Corrig called for the bags to be slit. The English officer in turn, ordered one of the foot soldiers to the task. Try as she might, Teagan couldn't find the strength to escape his grip.

Adrenaline rushed through her veins. The only surge it created was in her pulse and in the amount of sweat rolling down her neck at the moment.

Where was Darius? Why hadn't he zapped something and made it all stop? *Come on, damn it, flash, and make everything stand still.*

"Barley, sir," the soldier called out to the officer.

"And who do you travel with, madam?" the officer asked.

She looked at Corrig whose posture seemed different. He watched her with bold curiosity, which made her all the more self-conscious. The man didn't seem to recognize her.

He removed his hand and allowed her to answer the question. Rather than scream, which so much of her wanted to do, she tamped down that inclination, and tried to regain her voice.

"I travel with my…husband."

"What business brings you and your husband out before the sun breaks dawn?"

Time to lie. What would make them travel by moonlight?

"I am with child. The sun and late summer heat make me ill. The night air is cooling, and if I vomit along the night road, I am none the worse for it."

Both the man in charge and Corrig stared at her, trying to gauge the accuracy of her story.

"Where is your husband, now? Why does he leave his wife alone so close to the road?"

"I do not know where he is. I am weary and needed to rest. Perhaps he wandered to stretch his legs. Or perhaps he needed privacy." She hoped her insinuation at his whereabouts would stave any further interrogation.

"Sir!"

The call from the soldier caught them all off guard.

The anxious rush Teagan had felt a moment ago, sank like lead in her chest as the officer moved toward her horse, and examined the grain bag.

The aroma of tobacco did make her gag, as Corrig continued to hold her by the arm. Her body convulsed in a wretch which made her double over in a dry heave.

Method acting. Damned by her sense of smell.

She yanked her arm from Corrig and sank to her knees, covering her face with her sleeve. She needed to get away from him, or the wretching would continue.

Great. One realm walker produces an electrical effect upon her, the other an emetic.

In spite of her queasiness, she laughed. *He makes me sick.*

"Who, your husband?"

Teagan's head snapped up. She stared at Corrig. "Excuse me?"

She hadn't spoken the words, only thought them. Corrig had heard her thoughts and replied to them.

Before either of them could do or say, or think, anything else, the officer returned. "It seems you and your husband are attempting to smuggle goods."

"What?"

Teagan peered at the soldier who was tethering the two horses together, and leading them from the trees, toward the road.

"What are you doing? You can't take—"

"In the grain sack," the officer said to Corrig.

"They've hidden a clock in the grain sack. Quite a nice piece of workmanship, from what we can see of it. Smuggling is a crime against the crown, Mrs.—?"

"You have no right to hold me."

Two more soldiers appeared and seized both her arms, preventing her from either running or attacking.

"I have every right, madam. In service to His Majesty, I cannot condone thievery and smuggling. I am arresting you." He turned to Corrig who continued to stare inquisitively at her.

"Clocks are a bit rare to find inside a barley bag, don't you agree, Mr. Corrig?"

Even in the darkness, Teagan recognized the flash in his eyes.

The clock.

Whether he recognized her or not, the man who had tried to shoot her on Oak Island six days ago and two hundred and sixty years in the future, had just found what he'd been looking for.

She struggled to think random thoughts—squirrel, baking bread, tea, rhymes with...tree.

A cup of tea beneath the oak tree with Friarforefiddle and Winky, and thee. A book, bell, and candle, and rhyming good song, will carry us thither and move us along...

The nausea from the tobacco, combined with the seriousness of the situation, made her head pound as if someone had taken a sledgehammer to her skull. She mustn't think of—think of anything.

Acetyl salicylic acid. Willow bark. Acetyl Salicylic acid is found in the bark of the willow tree, a plant with slender limbs, indigenous to temperate climates such as North America. The bark of the willow, from a

Germanic origin, is used in medicinal application. Acetyl salicylic acid application? Medication.

Nothing can be read that isn't in the air...Fuzzy Wuzzy had no hair...

A cynical smile crept across his lips. "Your husband. A clock maker, I take it?"

****

Teagan was gone.

The scent of mortals, their warmth, lingered in the air.

As did another trace.

Darius did not bother calling to the horses. That they were no longer tethered, told him they had been taken. Teagan would not have left him deliberately. Not after their meeting with Ranulf.

Someone had taken her. He tried to hear her thoughts and found nothing more than gibberish. As if she were dreaming. Or singing.

Or rhyming.

Danger.

She had been scared, or in danger, and her brain automatically began reciting in rhyme. A great device for diversion. Especially for someone whose thoughts might be read by realm walkers.

Tobacco. He might not have recognized it at once had it not been for Teagan's constant assignment of aromas to places and people. She classified every scent she had come in contact with since North Carolina. She now associated each aroma with a person, or experience. For a woman so new to the quirks of realm walkers, she did seem to be adapting.

If she were aware of her surroundings, she might have left him clues.

Tea beneath the oak tree…British. The British had taken her? Why had he not heard anything?

Because he had been busy with the troops at the roadblock, half a mile ahead. He had wandered up the road, cast the men to slumber, then attempted to discern their purpose.

Now, he knew. The roadblock served as a diversion. Which meant that no mortal had arranged this. Wily as they could be, the English would not have fabricated this.

No. A realm walker lurked.

Ranulf Deschamb would soon be in a prison cell, awaiting a hearing on the charge of treason if he couldn't get him and his daughter onto a ship within a day's time.

First, he had to find Deschamb's daughter. Then he would save Teagan.

Tobacco meant Corrig.

Procuring a horse from the soldiers had been as easy as three hands of cards. He could have merely stopped everything for a few minutes to take advantage of the situation and stolen the beast. Then, of course, there would be questions. A hand of cards, however, accomplished the same end, without significant suspicions.

As the creature plodded along the road, being driven by Darius, he considered the fate of his friend. Had their coming back saved Ranulf? Moreover, could he set in motion the actions he also planned to save Teagan?

Automobiles and planes really were much more convenient.

Originally, realm walkers had no need for

transportation services. These days, such things as automobiles served as simple conveyances, to fool spectators. And as meditational devices.

For thousands of years, he had existed, traveling in dreams, a voyeur to people's desires, their guilt, their hopes. For that time, he had been a timekeeper, ensuring that what humans deemed ethically "good" maintained a balance with those deeds which so easily sought a place in history.

For all that time, he had never questioned his own being or his task in the universe. Not until Ranulf took Reagan to wed and shed his immortal gifts. To see what it cost his friend pained him. Ranulf had lost his ability to protect, to manipulate, to control mortals at will. He could not know their thoughts, could not walk the realms between wakefulness and dreams, and could not affect anything there.

And yet, his friend had found love. Such an infantile emotion at the surface. Surely, the sexual appetite of a realm walker made a physical relationship with one mortal pale in comparison to the conquests, both metaphysical and corporeal. Mustn't it?

He had confessed no less than that same failed emotion to his friend not two days ago. How could he, a realm walker, be in love? Is it possible that his true motive in all this might be greed more than just saving the girl?

Not a girl. A woman. Both the girl he rescued his first time here, and the one who needed him now, were fully grown women.

Darius spurred the horse to gallop. Could it be that his true reason for all of this was not to redeem himself for the sin committed, but to keep her alive, for his own need?

She is not a doll. And I am not a child who needs a play toy.

Young women of this era had married by sixteen and met their deaths often before they had seen a century pass. Teagan had seen eighteen years when he rescued her.

He had watched her grow through each life, gaining strength with each incarnation.

Is that how the ancient ones began? With the simplest memories of past lives, until they had little need for the confinement of time and body?

Could he give up this existence to remain with the woman who had put her trust in him?

Ire and sexual need battled in his muscles for dominance, and he wished for some way he could vent his frustration. The horse would not offer him succor on either account.

Only two things could. Finding both Teagans. And finding the one who threatened her.

To finish this.

Chapter Twenty-Nine

Teagan sat with her hands folded in her lap and straightened her spine. "I don't know what you are talking about." Lieutenant Monckton paced back and forth, calmly, the clock in question, having been placed on a table between them.

"You say your name is Alexander, yet you have no travel papers, and I know of no family in this area by that name. Your accent is not French, nor is it English, and you obviously are not one of the natives who roams the continent, so who are you?"

"I told you. My name is Teagan Alexander. My husband and I were traveling to see friends in the north." Her given name would not incriminate Alwin or Deschamb.

"Why do you have a clock hidden in your belongings?"

"Lieutenant Monckton, have you not noticed there are thieves in the world? The grain provided a cushion to guard against damage to the internal mechanism of the timepiece. It also served to protect the clock from greedy people who would steal it." *Like the British.* "How many highwaymen have you seen steal a sack of grain, Lieutenant?"

"During a war, madam, people steal everything. Including food. And clocks. In fact, if you are not smuggling, perhaps you are yourself a thief, who poses as a pregnant wife to thereby gain the trust of your intended victims. Either way, you do seek to rob King George."

"I do not. I can prove ownership of the clock."

The lieutenant raised an eyebrow in interest at her assertion, and she immediately regretted saying it. No matter what she said, someone would be implicated in a plot of some sort.

Please, give me strength. And guidance.

"Who built the clock, Mrs. Alexander?"

"I do not know the man who crafted the clock, sir. He is an acquaintance of my husband's from many years ago, I believe. The clock was a gift. Consider it a token of congratulations on our recent marriage." She did not lie, merely manipulated the truth.

A brief knock at the door heralded Corrig's arrival. Teagan bristled at his interference. Stupid realm walker didn't even recognize her. That, at least, offered something to relieve her anxiety.

The two men whispered conspiratorially, then Corrig turned his attention to her. "A wedding gift, you say?" he asked. "Our congratulations to you on your nuptials, dear lady. How long since your vows?"

Teagan stared blankly at him. How long? She had told them earlier that she was pregnant. How long ago would they have had to marry for her to know she was pregnant?

"We were married at the end of June."

"And yet your husband seems to have lost you already."

"Not so much lost me, as had me stolen. And while we are discussing identifications…who, sir, are you that you travel with British troops, yet wear no uniform yourself?"

Corrig smiled yet did not reply.

"Who are you to abduct a woman with the permission and assistance of the English army, to steal her belongings, her horses, and to squander her livelihood upon the ground to feed the birds and vermin? You have no title, or rank, or purpose here for all that I can see."

She had paid attention to everyone she had come into contact with over the past weeks. She'd be damned if she would let him win because she couldn't play their game.

"Tell, me, Mrs. Alexander, what game are you playing at? A woman, alone in the dark of night hiding among the trees, with contraband."

"What?"

The corner of his mouth twitched slightly, and he stroked the curve of the clock that sat between them. "You know time is of the essence in any war. One wrong move for the lieutenant and his men, and their lives could be gone, like that." The snap of his fingers jolted Teagan. Whatever she might have expected from him, a time freeze was not it.

The lieutenant was in mid-step.

Teagan realized immediately that she was not in mid-movement. Her movements were still fluid. She slipped her hand beneath her skirt and drew the knife Darius had insisted she strap there, then rose from the chair and readied herself to run for the door.

"You son-of-a-bitch! Let me go."

"You say that as if you and I have met before." Corrig tilted his head and studied her for a moment. "And you are the second woman this week whose opinion of me puts me in company with dogs. Tell me, are you and this other woman friends?"

While Teagan imagined there could be ample women who would consider Corrig's origins to be questionable, she could name one immediately whose accent matched her own.

Dana had made it through the vortex and was somewhere nearby. Which meant the clock that brought them here was nearby.

Alive?

"For the moment," he replied, "you are. As is your friend, the brunette with interesting appetites."

He stood and moved around the table until he stood no more than an inch from her. Menacingly close.

"She did entertain me a bit. She had a key that I was particularly interested in. Can you imagine what kind of key it was?"

Teagan tried not to wretch at the thick tobacco musk that clung to the man. He trailed his hands down her forearms and grabbed both wrists. "I wonder what enjoyment and enlightenment you can offer."

Teagan swung her arms away from her body, so violently, Corrig flew across the small room, and hit the wall. An action neither of them expected, but one for which Teagan, at least, was grateful.

"Who are you?" Blood droplets laced his cheek. "Only a realm walker has that kind of mental and physical power," Corrig said as he righted himself.

The force of her movement made her arms tremble. She ran toward the door, but Corrig tripped her. She fell to the floor as he straddled her, the blade scattered under the door.

She attempted to throw him off, unsuccessfully. He

bent over her and grabbed a handful of her hair, yanking her head to the side as he whispered in her ear. "I do not know whence you come. But I am willing to bet you won't be using that clock, soon. Certainly, not without the key."

"I don't need a key."

"Ah. I take it, then, that you are not Ranulf Deschamb's daughter. Pity. I was hoping I could finish my work here and leave this forsaken place. Still, we could have some fun, before I take your life."

"Because Zahra and the others would say nothing of you committing murder against another realm walker?"

That stopped him.

She actually felt the flinch in his muscles through the layers of cloth.

"Who are you?"

Teagan laughed at that. For the moment, she didn't quite know herself. Like Alice down the rabbit hole, her life had been turned upside down.

"I know what you want Robert Corrig," using his given name, which he had not yet shared with her. "And I also know that if you have me here, in a cell, you are never going to find that damned key. And without the key, you cannot destroy the clock completely." Two could play the mind-trick game.

She couldn't stop time, but she had just stopped a realm walker.

****

Darius watched the ship drift away from its moorings. At the rail, the tawney-haired beauty waved down to him. Her face, pale as porcelain, except for the two feathers of pink, where wind and tears had chaffed.

Like the Acadians, forced from their land, she, too, would find a new home. This time, however, she did so without the intervention she had received from her family's friend of so many years. This time, she left Nova Scotia with all her memories, with the knowledge that she most likely would never see her friends again, and with the knowledge of her true ancestry.

Darius tapped the cadence that thrummed in his head against his thigh as he considered the actions he had set in motion with this singular act. He had vowed to protect her. He had come back to release her. He could not guarantee she would not meet death in this lifetime, but he had made sure she did not meet her death prematurely because of the clock, or because of her father.

He had guaranteed she would be prepared when next she met a stranger who stared too long or smiled knowingly at her, or who tried to sift through her thoughts.

For his friend, for himself, or for the woman he meant to save in the future, he had sacrificed his greed, and now sent her forth to a new adventure. Whoever she became from here, he would find Ranulf Deschamb's daughter in her dreams, keeping a protective awareness of her as he had done before.

The young Teagan turned to the figure beside her at the railing, and linked her arm through his, kissed the grey-haired gentleman upon the cheek, and whispered something to him. The two shared a smile as they waved one last time.

Darius watched Ranulf and Teagan Deschamb, clockmaker and his daughter turn away from the railing, and walk toward their uncertain future.

Together.

The grey-haired gentleman waved to him and the two shared a smile as they waved one last time. Darius watched Ranulf Deschamb turn away from the railing, as the ship moved away from the mooring, toward a new future.

****

The makeshift prison cell was not part of any travel brochure Teagan had ever seen for Nova Scotia. At least there was a cot. She did worry about the former resident, and any souvenir pests that might have remained.

Corrig's inability to destroy the clock didn't stop him from releasing her to the local officials, planting in their minds that she was smuggling moneys in the clock to French troops. He also implied that she, by her very association with the Reverend Morreau, might be viewed as an Acadian sympathizer. Both charges marked her a treason suspect.

Thank goodness, he had not recognized her. He had not been able to halt her mobility or her thoughts while he held the rest of the room in suspension. That alone intrigued him enough to let her live for a short time more. However, he had slipped some European gold coins into the clock before vanquishing the spell that held the others in the room frozen.

When everything began to move, the sentry at the door caught her, Lieutenant Monck found the gold, and Teagan found that she could not escape arrest.

But Darius had.

Deliberately, she had manipulated her own thoughts so that Corrig would not know Darius had been with her. Even as she paced the floor of her cell, she expected he watched her from somewhere nearby.

She needed Darius to know that Dana had made it through the rabbit hole, and that she had the key. That begged the question, if the British guard was in possession of the original clock, where was the clock that had brought them here? For now, the original version of the clock, which sat in Monck's company, had little time-bending protection power if the only person who had the key was off in the country doing housework. As long as the *other* Teagan stayed hidden, and out of Corrig's reach, everyone remained safe.

Everyone, that is, except she, herself, who finally succumbed to fatigue and collapsed upon the mattress.

How could she be here now, in an English gaol? And where was her realm walker?

What seemed like hours later, she heard shouting from somewhere down the corridor. A woman's voice yelled, "She's lying! I didn't steal anything. If I had, it would be something of real value, not letters!"

She recognized the voice immediately. American accent. *Dana.*

The woman screaming about not being a thief was just that, and more. Dana literally held the key to the clock—a key to the solution to all their problems.

A rattle at the door heralded someone's presence, and Teagan looked up to see Monck speaking to a soldier in the corridor. After a moment, the bolt on the wooden door was thrown and the lieutenant stepped in.

She sat up.

"Mrs. Alexander, I have checked with the town's officials, and no one has heard of you or any gentleman with you. There is no record of your name in the church records or in any business ledgers locally."

"Of course not. We are just visiting." She couldn't very well give Darius's real name, could she? Corrig would have recognized that immediately.

"Furthermore, the invisible husband you claim to have been with in the woods has not materialized to either validate your story, or to claim you as his bride and the mother of his as-of-yet-unborn children."

"And?"

"Thus, based upon the contraband discovered in your possession, the gold hidden away, and your reluctance to assist in our investigation, I hold the authority to treat you as a hostile prisoner, a spy, and a traitor to the crown."

"A what?" Teagan knew enough history to know that during the eighteenth century, in a time of war, there were many people who were treated as traitors. That had been Ranulf's Deschamb's demise, hadn't it?

Traitors died by execution.

"Teagan Alexander, as a servant to King George, the crown of England, I do hereby charge you with treason, and with smuggling, a crime against his Majesty's realm. In accordance with my duty, I sentence you to death by hanging in two days' time."

Nausea flooded through her. The room began to spin as she sat clutching the edge of the cot. Death by hanging? Two days? What sick joke was this?

"No. You can't. I haven't been given a trial. I am due a trial of my peers. I'm not even—"

Not even what? Canadian? Nova Scotia, like the colonies to the south, existed in 1758 as a province of the British empire. She couldn't even claim citizenship of the United States, as they would not exist for another twenty-five years.

"Not even what?" The voice that posed the question came not from Monck's throat but from the man who stepped from the shadows, into the room. "What are you not?" Corrig asked. "*Mortal?*"

She read this thought loud and clear, just before she threw up all over the lieutenant's boots.

***

The sun had fallen behind the horizon, when Darius found the building that the English were currently using as a command post and gaol. Morreau and Frau Koehler made no short work of telling him that the English had been making inquiries about a young woman traveling alone who fit Teagan's description.

He watched as Corrig departed with commander of the local regiment. The building currently was guarded by mortals, nothing more.

If Corrig had abandoned Teagan, it meant he hadn't figured out who she was. It also meant that he might be onto another lead. He already had the clock. Now, all that remained hidden was the key.

He hadn't meant to leave Teagan at all, along the road that night. When he had hidden her and set off toward the troops, he didn't know Corrig had set a trap. Once he realized the threat, he knew he had to get to Deschamb. If his friend had met British soldiers along that road, then history would literally have repeated itself.

This time, he had not been too late. This time, he had saved Ranulf Deschamb and his daughter.

Now he had to tie up the loose ends.

It shouldn't take long to find her and release his Teagan. The woman he had saved, the woman who had lived more than a dozen lives was in there, awaiting the fate that so many faced.

When had he fallen so in love with her? Had he always loved her? Had his vow to his friend sealed his fate to be forever connected to this woman?

She doesn't even know what she truly is. Then, together, they could reclaim the clock. Once they found the key, and made their way back to the island, he could end this nightmare.

Chapter Thirty

He found Teagan easily enough in the shabby shell of a prison, curled up on the ticking of the cot. Someone had considered her interesting or important enough to give her a cell with a cot. She did not budge as he moved through the doorway.

Exhaustion marked her features. Her face was smudged, and she was crumpled, but she looked no worse for the wear she had suffered. As an enigma, she had garnered some respect...or fear. Either served her well for the moment. He knelt beside her and brushed the hair away from her face. "I heard you ran into an old acquaintance."

She blinked timidly, then her eyes widened, and she leapt up and grabbed him. "I knew you'd come."

The sun sat low in the sky, now. Daylight lingered, but their proximity to the coast chilled the air. He wrapped his arms around her to warm her. Even through the layers of clothing, she was cold to the touch. Neither of them spoke for a long moment.

"You took care of him. He is safe, then? He is alive and safe, and you didn't have to break any rules?"

"They both are. I saw Ranulf and you—her—onto the ship. I convinced the captain that they are traveling *for* the governor, back to England, and that their passage was fully paid. I made certain that they have a fair amount of gold to cover their expenses, so they do not have anything to worry about from prying realm walkers."

Despite her best efforts, she shivered. Is this how her other self, Teagan Deschamb, had spent the last days of her life two hundred and sixty-five years ago?

Teagan broke the embrace and pushed herself to a stand. She moved to the window and stared out, toward the scaffolding. He didn't have to wonder at her thoughts.

She turned to face him. "What happens to me now? Do I merely cease to exist? Do I go into hiding? Wait to be captured? Do I fade away with the sunset?"

She stared out the cell window again. "That is how he died, isn't it? By saving Deschamb, this time, aren't you committing the same crime you committed the first time? Stopping a natural death?"

"Execution is not a natural death, Teagan. Realm walkers maintain an order, a balance. Ranulf Deschamb should never have been executed. He was no spy. He was merely a misguided man who sacrificed everything for his family."

"What of me? How do you rectify me? I cannot exist here, while she does, can I? That's the conundrum, isn't it? We can't both occupy the same space. Do I die on that scaffolding tomorrow just to maintain that balance?"

"You will not die, Teagan. I will make certain you do not."

A life for a life. Wasn't that the balance? Deschamb lived. Tomorrow she would take his place.

****

Darius crossed to her and stood behind her, so close that warmth radiated from his body. He gathered her into his arms and pulled her back against his chest as his breath kissed her hair.

"Do you remember it all?" she asked. "Do you remember everything you ever experienced? Do you remember saving her that day when she fell into the water?"

"Yes."

"And? What about that night before she escaped her cell? Did she—did I—take refuge in your arms the night before we escaped?"

"She did not meet me until I pulled her from the ocean's grasp."

"Oh." She stayed very still, too scared to move away from him, too wary to turn around. She had longed for him to find her, to allay her fears of what came next. Now, what came next would change everything.

His embrace tightened. "Everything will be alright, Teagan. Trust me."

"I do. But I cannot walk through walls, or people's dreams." She leaned her head against his chest and listened to his heartbeat. "Do you regret that she didn't know who you were? Or that you weren't there to prevent her father's death that night? You might not be risking your life and mine if you had been able to fix everything that night."

He turned her around and wrapped his arm around her waist as his other hand cupped her chin and tilted her face so she could look at him. "If things had been different then, I suspect we might never have met in this—your present lifetime."

"But you knew me in other lifetimes."

"Only because of that first encounter when I broke

the rules."

He had spent eternity, literally, trying to correct an error that had not been his to begin with. If Deschamb's daughter hadn't been in the water during the storm, then he would not have had to intervene.

She asked, "Do you wish you had never met me?"

He lowered his head, and pressed his lips to hers, stealing her breath and her words as he kissed her. She had grown accustomed to the static charge between them, and so did not pull away as the current pulsed through both their bodies.

He grew more demanding, both in his kiss and in his embrace. He pulled her closer, as his mouth punished her for her question, until she gave in and answered him. She met the passion in his kiss, reaching up to cup her hand around his neck as she pulled him closer.

For her entire life, she had never wanted anyone as much as she wanted Darius at this moment. Regardless of what fate had in store for her, she wanted this chance, this ridiculous opportunity to be with him. This intimacy, this electricity, this passion that had smoldered between them for two and a half centuries, waiting patiently for its time.

His hands clenched at her bodice, clawing at the fabric, grabbing and wrenching the laces, until he moved his hand one layer closer to her body.

The fact that they were inside the gaol, instead of a posh hotel, or even a drab inn was not lost on her. There was no time like the present, for there would be no tomorrow. Either she would be hanged, or the clock would be destroyed.

The warmth of his flesh, his hands tugging the

chemise away from her shoulders, burned her now. Her body surged with a hunger she did not remember experiencing before, even in the pit. He railed his mouth down her neck and across her collarbone. Her tremble at his heat only encouraged him, and he held her firmly against himself as he explored her body with his lips.

The fabric pulled away from her skin, and his breath became ragged. He moved her to the cot and guided her onto the mattress.

The mustiness of the ticking dissipated under his persuasion as he gave his attention once more to her mouth.

His hands worked fervently to free her of the binding layers of fabric that protected her from him. When he slid the chemise away from her, her body convulsed with enthusiasm, and he groaned in reply.

Her breasts swelled, and she pulled him to her.

"I want this."

"To give into your passion could mean madness for you."

She reached for him. "To deny it any longer certainly will."

"You don't know the evil of it. A mortal woman never recovers from it. I know. I've seen what it does. Firsthand."

"Whether I suffer gloriously in your arms, a madwoman, or I die on the scaffolding, this suffering is of my choosing. Besides, I am only as you and Corrig admitted, part human. Somewhere, inside me lies something of my origin. Something of Ranulf."

"I would forfeit myself before I would see you broken."

"If I am mad beyond this, then death won't mean anything to me. It will merely release me."

He pulled back from her, his breath heavy against her flesh, his cock swollen and firm against her thigh.

Her own slickness and desire drove her now, pushing him harder, stoking his lust and his desperation.

She knew the danger of her threat. She knew also that now she had little choice. Intercourse with the realm walker might push her to the brink of insanity, and she would die a mortal death with no clock, no memory, and no ties to her past, or she would survive. Three hundred years of deprivation had removed so many of her memories. Why not finish the task?

She stole the moment of his doubt to wriggle free and make for the cell door, intent on calling for the guard to sound the alarm, to force him to action.

Darius caught her by her shift, and flung her against the wall, slamming his own body against hers eagerly.

"Never."

"Never, what?"

The growl emanated from deep within him, roiling through his limbs as he held her, fingers bruising flesh. "You are mine. Always have been."

She stared into his eyes and watched the silver lining flash like lightning as he descended upon her.

He pushed her to the cot again, not bothering with gentility. Passion sought purchase with her reason, and she briefly fought against the lunatic she found hidden deep inside her own form.

Cloth ripped beneath his fingers, and he shoved her legs apart, drawing her arms over her head as he braced himself over her. One hand held her fists as his free hand caressed her flesh. His mouth laved first one nipple, then the other.

"Mine," he repeated. "Never another's."

Teagan relaxed her fists and arched against his mouth.

Her body ached, more so than it had in the cave, and she willed her spirit to bond with his, to take him inside her fully.

Reason fled as she tilted her hips to meet his. He raked his hand over her abdomen, until he stroked the mound that pulsed between her thighs. Her own voice escaped in a squeal of urgency, and he fed on her encouragement.

No softness, no tender youthful foreplay. Darius slid his fingers inside her and chortled at her eagerness. "I've pleasured myself for three hundred years, waiting to claim you, and taking others in your place. I've stood by as you bedded mortal men, watched you weather their futile attempts to satisfy you. I've even entered your dreams to tempt you. I won't be denied, now.

"Neither will I," she replied.

He claimed her, sinking into her—velvety smooth within—demanding him in return. With a solid thrust he impaled her. He thrust against her steadily, forcefully, every moment demanding more of her as he slid in and out, heightening his pleasure and hers. His hands cupped her breasts, eliciting her cries of pleasure.

He dipped his head and greedily suckled her breasts. She wound her arms around his neck holding him close to her breast. As she wriggled one leg from beneath his and wrapped it around his hips, she dared him to give her more—then took him deeper.

His rhythm increased, as did hers, and she clung to him, striving to meld their two bodies, as he pumped harder and faster.

Lightning flashed. Electricity filled the room. The storm's ferocity permeated the cell, crackling the air with the intensity of their lust as they moved against one another.

He lifted his head, capturing hers in his hands and gripped her with a villainous stare. The moment seared her to her core as she began to melt against him.

"Never," he commanded. "Never another. Swear it."

Fire, heat, a thousand times hotter than either of them could stand, opened within her, consumed her, burning her as everything began to swirl out of control.

"Say it. Swear it, Teagan. Never. Another. Only. Me."

She knew what he demanded. Knew what it meant. Knew there was no escape. Only salvation for them both.

"Always," she replied. "Only you."

She melted from the inside out, flowing around him, swirling into him as he exploded into her, filling her. Claiming her.

Time, wind, rain, static, all roared in her ears as she held on to him. His flesh melted into hers, their pulse synchronized to one throbbing drum.

Despite trying to stay in the corporeal shell, She rose out of her body, gliding up through the magnetic storm that illuminated the tiny room. She tried to force herself back down and found it impossible to do. Another surge of white heat enveloped her, and she found herself joined by a shimmering light.

His.

Darius held her tight, caressing her as gently as if she were a newborn kitten.

She attempted to kiss him and found she could not grasp him. Panic welled when she felt herself moving through him as if she were a ghost.

He'd been right. She couldn't survive.

"You are fine. Just weakened by the force of it."

She peered down at her form on the cot, naked and still. *"Not dead?"*

"Not yet."

"Say it, then. Say it now, Darius."

"Mine. Never another. Always mine."

She drifted heavily downward toward her body, sinking through his flesh, reveling in the testosterone charged bulk of him as he lay, still half swollen inside her, refusing to release her. Never had she known this pleasure. Never would she forget.

The *petit mort*, some called it.

Tomorrow's death would be real.

Chapter Thirty-One

Dana stood on the scaffolding with her hands tied behind her back. Around her neck hung the key that Darius, Teagan, and Corrig all coveted. Fine. They could have it after they ripped it from her cold, broken neck.

She smirked at the crowd of onlookers. A few paltry soldiers and some young boys were all that filled the space below.

Like a roll of the dice in Vegas, she had taken a chance, and had lost everything. Or was about to.

Stupid soldier. A few coins and a mention of Deschamb's name, and suddenly she'd been charged with treason. She stared at the back of the crowd. Several of the onlookers resembled those she had seen at the dinner party. She knew the mayor's wife had a hand in this. Women were much more clever when it came to such games.

Had the roles been reversed, she would have done the same.

A figure lurked in the shadow of the doorway. A memory flitted through her mind. A man with a velvet touch, and the scent of tobacco…like a dream.

The executioner murmured something in her ear that sounded like a promise of mercy should her neck not break on impact of the fall. She pushed aside the flutter of fear that gnawed at her belly and stepped onto the planks of the trap door.

She wondered briefly if she would come back. Did reincarnation exist? If she did return, perhaps she would become a clock maker. *Tick-tock, I could rule time.*

****

"The woman you sought is dead," Darius said to Corrig.

As evidence, he pulled back the canvas and revealed the corpse's auburn hair and pale features. Oddly, even in death, despite a murder's nature, she was a remarkably beautiful woman.

"This is Ranulf Deschamb's daughter?" Corrig's face registered surprise.

Which pleased Darius significantly.

"Does she not match Deschamb's daughter's description? Petite build, brown hair, alabaster complexion?"

Corrig's brow furrowed momentarily as he, the realm-walker who had hunted this woman for so many months, processed what he saw before him.

"And see," Darius continued, "she wears it around her neck. Deschamb's key."

An eager smile spread across the realm walker's face. He reached out and brushed his fingers across her flesh. No doubt ensuring himself she held no pulse, he stroked the metal that kissed the skin beneath her bruised neck.

"Ah, yes, the key. I asked her about it, and she would not tell me where she had gotten it."

"No doubt, she hoped to protect her father."

"Mortals are peculiar that way."

Darius smiled inwardly. Yes, they were.

"Now that I have kept my part of the bargain, it is

your turn. You have the clock. You have the key. You have the body. You and I are both exonerated as soon as you destroy the clock."

Corrig snapped the chain that clung to the key and palmed the metal object. Then, turning a smile to Darius, he asked, "What will you do with her?"

Darius did not miss the hint of lust in Corrig's voice and knew the answer that could best ensure Teagan's release.

"I shall enjoy her."

****

Teagan sat in the skiff, a blanket wrapped around her shoulders, and watched the man who sat across from her, oars in hand, as the waves rocked against the hull of the craft.

His muscles rippled beneath the fabric of his shirt as he applied the oars repeatedly to the water, moving them farther and farther away from the pier. "Are you sure you wouldn't prefer to stay?"

A shiver moved through her chest at the timber of his voice. "I'm sure." As beautiful as the coastline was, she had little desire to stay here, now. Perhaps in another time.

Sassafras wafted on the breeze, and she inhaled deeply, trying ardently to focus on where they were headed, instead of focusing on the tanned expanse of chest that showed from the neck of his shirt, or the piercing, hungry blue of his eyes.

Latent sexual desire raged inside her as they inched toward the speck of an island in the distance. "I prefer the comforts of a modern shower, and a coffee shop on every corner. And a king-sized bed."

His eyebrows arched.

"I am new to this whole realm walker thing. I think we will have to practice quite a bit to help me hone my abilities."

"Abilities or appetites?" he countered.

"Hmmm. Perhaps, Mr. Alwin, you may have to aid me with both."

He paused his rowing momentarily, found his jacket, and reached into the inside pocket, then tossed something into her lap. Teagan looked down at the shimmering gold metal key.

"Do you think it will work?"

"Different clock. Same use. Your father was a very clever man."

"And once we are back?"

"We won't need it anymore, will we?"

"No. But it seems a waste to destroy it. A family heirloom, and all."

"And yet, you no longer need what it offers."

"Why not?"

He carefully placed the oars beside him in the boat, then reached across and pulled her to him. "Have I not told you repeatedly?"

"You've told me a lot of things."

"You no longer need the clock because you have your own realm walker to protect you."

"You?" she asked.

"If you will have me?"

"But you can't, can you?"

"I cannot bond with a mortal and relinquish my own powers without forfeiting my own immortality."

"You would give that up for me?"

"I do not have to."

Teagan's heart skipped a beat. "Why not?"

"You, Teagan, are not a conventional mortal. You are a hybrid. You bonded yesterday with a realm walker, so I would say you've just about hit your own realm walker puberty."

"Oh, no. I couldn't stand puberty the first time. I am not going there again."

"This time will be different."

"How so?"

"This time, you will have me at your side, in your king-sized bed, and even in your dreams."

"What of the others? Won't they come looking for us? Don't I pose some kind of threat?"

He kissed her lightly on the lips, and thunder trembled in the distance. "You, my dear, offer Deschamb's greatest gift to the realm walkers. A glimpse of our humanity returned to us. The only true problem they might find is with the pleasure we offer one another, a human to realm walker union defies the rules and brings both worlds closer. I dare say, they'll all be very jealous."

A word about the author...

A 2015 Golden Heart finalist for historical fiction, Lori has spent most of her adult life traveling to faires and fields throughout the United Kingdom and North America searching for all things historical and literary. She lives in Florida with her husband and several very spoiled pets. http://www.lorifrancis.org